Lestrade and the Devil's Own

Lestrade and the Devil's Own

Volume XVI in the Lestrade Mystery Series

M.J. Trow

A Gateway Mystery

REGNERY
PUBLISHING, INC.
Since 1947 • An Eagle Publishing Company

Library of Congress Cataloging-in-Publication Data

Trow, M.J.
        Lestrade and the devil's own / M.J. Trow
            p.   cm. — (A Gateway mystery) (Lestrade mystery series.; v. 16)
        ISBN 0-89526-215-0
    1. Lestrade, Inspector (Fictitious character)—Fiction. 2. Police—England—London—Fiction. 3. London (England)—Fiction. I. Title. II. Series
        823'.914—dc21   00-065311

Published in the United States by
Regnery Publishing, Inc.
An Eagle Publishing Company
One Massachusetts Avenue, NW
Washington, DC 20001
www.regnery.com

Distributed to the trade by
National Book Network
4720-A Boston Way
Lanham, MD 20706

Printed on acid-free paper
Manufactured in the United States of America
Originally published in Great Britain

10 9 8 7 6 5 4 3 2 1

Books are available in quantity for promotional or premium use. Write to Director of Special Sales, Regnery Publishing, Inc., One Massachusetts Avenue, NW, Washington, DC 20001, for information on discounts and terms or call (202) 216-0600.

The character of Inspector Lestrade was created by the late Sir Arthur Conan Doyle and appears in Sherlock Holmes stories and novels by him, as do some other characters in this book.

Miles – thanks from Sholto

'Needs must, when the
Devil drives.'

1

'Sholto Joseph Lestrade, you have been found guilty of the most abhorrent of crimes short of joining the Labour party – the foul crime of murder. You, a guardian of the people, a champion of the peace . . . That you should fall so low from your position of trust is inexcusable. I doubt you have a mother living, but if she should hear of this . . . Do you have anything to say why judgement of death should not be passed upon you?'

The old man in the black cap peered through his pince-nez across the crowded court of the Bailey where the morning sunlight threw its shafts on the parchment-yellow face of the man in the dock.

'I believe there's been some mistake, My Lord.'

'Indeed there has, Lestrade,' His Lordship replied, leaning back. 'And it was yours the day you left your fingerprints all over the bombazine of Mrs Millicent Millichip. Not only a bestial murderer, but an incompetent one. Did you learn nothing from your years at the Yard? I can forgive bestiality, Lestrade, but gross stupidity, never.'

His Lordship straightened in his high-backed chair, the sword of justice gleaming in the sunlight over his head. 'The sentence of this court is that you be taken from hence to the place from whence you came and from thence to a place of lawful execution; and that you there be hanged by the neck until you be dead; and that your body afterwards be buried within the precincts of the prison in which you shall have been last confined. And may the Lord have mercy on your soul.'

The man in the dock blinked. There was a stir in the gallery behind him. He turned his head once to see a veiled lady being helped out by a tall man with blond hair. His faithful Harry supporting his darling Fanny.

His Lordship stood up, bellowing 'Take him down' and he felt the tug of steel on his wrist as he vanished below into the bowels of the building.

'Missing you already,' muttered His Lordship. 'Clerk of Assize? Got a spare pair of trousers there by any chance?'

The man in the dock didn't even pass 'Go' on his way to Pentonville. The matched greys clattered up the long ramp off the Caledonian Road, pulling the dark police wagon with its solitary occupant under the false portcullis and the great arch. Sir Charles Barry, fresh from his Gothic excesses in the Houses of Parliament, had erected the radial wings and Italian clocktower in 1841, when Sholto Joseph Lestrade was rather less than a twinkle in his father's eye and his father's bull's-eye had been gleaming on his Pimlico beat in C Division, Metropolitan District.

The wagon lurched to a halt in the central exercise yard and the door was unbolted and swung back. Warders whose bulk blotted out the weak December sunshine flanked the condemned man along the dark corridors, through grilles and gates without number. But for two months this, for Lestrade, had been home. He'd even stopped scratching in the rough prison grey and had come to miss the broad arrows on his shirt. This, as they locked him back in the cell with grins and sneers, was the place from whence he had come. And as he turned to the wall, he knew that just down that corridor, where the green and cream of the morning turned black in the shadows, lay the place of lawful execution His Lordship had talked about. It would have a wooden floor and in it, a trap with hinges and bolts. There would be an upright post to his right, a horizontal beam above his head. A fervent chaplain would be mumbling at his elbow and he'd feel his feet pinioned together and his arms locked behind him before they threw the white hood over his face. And Death would come to Sholto Lestrade.

And he suddenly realized that it was *his* fists banging on the cold, unyielding iron of the door. *His* voice shouting, 'Wait a minute! You don't understand! I believe there's been some mistake!'

'Mr Lestrade?' a whiskered face peered in through the grille of the door.

'Not today, thank you.' The condemned man hadn't moved from his bed, but the door squealed outwards anyway. A thin man stood there, with grey, twinkling eyes and an awful tweed suit somewhere below his ginger moustaches.

'I'm . . .'

'I know who you are,' Lestrade said. 'John Ellis, the hangman. And you'll forgive me if I don't shake your hand. To save you any mathematical problems, I'm a little over five feet nine and I weigh approximately twelve stone one.'

'How kind,' Ellis purred in his soft Rochdale. 'You're very understanding. But.' He patted Lestrade's hard, bug-ridden bed and sat on it himself. 'I were just going to say I'm glad I caught you in. The fact is, we don't use the term "hangman" these days. It has . . . well . . . connotations. No, think of me, if you will, as Charon, a sort of ferryman what's going to take you to t'other side, as it were. I'd just like a brief chat with you first. Oh, don't worry, you've got a day or two yet, haven't you? The 'Ome Secretary's been in touch, 'as 'e? You'll 'ave 'ad the letter? Next Tuesday. Nine o'clock all right? Shame you'll miss Christmas, but it's gettin' so expensive these days, you're probably better off. Now, I don't want you to worry.' He patted Lestrade's hand. 'I've been ferryin' folks about now, as senior ferryman, you understand, for nigh on seven year; served my apprenticeship, you might say.'

'Oh good.' Lestrade found it quite difficult to smile, under the circumstances.

'My first were at Warwick. Lovely place. Nice old castle by the river. Perfect drop of five feet nine. Not even a quiver of that rope.'

'Get away.'

But Ellis didn't. He just kept on reminiscing.

'Two year ago, I took Henry Thompson across. He were the most callous man I ever met. We had to wake 'im up on the morning of departure and you know what 'e said?'

'No.' Lestrade sighed. 'But I have a curious feeling you're going to tell me.'

'Aye, I am.' Ellis nodded, producing a pipe. 'Shag?'

'Not at the moment,' Lestrade said.

'Thompson said, "Well, I shall be senior to Crippen in the other shop." Fancy that! You knew Crippen, didn't you?'

'I interviewed him, yes, along with my old friend Chief Inspector Dew.'

'Well, that was the first time I waited at the place, as it were, rather than walking ahead of the traveller. Less distressing. Do you know, if I'd been allowed to keep the rope, I could've sold it for £5 an inch.'

'Bothers you, does it?' Lestrade asked him. 'Distressing people?'

'Well, we in the removals business 'ave our sensitive side, you know. I were fair touched by poor old Seddon.'

'So was Eliza Barrow,' Lestrade commented.

'No, you see.' Ellis glanced from left to right, to make sure they

9

were alone in the nine foot by six foot cell. 'I shouldn't be tellin'
you this, but I am a Royal Antediluvian.'

'Really?'

Ellis nodded, inhaling noisily on his pipe stem. 'I was at Seddon's trial – in fact, that's where I first clapped eyes on you. You
remember he made the sign?'

'The sign?'

'The Masonic sign.' Ellis's voice had dropped to a whisper. 'I
can't be too graphic, you understand, but the judge, 'e were the
Provincial Grand Master of Surrey. It's like cuttin' your own
throat. I did my best for 'im, though – twenty-five seconds it took
to take 'im over. Cool as a cucumber 'e were. Ooh, bloody 'ell, this
psittacosis is giving me gyp!' And he scratched furiously at his
hand. 'That's bloody parrots for yer. Are you an animal lover, Mr
Lestrade?'

The condemned man shook his head.

'No, only I read the judge's comment at your trial, you know. I
like to take an interest in my passengers. I've all the cuttings.
When he said your crimes were bestial, I wondered if . . . No, no,
well, I didn't think so. I mean you bein' Church of England an' all.
But, you know what they say, there's nowt so queer as folk. By . . .
is that t'time?' The executioner had found his watch. 'I must fly.'
And he was at the cell door.

'By the by.' He paused once he'd thumped on it. 'I do occasionally – just occasionally, mind – get a bit of the jitters; like yer do.
What wi' t'neuritis an' psittacosis an' what yer might call stage
fright. But dinna mind. Look into my eyes next Tuesday morning,
Mr Lestrade and I'll get yer across all right.'

He beamed at the condemned man. ''Til Tuesday, then. Lookin'
forward to it!' And he was gone.

'Twenty-one,' Lestrade said, resting his head on his hand.

'Oh, bloody 'ell, Mr Lestrade.' The warder threw down his
paltry hand in disgust. 'What's that I owe you now?'

'Er . . . eight thousand four hundred and sixty-one pounds, one
and eightpence three farthings.'

'You couldn't wait 'til after Tuesday, could you? Only I'm a bit
short . . . oh, bloody 'ell . . .'

Lestrade smiled and shook his head. 'It's all right, Tom,' he said.
'There's many a slip. I'm not quite ready to meet my maker yet. By
the way, I'm prepared to waive the eightpence three farthings.'

'Sholto!'

Lestrade would have recognized that nasal twang anywhere

and sure enough, framed in the doorway stood Ashley Congleton, muscular in his Christianity and deep in his devotions.

'Chaplain! I'm afraid I've nothing for the collection plate this evening.'

'Ah, what doth it profit a man, et cetera, et cetera? Tom, be a good warder and bugger off, would you? I'd like a word with this sinner.'

'Very good, sir.' Tom scraped back his chair and jingled his way to the door. 'Cocoa at eleven, Mr Lestrade?'

'Delicious, Tom.' Lestrade nodded. 'Any threat of a Peek Frean?'

'I'll see what I can half-inch from the lads on D Wing.'

'You'll do me the honour of dining with me, of course?'

'Mighty big of you, Mr Lestrade.' Tom winked and he clashed and rattled his way out.

The Reverend Congleton was built like an outside lavatory. He wedged himself into the warder's chair, still warm from his penitential bottom. He surveyed the cards on the table. 'Ah, the devil's picture book,' he said, then suddenly leaned forward. 'Are you familiar with the rules of what our American cousins call Five Card Stud?'

Lestrade leaned forward too. 'Is the Chancellor of the Exchequer Lloyd George?'

'And while I'm dealing, Sholto, put that ace of diamonds back in the pack and tell me how the merry hell you came to be in this predicament.'

Lestrade smiled as he eased the offending card from his left cuff. 'Where did you serve your curacy, padre?' he asked.

'Sing Sing,' Congleton said. 'After Harrow and Brasenose it was a rest cure, I can tell you. Ready for a spot of confession, then?'

'All right,' Lestrade said, trying not to show his total despair at the lousy hand fate and the chaplain had dealt him. 'For days now you've been coming here, beating me hollow at every-game-known-to-man, and it's sneakily been leading up to this, hasn't it? Well, vicar, if you're sitting comfortably . . .'

Congleton eased himself back and smiled at the three kings in his hand.

'. . . then I'll begin.'

11

2

The fog lay over the city for two days that January. And traffic along the great artery that was the Thames slowed to a trickle, then a halt. On the roads it was different. To avoid anarchy and slaughter on the streets, the draymen had to deliver, no matter what. And cabmen, whose growlers stopped for nothing, sat hunched on their hansoms, like lines of ghosts, waiting for business.

But no one came. There was no milk for two mornings, for there was no milk train. The ladies of the Windmill Theatre, that never closed of course, sat in their sequins in the wings, filing their nails and talking about the weather.

Everywhere, there was an eerie stillness, like the muffling of a dream and solitary trams, empty save for their crews, clanked and clattered along their safe and silver lines.

Millicent Millichip, they'd remember later, got on at Marble Arch. She was a stout woman, jolly, middle-aged. She could have been the Madam of a brothel or a fishmonger – it wasn't possible to pinpoint her trade.

'Worst one I remember,' she said to the clippie as he took her fare. 'Can you change half a crown, ducks?'

'Seein' as 'ow you're the first body I've set me eyes on all day – other than the driver, o' course – it'll be my pleasure, Missus.'

'They ought to do something, you know,' she'd told him.

''Bout the pea-soupers? Too right. Still, it's quiet, you know. Bit like Christmas, really. You up for the sales, Missus?'

'In a manner of speaking. Do you know where we are?'

The conductor had pressed his nose against the window. 'Well, it's London,' he surmised. 'Beyond that I won't be drawn. Oh, 'ang about. There's Swan and Edgar. Must be Piccadilly Circus, or my nephew is a primate.'

'This is my stop.'

The conductor rang his bell and the tram lurched to a halt.

'There you are, then, Missus,' he called. 'Mind 'ow you go.'

Millicent Millichip thumped on to the pavement, treading on somebody as she went. Alighted was the wrong word for someone of her girth. Her own footsteps sounded like whispers on the pavement. Dim lights threw misty circles from lamp-posts and shop windows. It could only have been two o'clock, but it seemed like night. Damn Robert Peel. Damn the whole lot of them. She was on the telephone. Why couldn't they have called? Why did she have to come all this way up to town? And in this weather? With her asthma.

She was still tutting to herself, shuffling along the pavement, when she collided with a figure in the fog. She was aware of a thump in her chest, a sharp, sudden pain in her left side. She saw someone tip his hat, distinctly heard the word 'Sorry' and then she was on her knees on the pavement.

A man with a parchment-yellow face and sad eyes was crouching in front of her. She remembered the odd look on his face and for his face to be on the same level as hers, she guessed he must be a midget. She looked down at his hand. It was dangerously near to her left breast. A less worldly woman might have screamed. Then she noticed that his hand was dark red. He appeared to be bleeding. And the blood was warm now on her own hand. He was saying something. She knew that because she saw his moustache move. But she couldn't hear anything. Which was silly, because she knew she wasn't deaf. She blinked at him. His face was getting smaller, less distinct. This damn fog. This pea-souper. Millicent Millichip wondered again when they were going to do something about it all. Then she felt arms encircling hers and the parchment-yellow face was close again.

Then, Millicent Millichip did a very silly thing. Millicent Millichip died.

Detective-Sergeant Blevvins had come up the hard way. Everybody he worked with wished he hadn't and hoped he'd go the same way. There are some men born to be the flies in the ointment of life, the niggers in the piles of wood, the rub. Ned Blevvins was all of these and he sat that winter morning picking his teeth with Chief Inspector Froest's paper knife.

'So you're Lyall,' he grunted, reaching for his cocoa and scooping the skin from the top.

'Yes, Detective-Sergeant.' The young man stood stiffly before him, the bright January light reflected in his glasses.

'None of that round here, lad.' Blevvins frowned. 'This is Scotland Yard. You may address me as "sir" or . . . ' And he reached down to the trouser hem that encased the leg that was resting on the Chief Inspector's desk. He pulled it up slowly, closing his left eyelid, without taking his right eye off Lyall. ' . . . Should we be of the same affinity . . . '

Lyall stood even straighter. 'I'm a happily married man, sir,' he said.

Blevvins frowned and rolled his trouser leg down again. 'I was referring to the Lodge,' he growled. 'You stand no chance here unless you're affiliated.'

Lyall blinked disappointedly.

'You must be Tait.' The detective-sergeant threw down one sheaf of papers and picked up another.

'That is correct, sir.' The shorter man stood to attention.

'Says here you're a vegetarian,' Blevvins grunted. 'Think that's important, do you?'

'Sir?'

'Your star sign. Think it's important what sign you were born under?'

It was Tait's turn to blink. 'I . . . '

'I was born under the Ram, myself,' Blevvins volunteered.

The news came as no surprise to Tait and Lyall.

'All right; so, for the moment I'm stuck with you. You're on probation, of course. And I'll be watching. One gob in the wrong direction and I'll have you. You know what my view is on rookies?'

'No, sir,' the constables chorused.

'They belong in nesties, that's what they do.' Blevvins grinned his gappy smile. The constables did not. Blevvins stood up, scowling, looking both men in the eyes. He leaned on his knuckles on Froest's desk. 'You don't have to be crawling bastards to work here,' he told them, 'but it helps. And the first thing to do is to find Detective-Sergeant Edward Blevvins considerably funnier than George Robey and Dan Leno put together. Savvy?'

'Yessir.' And they did their best to summon up a muffled smirk.

'Right. Now, to cases. You'll need to know the higherarky here at the Yard. That means who's above you and who's below you. Except it's simple, really. 'Cos they're all above you and no bugger's below you. Got it?'

'Yessir.'

'Right. For day-to-day duties, tea-making, filing, tidying the office, you report to me. Any questions?'

Lyall looked at Tait. 'Who's above you, sir?'

The constables watched Blevvins turn a funny colour. 'Nobody,' he snarled. 'Nobody at all. Unless you're referring to those bastards with silver spoons in their mouths. Those blokes who got promotion 'cos their daddy's a nob or something. Yeah, we got a

14

few of them. The bloke on the door is "Buildings" Peabody on alternate days. The other one is Sergeant Douglas. Both tolerable coppers, but with the intellectual capacity of axolotls – that's those things that look like tadgers and float about in water at the zoo. Down the corridor you'll find the office of Chief Inspector Dew.'

'Is he the guv'nor, sir?'

'I told you, Tait.' Blevvins outstared his man. 'As far as you're concerned, I'm the guv'nor.'

'Yessir.'

'Chief Inspector Dew is something of a literary gent these days. He caught Crippen three years back and he's still dictating his memoirs. 'Course, it was my case really.'

'Was it, sir?' Tait and Lyall were all ears.

'What made you check the cellar in Hilldrop Crescent specifically?' Lyall asked.

'How did you know it was hyoscine?' Tait probed.

It was Blevvins's turn to blink. 'This office,' he said, 'when I'm not using it, is shared by the Head of the Serious Crimes Squad, Superintendent Froest.' And he spat expertly into the man's wastepaper basket.

'Don't you care for the Superintendent, sir?' Lyall pondered.

'My views on my colleagues are not a matter for public scrutiny, Constable. Aside from the fact that Froest is a fat, foreign bastard, I can take him or leave him.'

'What about Superintendent Lestrade, sir?' Tait leaned forward, eyes bright. 'I've been hearing about his exploits ever since I could shine my shoes.'

'Lestrade's off sick,' Blevvins told him. 'Not likely to be back. Old before his time. No, that bloke Conan Doyle had him pegged. What did he call him? "The worst of a bad bunch", that was it. He was wrong about the bunch, but right about Lestrade.'

'I'm not sure that's quite right, sir,' Lyall ventured. 'I think you'll find . . . '

'You couldn't find your way out of a paper bag without a ball of twine and a lot of help,' Blevvins snapped. 'And another thing . . . '

The door crashed back and a youngish man in a tweed coat and Homburg rushed in. 'Blevvins, why aren't you in the basement?'

'Er . . . ' The sergeant dithered.

'Tait and Lyall?'

'Yessir.'

'I'm Inspector Kane. Whatever this man has told you, forget it. Come on; Superintendent Lestrade is in the mortuary.'

And so he was. The world's second greatest detective was sitting on a green canvas chair, his parchment features lit by the dim and flaring lamps. There were introductions all round when the Yard men arrived.

'How's the leg, guv'nor?' Kane asked. He was a competent copper was John Kane, curly black hair, grim jaw, sense of humour to match. He was smart, resourceful and honest; and Sholto Lestrade wondered again what on earth he was doing at Scotland Yard.

'Floats like a butterfly since the cast came off yesterday,' Lestrade told him. 'But it stings like a b. I thought I'd pop into the West End, get my trousers refitted and would you believe it, first day off my crutches and a woman dies in my arms.'

'Had you broken your leg, sir?' Lyall asked, trying to make small talk and not look at the corpse on the slab.

'My, my,' Lestrade murmured, taking in his man. 'Got a good one here, then, John. Deducting with the best of 'em. Yes, young man. Twice in fact. The first time I fell off the *Titanic*, like you do. The second time I was knocked off a park bench by my daughter. There was no malice in it, of course.'

'The *Titanic* . . . ' Tait repeated.

'Yes, look, it's rather a long story.' Lestrade sighed. 'And there *are* more pressing matters – like Mrs Millichip here.'

'Ah.' Kane swept off his Homburg. 'The corpus delicti. I wondered when you'd introduce us. What's the score, guv'nor?'

Lestrade leaned back in the chair, clasping his hands across his waistcoat. 'Well, it's been rather a trying morning one way and another,' he said. 'If I tell you old Doc Hennessey is down with his usual . . . '

'Oh, God, no – it isn't?' Kane wailed, peering at the mortal remains.

Lestrade nodded and caught the mystified expressions on the faces of the rookies. 'The locum police surgeon here is Dr Benjamin Wentworth, known to all and sundry as the Doc Brief. You ask the man for all the detail he can give you and he's short to the point of dwarfism. "Cause of death?" I asked. "Stab," he said. "Where?" I cried – you see, it's catching. "Heart," was his lengthy rejoinder. "Weapon?" I queried. "Knife," he proliferated. Then he went to lunch.'

'What do we know then, guv?' Kane was looking at the dark, elliptical wound below the flabby left breast, the pale nipple lolling outwards. 'This looks neat.'

'Doesn't it?' Lestrade nodded. 'I've always maintained, if you want to kill somebody, do it in a pea-souper. I was close enough to see who did this, John, and I didn't see a bloody thing.'

'Where was this?'

'Oxford Street. Harry Bandicoot had insisted I go to his tailors – Proon and Ledbeater of St James's. The doctor had told me to exercise the leg, so I found myself strolling.'

'You were strolling along Oxford Street.' Kane couldn't help checking. 'Having been to St James's?'

'No, I was going to St James's. Twelve stone of Mrs Millichip in my lap rather scotched all that.'

'Were you going East or West?'

'Er . . . West.'

'Towards Marble Arch?'

'John!' Lestrade's voice rose for an instant. 'If I remember my history lessons at old Mr Poulson's Academy for the Sons of Nearly Respectable Gentlefolk, the Inquisition was in Spain, not Vine Street.'

'Sorry, guv.' Kane grinned. 'It's just that . . . well, what happened?'

'Damned if I know.' Lestrade shrugged. 'There weren't many people about, of course, on account of the fog. Odd how sounds change then, isn't it? I barely heard the tram she got off.'

'She got off a tram?'

'Oh, yes. The local beat man saw it all.'

'He did?'

Lestrade nodded, then shook his head. 'Not exactly. Name of Tressider. Brain like a differencing machine. He saw the old girl get off the Number Sixteen, hit the pavement at a trot and collide with her killer.'

'Can he describe him?'

'Ah.' Lestrade smiled. 'Constable Tressider is a sharp operator, Inspector. Commendations as long as a felt want, *but*, he only just passed the physical, eye-wise.'

'Yet he saw her get off the tram?'

'Felt, more accurately,' Lestrade said. 'She landed on his toe and caught him a hefty one around the penalty area with her handbag.'

'How did he react?'

'Well, naturally, he assumed she was a Suffragette and was about to frogmarch her off to the nick for a spot of the old tea and biscuits, when he realized that it was an accident and let her go on her merry way. At least, it was merry for a few seconds more. It can't have been longer than a minute before whoever it was stabbed her – clean thrust, single-edged knife – and she fell forward; on to me, in fact.'

'And no one came past you, in the fog, I mean?' Kane asked.

Lestrade shook his head. 'I don't think so. I tried to catch her as she went down and somebody shouted "Call the police". I hadn't time to tell him I was the police when Constable Tressider doubled back – at the double, of course. He called an ambulance, but what with the fog it was half an hour before they found us. She was dead as a doorstop by then, so we brought her here. Sorry it's your patch.'

'All in a day's work, guv.' Kane shrugged. 'Anything known?'

'The briefest of rummages in her handbag revealed her name and address. She was a publican – worth quite a few bob, I shouldn't wonder. Kept the Phlebotomist's Arms in Chiswick.' Lestrade ferreted in his inside pocket. 'Her card.'

Kane checked the address, nodding to himself. 'Nobody's done next of kin, I suppose?' he asked.

'Nobody's had time. With this fog, I doubt you'd make Chiswick by week Thursday.'

'You're right.' Kane sighed. 'Still, "a policeman's lot". Tait, Lyall, back on the wagon. We're going West.' Kane looked again at the dead woman, the full hips, the multiplicity of chins. 'Clean thrust,' he murmured. 'Single edge.'

'That's right, John.' Lestrade nodded. 'Any thoughts?'

'No, sir,' the Inspector admitted. 'Not at the moment. When do you expect to be back, sir? At the Yard, I mean?'

'When the fog lifts, John,' Lestrade said, smiling. 'When the fog lifts.'

The fog didn't lift that January. The evil, swirling blackness gave way to a wet winter, and biting winds. 'Too cold for snow' said the Meteorological Office, checking their dangling bits of seaweed. And they were right.

In Michigan, a surgeon implanted a dog's brain into a man, only to find the operation a failure – the man was barking mad. On February 5th, they found the bodies of Captain Robert Falcon Scott and his companions, stiff and cold in the Arctic wastes, only eleven miles from the nearest base camp. 'For God's sake, look after our people.' But the deaths of some brave men did not deter the women who were suffragettes and Mr Lloyd George's house at Walton Heath was blown sky-high by one of their bombs on the 19th.

And on the day that Lestrade returned to his old office, wedged between the latrine and the broom cupboard, they found, in

Sardinia, several tons of boxes, which Lord Nelson had amassed for his Trafalgar campaign. The archaeologists had to concede that, though the rum was still pretty good, the weevils were past their best.

By that day, John Kane had interviewed everybody he could find in connection with the murder of Millicent Millichip. It all looked quite impressive, fluttering in the draught on his office wall and it caught the eye of Superintendent Lestrade.

The guv'nor looked the picture of heath, all gamminess gone. And if he didn't exactly spring up the stairs two at a time in Mr Shaw's former Opera House, that perhaps had more to do with the fact that he had just stared his sixtieth birthday in the face and had turned away quickly from his own reflection. Sergeant 'Buildings' Peabody had saluted him at the front desk as usual and all was right with the world.

'Well, Inspector.' The guv'nor sat himself down in Kane's office uninvited. 'You'll have trained up your lads by now. Who's the teaboy?'

The words were no sooner from his lips than Constable Lyall was at his elbow, a handleless mug on a tray.

'Good.' Lestrade nodded. 'Good. And the biscuits . . . ?'

Tait was ahead of him, sliding a plate of Bath Olivers across Kane's desk. Lestrade chose one, felt it with his fingers, sniffed it, dunked it in his tea. 'Excellent,' he purred and caught the dripping biscuit just in time. 'It's good to be back, gentlemen. My Fanny bakes a cake like no one else in the world, but a good cup of Rosie and an Oliver of a morning is something a man could die for. Right, John. Fill me in on the Millichip case.'

Kane had it down to one of three men and he'd seen them all. There was George Potter, whose family had made artificial limbs since the Peninsular War. In fact, those three rather natty hinged jobs worn (though never simultaneously) by Lord Uxbridge after Waterloo were all lovingly hand-crafted by the Potters. And old One-leg was gratitude itself, able to ride, dance and get his leg over just like the old days. George still carried his Lordship's complimentary letter in his wallet. He had come to know Millicent Millichip when Albert Millichip was still alive. He had loved her then, but George was a gentleman and he'd admired her from afar. After Albert's demise, however, and a suitable period of mourning, he'd been round the Phlebotomist's Arms, Chiswick with a bunch of flowers and a proposal of marriage 'when the time was right'.

Millicent, still in her widow's weeds, had hesitated, however. Arthur Weston was not a gentleman. He was barely a man at all in the legal sense, but the strapping twenty-two-year-old had shoulders like drayhorses and a smile that reduced the resolve of Millicent Millichip to water. She wasn't proud of the fact that she had seduced the boy while Albert was languishing in the Infirmary, but he did take her mind off her impending bereavement. And she hadn't realized you could do such a thing on the tap room bar. Thank God it was well after closing time.

The third corner of this torrid triangle was Archie Emblin, landlord of the Dog How Are You in Craigie Street. John Kane's money was on this one. His greed was legendary throughout the Western suburbs. All Middlesex knew that if Albert Millichip hadn't died, Archie would have proposed marriage to him in order to gain control of the Phlebotomist's Arms, thereby doubling the size of his empire and his profits at a stroke. He had, however, proposed marriage to Millicent and only the day after Albert Millichip died.

'They all know about each other?' Lestrade asked Kane, clutching his teacup in both hands. They'd done nothing to lessen the draughts at the Yard while he'd been away.

'Oh, yes,' the Inspector told him. 'The lad Weston pulled pints at the Dog before he went to work for Mrs Millichip. Emblin's staff are very loyal to him, but a couple of his clients remembered harsh words between the lad and Archie. I distinctly got the impression that the boy wasn't fired for his work. It was something else. Something personal.'

'That something being that he was polishing Mrs Millichip's tankards?'

'In a manner of speaking, guv, yes.'

'Alibis?' Lestrade asked. 'For the day in question?'

'Wide open.' Kane shrugged. 'Archie Emblin was making a delivery in the City that day.'

'Where?'

'To the Inns of Court Regiment, Chancery Lane.'

'Did he normally do that?' Lestrade asked. 'Deliver beer, I mean?'

'No. But he was settling the accounts that day, apparently. After the Christmas knees-up.'

'And from Chiswick . . .'

Kane nodded. 'I'm ahead of you there, guv. He could have gone along Oxford Street, yes.'

'What about the others?'

'It was the lad Weston's day off. He says he didn't leave the house until mid-afternoon.'

'By which time, Millicent was dead,' Lestrade mused.

'Quite. Except there's no one to corroborate that story. The lad Weston's mum saw him in bed asleep at eight in the morning. When she got back home by three he'd gone. There's no telling when he left.'

'She didn't feel the bed or anything?' Lestrade asked, realizing the unlikelihood of the prospect as he said it.

'No, guv.' Kane shook his head. The old boy was rustier than he'd thought possible after his convalescence.

'Where did Weston go when he went out?'

'The dogs at Catford. Only they weren't running on account of the fog.'

'Too foggy for the doggies, hmm?' Lestrade was peering into the middle distance. 'So what did he do?'

'Visited another lady friend of his,' Kane said, consulting a piece of paper on the wall by his head. 'A Mrs Verricker of Laundry Lane. Husband's a merchant seaman.'

'Handy.' Lestrade nodded. 'She verifies this?'

'Oh, yes, but he didn't get there until half past seven in the evening. That gives him ample time to reach the West End, even in a pea-souper, do the business and go South again. Some of the trains were running again by then. We checked.'

'What about Potter?'

'Working in the machine shop on a special job – all day, he says.'

'He says?'

'On account of the fog no one else came in to work that day. Potter was on his own.'

'Where are these works?'

'Chiswick High Road, not a stone's throw from the Phlebotomist's Arms. And not a million miles from the nearest tram stop, either.'

'How would any of them have known that Millicent would catch a tram and at what time?' Lestrade wondered aloud.

'That we don't know,' Kane confessed. 'Because we don't know where she was going. It's the very devil, isn't it? Someone dies in an out-of-the-way place, somewhere they aren't supposed to be. No one's come forward on that score at all.'

'No luck with the murder weapon, I suppose?'

'Potter has access to sharp objects – a whole range of them in fact in his line of work. We've come up with nothing there at all though. No blood traces. Nothing.'

'And the others?'

'Mrs Weston has the usual kitchen implements – bread knife and so on. But not the right shape for what we're looking for. Same in the Emblin establishment – bread knife, letter opener, thingie for getting stones out of drayhorses' hoofs. Nothing that quite fits. No, we're looking for something like that chiv of yours.'

'Mine?' Lestrade blinked.

'Yes,' Kane said. 'You know, the secret one in that set of knuckles you carry. Can I have a shuftie?'

'Well, you could, John,' Lestrade said. 'Except I've lost it.'

'Oh?'

'Fanny, I expect. You know, I've been a widower for so long, I can't get used to a woman in the house again. Turn your back and she's washed your socks or darned your nightie or whatever. I think she's hidden my knuckles somewhere. For all she's a copper's daughter and a copper's wife, she's never really approved of that.'

'I see.'

'Well.' Lestrade sighed, finishing his tea. 'I wish you joy of this one, Inspector. Don't worry, something will break soon.'

'Yes.' Kane scowled, unconvinced by his guv'nor's optimism. 'I wouldn't mind, but Millicent Millichip wasn't the only fatality the day of the pea-souper.'

'Really?'

'Hit-and-run, Hyde Park Corner. Within what . . . an hour of the other death. Some bloke . . . er . . . Chief Inspector Froest's got it . . . Robert Peel, that's it. Minding his own business, crossing Park Lane, when, wumpf! Out, brief candle.'

'Driver didn't see him, I suppose.'

'But you know when you've hit somebody, guv. The callous bastard just drove off.'

'Witnesses?'

'Don't know,' Kane said. 'You'd have to ask the Chief Inspector.'

'Yes.' Lestrade chuckled. 'I was afraid you'd say that.' He got to his feet. 'Don't worry, I can find my own way out . . . I think.'

Edward Henry still winced a little every time he coughed. A mad cabman called Alfred Bowes had pumped a bullet into his chest the year before, convinced as he was that Henry, as Assistant Commissioner of Police, was withholding his vehicle licence out of pure malice. Edward Henry could be pretty good at pure malice, but he was innocent in Bowes's case. It was only the good offices and lightning reflexes of Sholto Lestrade that allowed

Edward Henry to stand where he did today, twirling his moustaches in front of his office mirror.

There was a thump and a rattle on the glass plate of the door behind him and Frank Froest burst in. The Head of the Serious Crimes Squad looked rather like one of the Navy's new Dreadnoughts. Only he and possibly Mrs Froest knew what his water displacement was in the bath of a Friday evening, but his broadsides were deadly.

'Assistant Commissioner.' Froest's Homburg was tucked formally in the crook of his arm.

'Lestrade's back.' Henry whirled from his mid-morning toilette and sat down.

'So I heard.' Froest did likewise, the *chaise longue* shuddering as his bulk hit it. 'As if he'd never been away.'

'Ah, but he has, Frank, he has. Two broken legs in the space of six months, it takes it out of a man.'

'I don't suppose it's impaired his judgement, sir.'

'Maybe not, maybe not.' Henry pursed his lips against his clasped fingertips. 'Even so, break him in gradually, I think. Is there anything . . . gentle . . . for him?'

Froest's face said it all. 'We aren't talking about Walter Dew here, sir,' he said. 'You can't palm a man like Lestrade off with dogs fouling footpaths.'

'There's no law against dogs fouling footpaths – is there?' The Assistant Commissioner thought he'd better check.

'No, sir, precisely, but Walter Dew doesn't know that. No, for Lestrade, murder is the only game in town, I'm afraid.'

'What about that hit-and-run?' Henry asked. 'Hyde Park Corner, wasn't it?'

'Yes,' Froest said warily. 'But that's traffic, sir. Department B2. Sholto's not going to . . .'

Henry thumped the desk. He didn't do that often and every time he did he remembered why. It hurt like buggery. Still, it had the desired effect even on crusty old coppers like Froest. 'Lestrade may have been a confidant of His Late Majesty,' the Assistant Commissioner said. 'He may have been the first copper to be given the Order of Merit . . .'

'First man, sir,' Froest corrected him. 'First man to get it.'

'Whatever.' Henry fluttered his fingers. 'He may have been instrumental in bringing to book every notorious criminal in Edwardian England. But this is 1913, Chief Inspector. The man can't go on resting on his laurels for ever. And prima donnas, if my Italian serves me aright, belong in the opera. The hit-and-run it is!'

'Hit-and-run?' Lestrade bellowed.

Froest's hands were already in the air, placating the man, calming him down. 'I know, Sholto, I know. Look.' He grabbed a packet of biscuits on the desk in front of him. 'Have a Peek Frean?'

Lestrade's scowl said it all. 'Every man has his price, Frank.' He nodded. 'But do you seriously believe that mine's a Peek Frean?'

Froest realized the hopelessness of his position and he sat down.

'Look, Sholto,' he said. 'You and I both know that you should be sitting this side of the desk and I should be over there. The point is that when Mr Henry set up the Serious Crimes Squad, well . . . you weren't here. You'd fallen off the *Titanic*, if you remember . . .'

'A thing like that does tend to stay with one,' Lestrade growled.

'Yes, of course. I can see that. Of course. It's just . . . well, that's how it goes in this business. You know that. The Assistant Commissioner just wants to ease you back in gradually, that's all.'

The silence was positively deafening.

'Of course,' Froest felt brave enough to continue, 'the Assistant Commissioner did mention a month or two with Paddy Quinn in Special Branch . . .'

'Hyde Park Corner, I think you said,' Lestrade muttered, snatching up his bowler. 'I'll get right on it.'

Hyde Park was one of the lungs of London. A little consumptive perhaps in that winter of 1913. The rain bucketed on to Lestrade's bowler brim and bounced off the tarmac. Overhead, the pigeons nestled together on the window ledges and a solitary growler clopped its way South. Every now and then, the harsh, jarring bray of a klaxon reminded the three coppers that the motor car was now king of the road.

'Here, then.' Lestrade's eagle eyes followed the curve of the grass.

Constable Tait stood up, his fingers soaking from their recent immersion in the tire tracks that curled like parallel snakes over the green. 'Definitely, sir.'

'All right.' Lestrade faced his rookies. 'Tell me what happened.'

'Er . . . hit-and-run, sir,' Lyall ventured, convinced now that the guv'nor had cracked more than a leg bone when he fell off the White Star Line's pride and joy.

'Yes, yes.' Lestrade sighed. 'Give me details, man. You've read the reports.'

'Yessir.' Lyall straightened. 'The victim was Mr Robert Peel . . .'

'Robert Peel?' Lestrade cut in. 'I thought that's what John Kane said. Are you both having me on?'

'As I live and breathe, guv,' Lyall assured him. 'Robert Peel, aged forty-four. Lived in Maida Vale.'

'I suppose somebody has to.' Lestrade nodded. 'Which way was he going?'

'Er . . .' Lyall stalled.

'Look at the grass, man,' the Superintendent hissed. 'What does the evidence tell you?'

'Umm . . . ?'

Lestrade flapped his hands in the air and all three of them crouched by the roadside. 'Here. Look. The car came off the road from over there, behind us, it ploughed over the grass along here, flattened that sign that told him explicitly to keep off it and hit Mr Peel here – see how the mud splays out? That was the point of impact. He must have been walking that way. South.'

'How do you know?' A voice made all three get up.

'Who are you?' the Yard men chorused.

'I'll ask the questions.' Lestrade thought it best to establish the fact. 'Who are you?'

'Allardyce.' The stranger shook his hand. 'Tom. Well, actually Bayard, but that's a cross I have to bear.'

'Mr Allardyce.' Lestrade nodded. 'Do you always barge your way into private conversations?'

'I'm sorry, Mr Lestrade.' He grinned. 'Couldn't help myself.'

Lestrade's eyes narrowed. 'I don't believe I've had the pleasure.'

Tait and Lyall could believe that. The guv'nor must be knocking a hundred.

'I'm sorry.' Allardyce beamed. 'You don't remember, do you? The case of the Warminster Thing. '09. I was a cub reporter on the *Gazette* in those days.'

'Of course.' Lestrade nodded. 'I never forget a face. You were first on the scene.'

'Eighth.'

'You were working with Inspector Parsons.'

'Ransome.'

'That's right.' The Superintendent smiled. 'It's all coming back to me now. You had the Shin Fane theory.'

'The Mafia.'

'Of course. Like I said, I never forget a face . . . Weren't you blond?'

'Slightly,' Allardyce confessed. 'I'd spent three years in Natal. It does that to you, the sun.'

25

'Yes.' Lestrade peered up into the rain. 'So I believe. What brings you here, Mr Allardyce?'

'Well, I'm a witness.'

'A witness?'

'Yes. I saw the whole thing. The hit-and-run, I mean.'

'Didn't you report it?'

'Yes. I gave all my particulars to a constable then and there . . . I mean then and here. To Constable Smith. I was a little surprised not to have a visit.'

'Did you notice which Division?' Lestrade asked. 'The badges on the collar?'

'Er . . . oh, Lord . . . F, I think.'

'Ah.' Lestrade sighed knowingly. 'Listen and learn, gentlemen.'

'No, I work for Constable these days.'

'Do you mean you're a police officer, sir?' Lyall asked.

'Good Lord, no.' Allardyce laughed, flicking his muffler off his moustache. 'Constable the publisher. I'm an editor.'

'I see.' Lestrade nodded.

'Ever read a novel, Mr Lestrade?' Allardyce quizzed him.

'I tried something by George Eliot once,' the Superintendent remembered.

'Couldn't put it down?' Allardyce enthused.

'Couldn't pick it up,' Lestrade confessed. 'Not after the first time. He ought to stick to whodunits.'

'Who?'

'George Eliot. So you saw the whole thing?'

'Well, yes. I take my morning saunter to Dame Vera . . .'

'Dame Vera?'

Allardyce became confidential. 'Dame Vera Krupskaya, lives round the corner. You know, the Byelorussian Krupskayas?'

Lestrade didn't, but years of bluffing intellectuals like Allardyce gave him an edge. 'Of course.'

'Well, I shouldn't be telling you this,' the editor admitted. 'But she's writing her memoirs. Did you know, for instance, that she had a thing with Tolstoy?'

'Is that like the Warminster Thing?' Lestrade asked.

Allardyce frowned at him. 'I shouldn't think so for a moment, no. *And* it's rumoured she was the mistress of King Ludwig of Bavaria.'

'Tsk, tsk.' Lestrade shook his head.

'Which is odd because I always thought that was Wagner.'

'So did I.' Lestrade nodded sagely. 'Now, about the hit-and-run.'

'Ah, yes. Well, this was last Thursday. I was on my way to Dame

Vera's when I heard this dreadful squeal of brakes and a thud. Rather like . . .'

'Yes?' Lestrade asked.

'Well, rather like a motor hitting a person, really. I spun round.' And the editor suited his actions to his word. 'I spun round.' And he caught Lestrade in the eye with his scarf. 'And there he was, lying in a heap on the grass. Just where you are, Constable.'

Tait instinctively shifted to one side.

'It was the fog, I suppose,' Lestrade said.

'Fog?' Allardyce frowned.

'The reason for the accident. The driver couldn't see in the fog.'

'Oh, no, Mr Lestrade.' Allardyce shook his head. 'I told your chappie. The constable who came rushing over moments later. I told him. That was no accident. The driver swerved off the road deliberately. He was *aiming* at the poor fellow. What I witnessed was a murder.'

3

That was the February that somebody blew up the house of Mr David Lloyd George at Walton Heath. Scotland Yard received a telephone call later the same day from 'someone with a female accent' as Sergeant Blevvins put it. Estate agents were heckled in the street – the cost of property, especially in Walton Heath, was going through the roof.

Sholto Lestrade was having a rest day when it happened, sitting in the armchair he had made his own, his Fanny dozing beside him on the *chaise longue*, the fire crackling in the grate.

'What do we know about the late Robert Peel?' Lestrade fixed a point in the middle distance, in his mind's eye the green baize wall at the Yard, where his case notes flapped in the breeze off the river.

'Who, dear?' he heard Fanny say.

'Robert Peel.'

'Wasn't he Home Secretary?' she asked under the veil she'd draped across her face. 'And didn't he found the Police Force of which you are the doyen?'

'Not him, heart,' the Superintendent hissed, expertly whisking the skin off his cocoa. 'The hit-and-run victim.'

'Ah,' she said. '*That* Robert Peel. Something in the City. Worked at Hoopers and Firebrands.'

'Married?'

'To his job.'

'Aren't we all.' Lestrade beamed. He was aware of Fanny lifting her veil out of the corner of his eye. 'So, a bachelor.'

'Confirmed?' Fanny asked.

'Don't think he had much time for church,' Lestrade surmised.

'I mean, was there anyone in his life? A woman?'

'Ah, yes.' Her husband stretched out his legs before the fire. 'A Miss Larbalestier.'

'That means crossbowman,' Fanny told him. Years of attending lectures at the Women's Institute had left their mark.

'Be that as it may,' Lestrade said. 'They had been engaged, on and off, for four years.'

'Do you think she was tired of waiting?'

'And drove her car at him?' Lestrade asked. 'No, dear.'

'You're right,' Fanny said. 'Rather a thin motive.'

'Oh, it's not the motive,' Lestrade told her. 'It's the technicalities.'

'What *are* you talking about, Sholto?'

'Well, Tom Allardyce said the driver made straight for him. A perfect hit. No woman could do that.' And he patiently waited the requisite number of seconds before the flying cushion hit him around the head.

'Where did you say you'd met Allardyce?' Clearly Fanny was still speaking to him.

'Warminster,' Lestrade said, dunking his Rich Osborne. 'In Wiltshire. Back in '09. You were still a slip of a thing and I was . . . a Superintendent. The Wiltshire Force had called us in. Something frightening the sheep.'

'What was it?'

'A Thing.'

'A Thing?'

'Ah.' He smiled. 'Not just any old Thing. Peculiar shapes were appearing in cornfields – circles, spiders' webs, mazes. Most odd.'

'Who was doing it?'

'We never found out. The local bobby was an Inspector Ransome, known to his lads as "Esther" – I didn't pursue that one too far for obvious reasons. He thought it was a local farmers' feud; what I understand they call in America a range war.'

'And was it?'

'Well, certainly, there were punch-ups at the Corn Market and some very unpleasant name-calling at the Harvest Supper, but I think the local paper blew it up out of proportion.'

'And what had Allardyce to do with it?'

'He worked on the local rag. The *Gazette and Remembrancer*, if I remember aright. He thought the Mafia was involved. Or was it Shin Fane?'

'The Irish? Why?'

Lestrade shrugged and his Osborne plummeted into his cocoa. 'Damned if I know. Other than trespass, I couldn't see what crime had been committed. For a day or two we considered charging "Esther" with wasting police time – his own as well as ours. No, come to think of it, it *was* the Ities Allardyce favoured – the Mafia.'

'And Allardyce just happened to witness the hit-and-run?' Fanny's veil puffed up and floated back on to her face, landing like linen. Her husband looked at her with the raised eyebrow that

29

had sent tremors into the hearts of men. 'Yes,' he said slowly. 'Why is that odd?'

She took the cloth from her face. 'Did I say it was odd?' she asked him.

'I've known you, woman and girl, for more years than I care to remember, Fanny Lestrade,' he told her. 'I know that tone.'

She laughed. 'I'm a copper's daughter and a copper's wife,' she said. 'I've got to know over the years when something doesn't smell right.'

'And Allardyce . . . ?'

'Doesn't smell right.' She nodded.

Lestrade stopped fishing for his Osborne, pap as it was by this time. 'You're a deeply, deeply suspicious woman, Mrs Lestrade,' he said.

'You've made me what I am today.' She beamed. 'How did Allardyce describe the driver?'

Lestrade gave up his inquiries in the bowels of his cocoa. 'Male,' he told her. 'Average height – but of course he was sitting down. Average build – but of course he was wedged in the front seat of a motor.'

'Goggles and helmet?' she asked.

'Yes.' He nodded.

'A serious driver, then?'

'The weather was awful, remember. A real pea-souper.'

'You're looking for a woman.' She sat up.

'Fanny . . .'

She held up her hands. 'I know, I know,' she said. 'A woman wouldn't have the skill. I don't suppose you'd like to repeat that to Mrs Pankhurst, would you? I've a sneaky feeling that whoever the lady was who spread Mr Lloyd George's house over a few adjacent fields had a *certain* amount of technical know-how.'

'So you're saying I should start with . . . ?'

'Miss Larbalestier,' she told him. 'The crossbowwoman.'

But Superintendent Lestrade did not start with the crossbow-woman. Instead, he made another of those insignificant little mistakes with which his career was littered and nearly caused an international incident of the first water. He sent Sergeant Ned Blevvins to talk to Dame Vera Krupskaya, just to confirm the fact that Tom Allardyce, of Constable and Company, really did pay her a visit on that foggy day in London town, in that year of the Lord 1913.

Lestrade was still waiting for Blevvins's report the next day when Constable Lyall, in the middle of an announcement, was swept aside by a huge man in a fur coat. He looked like a bear, but was actually a Russian steamroller.

'Count Vladimir Sonofavitch Varutchin,' he boomed. 'My card.'

'My chair.' Lestrade waved him to it. 'That will be all, Constable.' He nodded at Lyall.

'This is not a social call,' Varutchin said, his fur cap tickling the ceiling. 'I will be blunt to the point of dullness.'

Lestrade didn't doubt it for a moment.

'Yesterday, one of my countrywomen was assaulted by one of your Okhrana.'

'My . . . er . . . ?'

'Your policemen. His name was . . . ' The Russian fumbled in his fur pockets for a note. 'Edward Ivanovich Blevvin. Blevvin in my country means idiot.'

'What a coincidence.' Lestrade smiled. 'That's exactly what it means in mine. Can't I get you a cup of tea?'

'You have samovar?' the Russian asked.

'Er . . . only Darjeeling, I'm afraid.'

'As you see, I am Cultural Attaché . . .'

'Bless you.' Lestrade nodded.

'An official letter of complaint will be lodged this morning at your Number Ten Downing Street. His Imperial Majesty will be most displeased.'

'Count . . . er . . . Varutchin.' Lestrade leaned back in his chair. 'I'm afraid I don't understand what has happened.'

The Attaché dispensed with the formalities and scraped back Lestrade's other chair. 'Here I am quoting word for word what Krupskaya has told me,' he said. 'This Blevvin called yesterday at her home in Hyde Park. He said – and he spoke very loud – "Speaky Englishsky?" Dame Vera has lived in London for many years. Her English is vastly superior to that of this Blevvin. He asked her if an Englishman named Allardyce had been to see her.'

'He was working on my instructions,' Lestrade said. 'On a case.'

'This Blevvin is a case and a half,' the Attaché rumbled. 'In Russia he would be chained to a wheelbarrow in Siberia.'

What a good idea, Lestrade thought – perhaps a wheelbarrow in Furness?

'If Sergeant Blevvins offended Dame Vera . . .'

'If?' Varutchin bellowed. 'You speak to me of "ifs"? Do you doubt the word of his Imperial Majesty's Cultural Attaché?'

'No, I . . .'

'My card.' The Attaché hurled it down on Lestrade's desk.

31

'Thank you,' the Superintendent said. 'You've just given me one of those.'

'*Nyet*!' the Russian snapped. 'That was my calling card. *This*', and he tapped it imperiously, 'is my calling out card.'

'You mean . . . ?' Lestrade was confused.

'My seconds will call on you tomorrow.'

'Tsk, tsk,' Lestrade said. 'All this calling out. It won't do, Count. We have laws against duelling in this country.'

'You also have laws against women voting,' Varutchin commented acidly. 'Yet you allow them to blow up the houses of your politicians. At least our terrorists are Bolsheviks. And mostly male.'

'I am sorry if Sergeant Blevvins overstepped the mark . . .'

'He would not know a mark if it bit him on the leg,' the Attaché snarled. 'Are you refusing to face me?'

'In a duel, yes,' Lestrade said. 'But I can put you in jail for threatening a police officer, if you like.'

Varutchin was horrified. 'My God.' He crossed himself in that curious way that Russians do, from right to left. 'I thought *our* policemen were a little harsh. You would risk an international incident by arresting a member of the Russian Embassy?'

'Is Rasputin a peasant?' Lestrade asked, suddenly doubting that he was. Perhaps the *Graphic* had got it all wrong.

Varutchin was silent for a moment. 'You are sorry that this Blevvin went too far?'

'Truly.' Lestrade nodded.

'Madly?' Varutchin checked.

'Deeply,' Lestrade vouchsafed.

Varutchin stood up to his full Ukrainian height. 'Very well,' he said. 'But there will be rumblings in St Petersburg. Krupskaya is the aunt of Prince Dolgorouky, who has the ear of the Tsar.'

Lestrade nodded. No wonder the Duma's pleas to Nicholas II had fallen on deaf ears.

'I must still register my complaint with Downing Street,' the Count said.

'And I shall see to it that Sergeant Blevvins is demolished,' Lestrade promised.

'You have firing squad?' Varutchin asked.

'Er . . . not here,' Lestrade assured him.

'Knout?'

Lestrade was surprised to hear broad Yorkshire from a Russian. 'Nothing at all,' he confirmed.

Varutchin sighed. 'I have been here too long,' he said. 'It's time I went home to a civilized country.'

'All right, guv.' Blevvins had been on Lestrade's carpet before. In fact he was as at home there as the rather awful pattern. 'I may have raised my voice a little, but the old bat . . . the old lady was hard of hearing.'

'Did you lay a hand on her, Blevvins?'

The pug-nosed sergeant grimaced. 'Have a heart, guv,' he said. 'She's got to be knocking seventy. Last time she had a roll in the hay they were building the pyramids.'

'The Russian Attaché is talking to the Prime Minister as we speak,' the Superintendent said.

'That's nice.' Blevvins scowled.

'About you, Sergeant,' Lestrade snapped. 'I nearly took a bullet for you today.'

'What?'

'Never mind,' Lestrade said. 'It's one of those little things that goes with the territory, I suppose. What did you find out?'

'Nothing.' Blevvins shrugged. 'Allardyce was there all right. Like he said.'

'Time?'

'Two thirty. He left at three or quarter past. The old girl couldn't remember. She wouldn't remember her teeth unless they happened to be in a glass by her bed.'

'This was on the Thursday?' Lestrade checked.

'No, guv.' Blevvins blinked. 'The Tuesday.'

'Tuesday?' Lestrade blinked as well. They were a pair of blinkers.

Blevvins rummaged in his pocket for his notepad. 'Yeah.' He found it. 'Tuesday. Tuesday January 2nd.'

'January 2nd!' Lestrade shouted. 'Then he's got no alibi.'

'What?'

The Superintendent slid back his swivel and crossed to the wall where Messrs Parslow and Minch, Purveyors to the Met, had pinned their gratis calendar for 1913. 'January 13th was a Thursday. The day Robert Peel was killed. And the day Mrs Millichip went down. I know. I was there. Allardyce says he saw Peel die on his way to visit Dame Vera Krupswhatever. And she tells you she last saw him eleven days earlier. Is she sure about the date?'

'She seemed to be,' Blevvins said. 'Before I knocked over that fancy egg thing she had on her mantelpiece.'

'Egg?'

'Yeah. Flash, it was.'

'You mean, pearls and diamonds?' Lestrade had gone pale.

'Oh, yeah.' Blevvins grinned. 'Paste, guv. Believe me, I've been around. More paste in that than Shippams. She went a bit spare, shouting at me in Russian . . .'

'You . . . *didn't* hit her, did you, Blevvins?'

The Sergeant looked affronted. 'Well, really, Mr Lestrade, sir,' he said. 'Can you seriously believe I would misuse my constabulary powers to harm the head of an elderly – if deranged – member of the fair gender?'

'Well . . . ' Lestrade had had experience of this man before.

'No,' Blevvins assured him. 'For her own safety, I tied her up in the window-sash-cord, trod on her cat and left.'

Lestrade sighed. 'For a moment there', he said, 'I thought the Attaché's complaint might have some substance.'

'Nah,' Blevvins said. 'They've all got complaints, these Ruskies, most of 'em picked up in Greek Street from some gyppo. Shall I nail this Allardyce, then? He obviously did it.'

'No, thank you, Blevvins,' Lestrade said quickly. 'Not just yet awhile. I want to know more about the constable he reported the hit-and-run to.'

'Yeah, well.' Blevvins chuckled. 'F Division. Not much mileage there, I wouldn't 'ave thought in the solving-of-crime stakes.'

'Ah, but that's where I think you're wrong, Sergeant.' Lestrade returned to his desk.

'Oh?' Blevvins frowned. 'In what way?'

'Where did Mr Peel die, Blevvins?' Lestrade asked.

Blevvins gave his guv'nor an old-fashioned look. Those two broken legs must have taken their toll of the old bugger after all. 'Hyde Park Corner, guv,' he said.

'Precisely,' Lestrade said, swinging his feet up on the desk. 'And where is F Division's patch?'

'Er . . . oh, blimey,' Blevvins said. 'Paddington.'

Lestrade nodded. 'So, either our man was patrolling the beat the pretty way, or . . .'

'Or 'e done it!' Blevvins clicked his fingers.

'You know, Blevvins.' Lestrade sighed. 'We *might* make a detective of you yet.' He looked up at the ox-like shoulders, the bulldog jaw. 'There again, Winston Churchill might take Mrs Pankhurst out to the Palais.'

Alexandra Larbalestier was a Gibson girl, as radiant a creature as Lestrade could remember. Her chestnut hair was swept up over her broad forehead and her eyes were deep enough for a man to drown in. She sat in the drawing-room on that bright February morning with the sun gilding her lilies. Her brother Gerald was there too, a perfect pig of a man with short-cropped caroty hair and matching moustache.

'When did you last see Mr Peel, Miss Larbalestier?' Lestrade asked. He had not been offered tea and the great house in Chiswick was as cold as a Highlander's sporran.

'The day before he died,' she told him, staring resolutely ahead. Her fingers were tight on a handkerchief knotted in her left hand, but her voice was steady and her eyes were clear. 'We went to Brooklands.'

'Brooklands?'

'It's a racing track, Superintendent,' Gerald told him, somewhat short-temperedly. 'In Surrey.'

'Thank you, sir.' It was Lestrade's turn to stare resolutely ahead. 'You went to watch the races, Miss Larbalestier?'

'To watch Bobby race, yes.'

'Mr Peel was an automobilist?'

'Surely you knew that.' Larbalestier got up and poured himself another brandy. 'Honestly, I don't know how you police chappies get your jobs. It wouldn't do at Raleigh Harman.'

'Raleigh Harman?'

'Raleigh Harman, Superintendent,' the young man repeated with what little patience he could muster. 'Lombard Street. One of the foremost brokers in the City.'

'You work there?' Lestrade checked.

Larbalestier winced at the mere mention of the word. 'Let's just say that Sierra Leone groundnuts are us, shall we?' And he patted the side of his nose.

'So you knew Mr Peel through the City?' Lestrade asked.

'Of course,' Larbalestier returned to his seat on the sofa, taking his sister's hands in one of his, the other not relinquishing the brandy. 'I introduced Bobby to Alex, didn't I, darling?'

She nodded. 'It was the day Anglo-Saxon Petroleum hit oil in Borneo.'

'Lord, yes,' Larbalestier remembered. 'Old Brookie made a killing that day. The old wires were red hot. Eight hundred and sixty feet down and the entire Brooke family covered in clover.'

'Mr Peel worked for Hoopers and Firebrands?' Lestrade checked.

'Yes.' Larbalestier sneered. 'Not a bad little House, actually, although he was capable of better things. Allie was trying to woo him across – own office, company motor, salary in triple figures, you know the sort of thing.'

'Allie?'

'Alaric Bligh, the M.D. And please, Lestrade,' Larbalestier held

up his hand, 'Spare us the "captain of the ship" joke. I rather
suspect old Allie's heard it before. I know I have.'

'Can you think of anyone who would like to see your ex-fiancé
dead, Miss Larbalestier?' Lestrade thought it time to ask.

Brother and sister exchanged glances. 'What are you saying,
Lestrade?' Gerald asked.

'I am saying that I have reason to believe Robert Peel was
murdered, Mr Larbalestier.'

Alex breathed in sharply. 'Oh, God.'

Gerald stood up suddenly. 'Why weren't we told before?' he
asked.

'You are being told, sir,' Lestrade said. 'Now. Will you answer
the question, please, Miss Larbalestier?'

'I . . . I don't know. He was charming. Utterly charming.'

'Now, Alex . . .' Gerald raised a finger.

'He was, Gerry.' She rounded on him. 'And I won't have you
saying otherwise.'

'Oh, in a social sense, of course. Good Lord, I even lent him my
gaberdine on the day he . . . passed over. But in business . . . Well,
frankly, my dear, he didn't give a damn.'

'You mean . . . ?'

Gerald took Lestrade's arm and escorted him across the room.
They stood by the window where the morning sun filtered
through the shrubbery. 'Ruthless was his middle name,' he said.

'Oh?'

'I could give you a list as long as my arm of brokers who could
cheerfully have wrapped an automobile around Bobby's head.
His personal charm made him all the more lethal.'

'Gerald, stop that at once!' Alex had joined the men at the
window. 'How dare you say these things now that dear Bobby's
not here to defend himself.'

'I'd start with old Griffin,' Larbalestier said, ignoring her. 'You'll
find him at the Shop.'

'The Shop? You mean he's in the Artillery?'

'No, no.' Larbalestier tutted. 'He's in charge of South American
Guano at Raleigh Harman. Lombard Street. You can't miss it. I'd
take you myself, but we're still in mourning, of course. Aren't we,
Alex?'

But the swish of her skirt told them both that she had gone and
had no intention of answering his question.

In those days, all roads led to Lombard Street. Those crafty little
Northern Italians who had come across in the twelfth century had

set up their little stalls on the edge of the City and had cornered the market. The Fuggers were out and the Lombards were in. And long before they made ice-cream, they made money.

Lestrade took Tait and Lyall with him on this one. Blevvins was grounded. If Lestrade had had his way, he'd have grounded him into the carpet, but he'd decided to bide his time. The three of them strolled along the shady side of Lombard Street, where walk clerks in bowler hats scurried like rats in a maze and silk-hatted gentlemen came and went in landaus and Victorias. Now and then, a Napier would snarl and belch as its chauffeur nudged it through the dense mass of money-makers. They passed the great Houses – Lloyds, where the black horse reared; Roberts and Lubbock, Gresham's with its golden grasshopper; the Credit Lyonnais and on to Raleigh Harman, gaudier and loftier than the rest.

They were shown to the lift and up to the eighth floor by an ingratiating young man with a nervous tic. Both Tait and Lyall had already returned his winks before they realized he wasn't really trying to be friendly. Lestrade, who had seen more afflictions than his rookies, ignored it. It was possible of course that the man was a mason, but Lestrade would need more proof than a wink before he'd respond to that one. A prominent nipple might do it.

The Otis elevator juddered to a halt and the Yard men spilled out. A door opposite them had 'Consoles' etched into the glass. Lestrade wondered what did. The first part of the sign must have fallen off. At the high desk inside, an ancient walk clerk who seemed to be having difficulty meeting the requirements of his job, tottered about between ledgers, still balancing the books after all these years.

'Superintendent Lestrade', said Lestrade, 'to see Mr Worsthorne Griffin.'

The ancient accountant looked over his pince-nez. He took out his watch. 'Oh, dear, it is a *little* early for Mr Griffin,' he mumbled.

'It's half past three,' Lestrade said. 'Is Mr Griffin still at lunch?'

'No, no. He attends service at St Mary Woolnoth each afternoon,' the clerk explained. 'I haven't heard him come back. But then, I haven't heard him go out either, come to think of it.' He glanced at the clock on the wall. It said twenty to eight. The ancient clerk saw the policemen's faces. 'Oh, that's the time in Buenos Aires,' he said. 'We deal with South American Guano here and similar conglomerates.'

'Could you check whether Mr Griffin is in?' Lestrade asked. 'Otherwise we will go to St Mary Woolnoth.'

'Of course.' The clerk bowed and staggered into the bowels of his office. Above the clack of a solitary Remington, they heard the knock at the door. They heard the door open. They heard the clerk's voice mumble in a low monotone. Then they heard a scream. Simultaneously, the Yard men dashed forward, Tait and Lyall leaping the counter in the manner of the Yard gym, Lestrade lifting the hatch and walking through. They batted aside the ancient clerk and pushed their way into the office of Worsthorne Griffin. The broker of that name sat in his chair, his head thrown back, his fists clenched.

'Tait,' Lestrade snapped to jolt the rookies out of their momentary freeze. 'The door. Mr . . . er . . . ?'

'It's Mr Griffin . . .' the old man rambled.

'Well.' Lestrade wondered at the confusion that coincidence must have caused over the years. 'Perhaps you'd like to accompany my constable to the outer office.'

'But . . . ?'

'Now, sir, please,' Lestrade insisted, jerking his head in the direction of the door for Lyall's benefit.

'Come along now, sir,' the constable said. 'There are just a few questions.'

And Tait heard the door click again behind them. 'The windows,' Lestrade said. The constable mechanically checked them.

'Locked, sir.' His face turned purple slowly. 'Or rusted. Anyhow, I can't shift them.'

Lestrade checked the dead man. He had been upwards of seventy years old, with the enormous Dundrearies fashionable in a bygone age. His mouth gaped open, like some hideous gargoyle pointing the wrong way and his sunken, sightless eyes stared at the ceiling. The Superintendent slipped a hand under the man's frock coat, feeling for his heart. Nothing. He lifted the clenched right hand. Still warm. He handled the cadaverous wrist and as his fingers closed around it, there was no pulse.

'Heart, sir?' Lyall stood facing the desk.

'That would be my guess, yes.' Lestrade looked at the desk, at the piles of paperwork. 'Perhaps the bottom's fallen out of guano,' he said, 'whatever that is. Hello, what's this?'

It was the most unusual calling card Lestrade had seen, lying near the dead man's left hand. It was scarlet and on the upper side was a devil's face with wickedly glinting eyes, spiral horns and a leering, lolling tongue. On the back, in pencil, was the single number 14. Or was that a double number?

'See if they've got a telephone out there, Lyall,' the Superintendent said. 'And call an ambulance. You'd better get on to the

38

City Force. They'll be furious that we beat them to it, of course, but that's the price you pay for being inferior. Hop to it, man.'

Lyall did and while he was gone, Lestrade draped his handkerchief over the dead man's face and ushered in the ancient clerk. Quite a crowd had gathered in the outer office and there was even the flash of a camera.

'Tait,' Lestrade roared. 'Get rid of these people. Who's that idiot with the camera?'

'*Money Monthly*,' the photographer introduced himself. 'My card.' And he pushed it through the jostling throng at the door. 'I happened to be passing. Good front-page stuff, this; Old Griffin stiff as a Clearing House.'

Lestrade whisked the confused old clerk inside and closed the door on the others. 'Tait, I want that outer office cleared, now. Confiscate that film and if he complains, trip over and make sure his camera gets in the way as you do. I want no publicity on this until we're good and ready.'

'Right you are, guv.' Tait snapped to it.

'Mr Griffin, I realize this has been a shock . . .' Lestrade said. The old clerk looked at him in a rather quizzical way.

'I'm afraid he's dead, Superintendent,' he said. 'He can't hear you now.'

'I was talking to you,' said Lestrade, returning the old boy's look.

'My name is Cuthbertson,' the ancient accountant said.

'Then why . . . ? Never mind. Sit down, Mr Cuthbertson.' And he waited until the old boy had. 'I expect Constable Tait will have asked you some questions.'

'Yes.' Cuthbertson's pale eyes kept glancing at the corpse to his right. 'Yes, he did. It's terrible. Just terrible.'

'Well, he's young,' Lestrade apologized. 'He'll get better.'

'No, I mean Mr Griffin. Dying like that.'

'Indeed. How old was he?'

'Eighty-one. No. I tell a lie. Seventy-nine. Wait . . . no, I'm wrong . . .'

It was encouraging that the old boy was so good with figures.

'How long had you known him?'

'I came to work here at Raleigh Harman in 1863. It was His Late Majesty's wedding day. I remember because old Mr Raleigh gave us the day off.'

'Touching. And Mr Griffin was here then?'

'Oh, yes. He and I were of an age. He was the first person I met in the lobby. Of course, we had no lifts in those days. And quill pens. We still had quill pens. And gas lighting, of course, none of these new-fangled . . .'

'Yes, quite. So you knew Mr Griffin well?'

'Very well,' Cuthbertson said. 'Why, only the other day, he said to me, "You may call me Mr Griffin, Cuthbertson. After all, we have known each other for fifty years." '

Lestrade was confused. 'What did you call him before?' he asked.

' "Sir",' was Cuthbertson's reply. It made a sort of sense in the world of Lombard Street.

'Tell me, Mr Cuthbertson, did Mr Griffin attend church every day?'

'Every day since the accident, sir, yes.'

'The accident?'

'Since his only son died. That would be five years ago now.'

'I see. And his son worked here with him?'

'No. He was a barrister. At Lincoln's Inn.'

'And you say you didn't see Mr Griffin go out today, to church, I mean?'

'No, sir. But he has his own back passage.'

Lestrade didn't doubt it.

'It runs into Yard Pound and directly to the church.'

'Through that door?'

'Yes.'

Lestrade had assumed the door in the corner was a cupboard. He crossed the room and tried it. It wouldn't give.

'Where is the key?'

'In Mr Griffin's pocket, sir,' Cuthbertson said. 'He always carried it with him.'

'Right or left?' Lestrade hovered at the dead man's shoulder.

'Right.'

Lestrade rummaged in the aforementioned pocket. It did seem a *little* much to do this, but it was one of those little indignities the dead must face. Old Worsthorne Griffin was beyond minding now. Lestrade found the cold metal and gingerly levered it out, careful not to obliterate too many prints. He placed it down on the desk.

'Tell me,' he said, 'what is this?' And he showed Cuthbertson the red card.

'It appears to be a calling card, sir.' Clearly fifty years at Raleigh Harman had not dimmed the old boy's faculties one iota.

'Have you seen it before?'

'No, sir. But it may have come in this morning's post. Or this afternoon's.'

'Where are the letters?' Lestrade asked.

'Here.' Cuthbertson did his best not to look at the white knuckles inches from the envelopes. 'Mr Griffin always placed his letters pending on his left. In the "out" tray.'

Lestrade picked up the envelopes carefully, handling them at the corners. One contained a standard letter of credit transfer from the Birkbeck Bank. The other was empty. Its address was typewritten, on an Oliver if he was any judge, and it bore a postmark of the City.

'Posted this morning,' he said. 'Ten a.m. Is this all today's post?'

'Yes, sir.'

'Does it come to you first?'

'It passes through my hands, sir,' Cuthbertson told him. 'But I never opened Mr Griffin's letters. I merely brought them through.'

'And what time did you bring these through?'

'At twelve thirty, sir. As usual.'

'Mr Griffin was here then?'

'Oh, yes.'

'Did he open the letters?'

'No. He just thanked me and carried on with his liabilities.'

'And that was the last you saw of him?'

'Alive, sir,' Cuthbertson said. 'Yes, it was.'

The door crashed back and a large, grey-haired man burst into the room. 'I've just heard that . . . oh, my God!'

Cuthbertson, who had that moment sat down, leapt to his feet.

'Who the devil are you?' the newcomer bellowed.

'Cuthbertson, sir. South American Guano.'

'Not you, Cuthbertson.' The whirlwind tutted. 'You.'

'Superintendent Lestrade,' said Lestrade. 'Scotland Yard.'

'My God!' He whisked the cloth away from the dead man's face and just as quickly whisked it back. 'My God!'

He spun to Cuthbertson. Then to Lestrade. 'Still,' he said, after a moment's thought. 'He'd had a good innings. Time for him to go back to the pavilion, I think.'

'Are you a cricketing man, Mr . . . er . . . ?'

'Bligh. Alaric Bligh. I am Managing Director of Raleigh Harman. In fact, it would not be straining a metaphor too far to say that I *am* Raleigh Harman. What has happened here, Superintendent?'

The faces had filled the open doorway.

'Could we . . . ?' Lestrade wondered.

'Gentlemen.' Bligh whirled towards them. 'A great broker is dead. You will pay your respects at the proper time, but . . . it is already nearly midnight in Tokyo and early morning in New

York. Do you think they're standing gawping on Wall Street? To work! Cuthbertson.' Bligh took the old man by his frail shoulders. 'If the Superintendent has finished with you?' Lestrade nodded. 'Then, take the rest of the week off.'

'But, sir . . .'

'No buts, Cuthbertson. This day has been long coming, but we none of us knew when. Give my best to Mrs Cuthbertson.' And the Managing Director saw out the ancient clerk.

'Devil of a thing,' muttered Bligh, turning back to the dead man. 'Heart, I suppose?'

'I'd say so, sir. We'll have to wait for the post-mortem.'

'Post-mortem?'

'The examination, sir. It means "after death", I believe, in the original Greek.'

'I know what it means, Lestrade,' Bligh said acidly. 'I merely wondered why it is necessary.'

'All cases of suspicious death, sir. It's routine.'

'Suspicious? Good God, Lestrade. Old Griffin was nearly eighty. Most other brokers of that age have long since gone to that great Brokers' Yard in the sky.'

'Perhaps so, sir. It's just . . . this I find odd.' And he held up the devil's card.

'What is it?'

'I don't know,' Lestrade said. 'No, don't touch it, sir, please.'

'Ah, yes, fingerprints, of course. Looks like a calling card.'

'The devil's calling card.' Lestrade nodded.

'No name, I suppose?'

'None.' Lestrade shook his head. 'Only the number "14". Does that mean anything, in monetary circles, I mean?'

'Well.' Bligh stroked his square chin. 'It invariably appears between thirteen and fifteen in monetary circles, but I don't suppose that helps you very much.' Bligh had supposed correctly. 'But what's it got to do with poor old Griffin?'

'I don't know,' Lestrade admitted. 'But I believe it arrived in this afternoon's post. And I also believe that whoever sent it knew the effect it would have on the old man.'

'Effect?'

'Yes.' Lestrade nodded. 'You see, it stopped his heart. Someone has made a killing, as I believe you say in the City.'

4

Alaric Bligh was one of those annoying people who have the knack of holding the receiver of a telephone in the crook of their neck, thus leaving his hands free. His hands were flicking through pages of bankrupt stock while he listened to a jobber on the other end of the line and now and then fired off a directive or two.

'Hm. Hm. Yes. No. Buy. Buy. Thirty-eight and fourpence? Some dividend! Sell. Right. Ha! Ludicrous. Tell him he's got 'til the end of the week. Buy. Buy. Bye bye.' And he put down the receiver. 'Now.' He frowned again at the Superintendent. 'Where were we?'

'Old Mr Griffin.'

'Ah, yes, yes. You're sure you won't take a double brandy? Does wonders for the complexion.'

'Thank you, no,' Lestrade declined. 'Mr Cuthbertson said something about an accident involving his son.'

'Accident?' Bligh frowned. 'Ah, that's just the old man's loyalty. No, George Griffin topped himself, I'm afraid. All very tragic.'

'Suicide?'

'The same.' Bligh rang a little bell before him. 'Oh, must be five years ago now.'

'What happened?'

'It was summer. Caused quite a splash at the time. He threw himself into the Thames at Battersea. The papers were full of it.'

'Five years ago,' Lestrade pondered. 'If my memory serves, I had my hands full with the Olympic Games that season. There wasn't time for much else.'

'Quite. Quite. Well, George was a rather melancholy chap. Given to visiting gyppoes at fairgrounds and taking them seriously. One of them told him his law practice wouldn't prosper. Alarmed, he visited another – sort of second opinion, I suppose. She told him he'd meet a watery end. And lo, he did.'

'Bit pat, that, wasn't it?'

'Ah, the power of suggestion, Mr Lestrade. Try it yourself. Fight your way on to the floor of the Exchange, if you can stand the bustle and the noise, and whisper in a jobber's ear that you've heard American Cotton's slipping. When he asks you how you know, tell him Woodrow Wilson's just been arrested in New York in a corset and lady's bloomers. The jobber will turn pale, start an avalanche and the international cotton market will collapse overnight. Oh, and as an added bonus, Congress will have impeached Woodrow Wilson by close of business.'

'The power of suggestion.'

'Exactly. Frightening, isn't it? No, between you and me, I was never particularly struck by George Griffin. He had no head for business at all. Thought a bull was something you kept to service the cows. As a lawyer he wasn't much better. Anyway, the upshot was that his death sent old Griffin off his rocker. He got religion in a fairly meaningful way and seemed to spend his every waking hour, when not here at the Shop, genuflecting in some tomb of a church. He blamed himself, I think, for George's death.'

'Is there a Mrs Griffin?'

'Consort of Worsthorne or consort of George?'

'Either.'

'Neither. George was too forlorn to attract a filly. Had no powers of conversation whatsoever. As for his mother, she long ago shuffled off this mortal coil. Died of embarrassment over George's abject career, I shouldn't wonder. Look here, Lestrade, are you suggesting in all this that old Griffin was murdered? Am I understanding you?'

'You are, sir,' the Superintendent said. 'I shall, of course, need to talk to your staff.'

Bligh sighed. 'Very well, but discretion, Mr Lestrade, please. Next to being caught in a corset and bloomers, having a fishy corpse in Guano comes precious close in the lack of confidence stakes. It does nothing for Raleigh Harman's reputation at all.'

Chief Inspector Walter Dew had tried not to let fame go to his head. But what can you do when you're the man who caught Crippen? That was three years ago and ever since then, he'd spent every moment when not at the Yard working on his memoirs. And here he was, three years later, on chapter four.

'Guv?' Old habits died hard in Dew. His hair had grown nearly white in the service of law and order and he was his own man now – as much as anyone ever really is their own man in the corridors of crime. But he had been a rookie on the beat when Sholto Lestrade had met him first, in the charnel house of Whitechapel in the year of the Ripper, in the Autumn of Terror. Old habits died hard and he found himself on his feet, back like a ramrod, in the presence of his old guv'nor.

'Walter.' Lestrade shook the man's hand. 'It's been a while.'

'How's the leg, guv?' Dew asked.

'Oh, coming along,' Lestrade said. 'I'm a bit ropey on the stairs but other than that . . . How's Mrs Dew? And all the little Dews?'

'Very well, sir, thank you. And Mrs Lestrade?'

'Fanny's fine, Walter. Emma's gone to Finishing School this summer. I don't know where the years have gone.'

'Cuppa tea, guv?' Dew asked.

Lestrade smiled. Walter Dew was an average copper, but his tea was the stuff of legend. The Superintendent threw himself into the wicker chair in Dew's office. 'I thought you'd never offer,' he said. 'Got a Bath Oliver?'

Dew rummaged in his drawer. 'Macvities only, I'm afraid.'

'Hey-ho.' Lestrade sighed. 'There are just some disappointments we have to live with. Nineteen O eight.'

Dew paused before he lit the gas. 'Good year,' he remembered aloud. 'We were tied up with the Olympics. The White City.'

'What happened in July?'

Dew looked blank. To be fair, he'd had lots of experience.

'The river,' Lestrade prompted him.

'Ah, yes. I was seconded to the Bluebottles.'

'Any suicides?'

Dew screwed up his face trying to remember. 'No, the River Police were a cheery bunch, if my memory serves.'

'Not the Bluebottles, Walter.' Lestrade sighed. 'Joseph public.'

'Oh, right you are, guv.' Dew grinned sheepishly. 'Yes. There were a few. Well, it was the heat, probably.'

'One name of Griffin.' Lestrade narrowed the search down for Dew in that vast, echoing head of his.

The Chief Inspector gave up and turned to the salvation of the rows of shoe-boxes, indexed neatly on the cupboard to one side. 'Griffin, you say?'

'George,' Lestrade confirmed. 'I don't have an address.'

'Gershwin,' Dew muttered, flicking through the files, 'Gerulaitis – oh, yes, that business in Greek Street. Gopping – the Case of the Ugly Girl. Ah, here we are, Griffin, George. Address in Maida Vale. Chambers at Lincoln's Inn. He was a barrister, guv.'

Lestrade's eyebrow rose by the regulation amount concomitant with exasperation with one's inferiors.

'He was found floating on July 9th, a little below Battersea. We estimated he went in at Lambeth.'

'Note?'

'Nothing. A few bob on him when he was found. Oh, yes, that was peculiar.'

'What was?'

'Well, a woman saw it happen. Or rather heard it.'

The whistling kettle told the detectives that tea was at hand. Dew did the honours.

'Heard it?' Lestrade cleared a few pages of Dew's manuscript to make room for the forthcoming cup.

'Yes. She was on her way home along the Embankment on the night of July 8th and she saw what she took to be a man standing on the parapet. He was partly screened by a plane tree, but he might have seen her. He shouted something and disappeared.'

'She heard a splash?'

'Yes. But she didn't actually see him go in. I've got it written down here.' He adjusted his glasses to read the small print. ' "Assumed victim was George Griffin. Short walk from Lincoln's Inn. Balance of mind disturbed." '

'Quite. What did he shout?'

'Er . . . Mrs Millichip wasn't quite sure. It sounded like Nill Aspairer. What's that? French?'

'What did you say?'

Dew turned a shade puce. 'Well, it's probably my accent, guv. I've got it written down here . . .'

'No, no. The name. The name of the witness.'

'Millichip.' Dew leaned over and poured the scalding water carefully over his hand. 'Mrs Millicent. Ow, that smarts.'

'Big woman? Bombazine armour?'

'Blimey, guv.' Dew began to wrap his knuckles with his handkerchief. 'We're talking about five years ago. I've interviewed a lot of women in that time.'

'Yes, yes,' Lestrade agreed. 'A lot of water under the bridge, of course. But think, man. This is important.'

'Well.' Dew sat down. 'She was quite large, I seem to remember. That's right. You remember old Malleson, Sergeant, A Division? We called him Vickers, because his stutter sounded like a machine-gun.'

'Yes.'

'He said – and I won't do the impression, because I don't suppose you've got the time – she must be what the Germans were building over at Kiel. The most heavily armoured things afloat.'

'You haven't got an address for Mrs Millichip?'

'Er . . .' Dew consulted his cards again. 'No, guv. Sorry. Oh, wait a minute. She ran a pub.'

'How do you know?'

'Well, old Vickers – he didn't care, did he? For a bloke with a speech impediment, I mean. He said to her – it's all coming back to me now, he said, "W-w-well, Mrs Mmmm . . ." never did get her name out. He said, "I bet you get those huge b-b-b . . . arms pulling p-p-pints." And she said "Yes." So, yes, she kept a pub. Or at least worked in one. Rosie Lee, guv.' He passed over the cup that cheers. 'What's all this about, by the way?'

'About?' Lestrade was already on his feet. 'It's about a circle, Walter, a circle of death that's tightening all the time. Like the spring of a watch that's overwound. And something's got to give. I'll have to pass on the tea, I'm afraid. By the way, is Vickers still on the Force?'

'He was in Lost Property, Railway Police when I heard last, guv. Vine Street.'

'Thank you, Walter,' Lestrade called from the doorway. 'A mine of information as usual. Give my love to Mrs Dew.'

'I'll do that, guv'nor.' Dew beamed.

On the day that Lestrade had plummeted over the rail of the White Star's *Titanic* in Southampton Water – like you do – they had installed the new cafeteria system at the Yard. Like all awful things, it was an American idea and did away with waitresses, in those days the only women allowed on the Yard premises. The Women's Political and Social Union had of course taken umbrage and threatened to march on the Headquarters of the Metropolitan Police.

Lestrade found himself there now, elbow to elbow with Inspector John Kane and some shifty-looking bloke from the Fraud Squad.

'May I recommend the Cottage Pie, sir?' the reptilian creature behind the counter wondered. Since Lestrade had caught a glimpse of the man moments earlier with half his arm up his nose, he doubted it and settled for the ham sandwiches. John Kane had not had that experience and was rash enough not only to go for the Cottage Pie, but the Spotted Dick as well. He washed it all down with a particularly entrancing Darjeeling.

'Eating with the riff-raff today, guv?' Kane smiled, reaching for the salt.

'I owe it to you boys to spend some time with you now and again,' Lestrade said, reaching for the Colman's. 'Produces a sense of well-being. Besides, I want to know how the Millichip case is progressing.'

'Shelved, guv.'

'Shelved?' Lestrade frowned.

Kane checked that the Yard's cafeteria walls did not, as rumour ran, have ears. 'Something pretty big and hush-hush is blowing up upstairs, sir,' he said solemnly. 'I can't say too much, of course, but it's foreign and it's fraudulent.'

'The fourth floor?' Lestrade probed.

'Not a million miles from there.' Kane nodded. Lestrade took in his man as the mustard seared his mouth. John Kane was one of the new school, clean-shaven, clean-cut, clean-whistled. Such men could run rings around the coppers of yesteryear, like Walter Dew. The question was, could they run rings around Lestrade? 'This is Inspector Dimsdale, Fraud Squad.'

'Inspector.' Lestrade reached across the artificial flowers and shook the man's hand.

'Chief Superintendent.' Dimsdale had the air of a chartered surveyor.

'So there's no progress on Mrs Millichip, then?'

'None.' Kane shrugged. 'I don't honestly know who it's been passed to now, but my money was always on Potter.'

'One of the suitors?'

'Yes. I had my lads give his gaff the once over. Nothing there, of course; clean as a whistle. Still, it's almost childishly easy to lose a chiv, isn't it? Did yours ever turn up, by the way?'

'My knife? No, it hasn't. Fanny swears she didn't take it to the cleaners, but her man Madison isn't exactly Mr Memory, so it could be anywhere. I feel quite naked without it. So, Inspector, "something big and foreign", eh, to paraphrase my old oppo. Can you shed any light?'

'Mr Lestrade.' Dimsdale took off his glasses to polish them. 'You know that we in the Serious Fraud Office are *most* discreet in discussing our cases. We have a reputation second to none in that respect. Why, the entire integrity of our operations depends on the need for absolute secrecy. What do you want to know?'

'Well.' Lestrade shrugged, merely filling in half an hour over lunch, having drawn a blank on the death of Millicent Millichip. 'Anything, really.'

Dimsdale leaned low over his Queen of Puddings. 'Does the name Lloyd George mean anything to you?'

Lestrade leaned back, thinking hard. 'Chancellor of the Exchequer, isn't he?'

Dimsdale nodded. 'Rufus Isaacs?'

'Er . . .' Now Lestrade was really stumped. 'Chief Rabbi?'

'Solicitor-General,' Dimsdale corrected him. 'Then, of course, there's the government's chief whip . . .'

Lestrade shook his head. He was sadly prepared to believe anything of the Liberals.

'. . . the Master of Elibank. What do all these have in common?'

'Um . . . politicians?' Lestrade had not risen to his exalted rank for nothing.

'Precisely. But what else?'

Lestrade shrugged. 'Do they all wear stockings and bloomers?'

Dimsdale gave him an odd look, then glanced at Kane. 'No, well, perhaps – and if they do, my money's on Elibank. But no, the common ground is that they all own shares in the Marconi Wireless Company.'

'So?'

'So?' Dimsdale leaned back, his glasses steamed anew by the emanations from his custard. 'Chief Superintendent, that is what we in the City call Insider Trading. It is illegal.'

'Is it?'

'Of course,' Kane cut in. 'These ministers of the crown have set up a contract with Marconi to supply a chain of wireless stations all over the Empire. If it can be proven that they are, shall we say, financially interested in the company, then that is fraud. And a Paris newspaper has already said so.'

'Has it?'

'It has,' Dimsdale assured him. 'The *Malodorante*. Of course, the Solicitor-General and the Chancellor are suing, but . . . well, there's no smoke without fire as we say on the Fourth Floor.'

'Indeed not. So the government is under inquiry by the police?'

'Sshh!' Dimsdale's beady eyes swivelled in all directions behind their frosted glass. 'Talk like that is highly inflammatory, Mr Lestrade. Remember "Softlee, softlee, catchee monkee" – it's a saying we have on the Fourth Floor.'

'Yes.' Lestrade nodded archly. 'It's one you pinched from us on the Second Floor.'

'The point is, guv.' Kane closed to the Superintendent. 'If only a fraction of what we hear is true, then this government's days are numbered. And you know what that means?'

'Suffragettes?'

'The Labour party,' Dimsdale hissed.

You could have heard a fork drop. In fact, one did, somewhere to the West of the canteen and all eyes momentarily swivelled to it and away from Dimsdale.

'That serious?' Lestrade asked after a suitable moment.

Dimsdale nodded.

'Well,' Lestrade said, 'I'm sure it will all turn out for the best. Are you getting the cigars in, John? I appear to have left mine in my other jacket.'

Spring gave way to summer. As a sign of the times and to prove how far the Great had abandoned Britain, Oxford University began offering diplomas in Business Studies. Furious Scholars from Tunbridge Wells and other bastions of civilization sent their degrees back in dudgeon, some higher than others.

The coroner confirmed it: old Worsthorne Griffin had indeed gone of a heart attack. And effectively, the trail ended there.

Silently, that summer, the hats came off. As the funeral cortège wound its way towards King's Cross, the policemen who lined the route stiffened. Ordinarily, they would have saluted. Except that they had been ordered not to salute. It would convey the wrong message to the world. And everywhere, behind the thin, scattered line of blue, was the green, purple and white of the Movement.

The muffled chattering in the crowd stilled to silence as the coffin slid past on its open carriage, the sleek black stallions plodding onwards under the nodding ostrich plumes. Over the coffin, the pall of purple velvet shone with gold lettering in the June sun – 'Welcome the Northumbrian hunger striker'.

Miss Emily Davison was going home.

June was like that in those days. Wedged by ancient Roman edict between May and July, it could be flaming one day and fog-bound the next. Detective-Sergeant Ned Blevvins shook his head with disgust as he read the *Morning Standard* at the end of his shift.

'Bloody Suffragettes!' he growled to himself as he took in the photograph of the great cortège. 'Look at those bloody vicars at the front. And that bloke driving the hearse! Call themselves men? Horse whipping's too good for 'em.'

No one was listening at that hour of the morning. No one else was in. It was that ghastly hour of the dog watch, when the sun was barely up over sleeping Westminster and the bargees stirred themselves as Blevvins stirred his morning tea. It had been a quiet night, all in all. Time to go home and get some shut-eye, before the guv'nor got in and found him something else to do.

Blevvins drained his cup, spitting out the odd leaf, and reached for his bowler. He whistled through his teeth as he left Lestrade's office.

'Lyall!'

The rookie of the same name sprang to his feet. Not for all the world would he have it said he'd been asleep on duty.

'There's a cup here,' Blevvins told him as his squat bulk crashed through the door. 'Needs washing, I'd say.' And he'd gone. He'd put the paper back as neatly as he knew how and took the stairs two at a time to the ground floor.

'Morning, Ethel,' he grunted at the desk man.

Ethelstan Douglas had the misfortune to have a father obsessed with the Anglo-Saxons. He was the lucky one, though. His little brother had been christened Witanegamot. 'Morning, Ned. Pea-souper again today. Still, it'll be a scorcher, shouldn't wonder, when it clears. Whaddya think of that funeral yesterday, eh? Bit over-the-top, wasn't it?'

'Bloody disgrace,' agreed Blevvins, signing out in Douglas's black book. 'You know my view, Ethel. A woman's place is in the kitchen and she ought to bloody clean it occasionally. Either that or spreadeagled over a . . . oh, my bleedin' bollocks!'

Sergeant Blevvins stood in the doorway, gripping the frame with both hands. The mist still lay thick over the river, swirling pale green around the railings of the Embankment and those verdigris dolphins that coiled around the lamps, only at that moment going out all over London. He thought they were trees at first, but there were too many of them. And they were too short. And they wore hats. Sergeant Blevvins spun on his heel and slammed the door.

'Ned?' Sergeant Douglas looked up. 'You've gone a funny colour.'

'Women,' Blevvins mumbled. 'Thousands of them.'

Douglas blinked. Then he grinned. 'Now, Ned, come off it. What did you have in your tea this morning?'

'Not the sort of women you're thinking of, Eth,' Blevvins snapped, dashing to the window. 'Massive ones. With biceps and moustaches. Jesus Christ Almighty. They've got a howitzer.'

Ethelstan Douglas left his desk to join his old oppo on the other side of the entrance lobby. Blevvins was right. Across the Embankment from the Yard, stretching to right and left into the eerie silence of the fog, stood a monstrous regiment of women. In a moment of bravado, Douglas slid up the sash.

'They can't be women,' he hissed to Blevvins. 'They're not saying a word.'

'My wife did that once,' Blevvins whispered. 'Didn't speak for a whole day. God, it was unnerving.'

'I never knew you was married, Ned,' Douglas whispered.

'It's not something I generally brag about, Eth,' Blevvins told him. 'We was incompatible. You know how it is, the job. The hours, the loneliness, the hatred in the staring eyes. In the end I told her straight. It's either the Sunday School or me, Bess, I told her – 'cos that was her name, see, Bess. You either give up that job or I walk.'

'So you walked?'

'I did, Eth . . .'

'Ned.' Blevvins felt the desk man grip his sleeve. 'One of 'em's approaching, in a North-Westerly direction. Coming our way.'

Indeed she was. A large woman in a vast motoring hat tied under the chin with a chiffon scarf, crossed the road under a white flag fluttering from a broomstick.

'We demand to see the senior man,' she trilled with a voice that could shatter glass.

'What time is it? Ned?' Douglas asked.

'Er . . .' Blevvins fumbled for his watch. 'I make it half past seven. Why?'

'Nobody above the rank of detective-sergeant on until eight.'

'That's you, then, Ned,' Douglas pointed out.

'Malcolm.' Blevvins clicked his fingers.

'Who?'

'Sergeant Malcolm. He's senior to me, in a manner of speaking.'

Douglas shook his head. 'Knocked off a quarter of an hour ago. Half-way to Islington by now.'

'Raynard!' Blevvins suddenly remembered.

'Laid off,' Douglas informed him. 'Fell out of that tree, remember? Getting Her Majesty's pekinese down at the Palace.'

'Oh, yeah.' Blevvins frowned. 'How it got up there in the first place I couldn't fathom.'

'Mr Froest's put a small prize up for the best answer to that one.'

'We're waiting,' the harridan shrieked, the mist swirling at her feet. 'Either you send out your senior man or we blow a hole in your wall.'

By now, there was a pallid face at nearly every window that fronted the Embankment; in some cases, two. And not one of them was more senior than Ned Blevvins.

'Sarge!' A startled voice made the sergeants turn. A wild-eyed constable stood there, helmeted and caped. His helmet was white with flour. So was his cape.

'Good God, man,' Douglas hissed. 'Look at the state of you. Where do you think you are?'

'Sorry, Sarge. It's the Suffragettes. They've blocked off White-hall. I only just got through. Billy Armstrong was lifted off of his feet by 'em. It's like the rush hour. 'Cept they're all women. The last I saw of Constable Clements was his trousers thrown over the heads of the crowd.'

'Sarge!' Another hysterical constable hurtled down the stairs. 'They're all around us, Sarge. We've had it! We've had it!'

'Now that's enough!' Blevvins bellowed. 'This is Scotland Yard. Get on the blower, Ethel. The War Office. Tell 'em what's going on. We need the Fusiliers. At a pinch, the Honourable Artillery Company. And tell 'em no fancy dress. None of those stupid pike things. This is a bloody war.'

'But they're women, Ned,' Douglas still had the decency to protest.

'Are they, Eth?' Blevvins's eyes narrowed at the sentinel who stood, legs braced beneath her white ensign. 'Sometimes I bloody wonder.'

'That's no good, Mr Blevvins, sir,' the assaulted constable panted, leaning against the desk to get his breath back. 'I've just come past the War Office. The rumour there is that the cleaners have turned on the clerks. There's blood everywhere, running in the gutters.'

'Dead!' Douglas said, tapping the telephone frenziedly. 'The corseted cows have cut the wires.'

Blevvins turned to the window again. A closer look gave him the view of the lone woman's left hand, closed around a massive pair of wire cutters. He saw her right hand lift the white flag.

'On the count of three!' she screamed and the howitzer crew scuttled around in the fog with shot and shell.

'Wait!' Blevvins bellowed. 'Just . . . just give us a minute, for God's sake.' He turned to Douglas. 'Eth, me ol' mucker, you know I'd never pull rank on you. All right, so I've got the civvy suit and you've got the pointed hat. Well, that's how it goes.'

'When's your commission?' Douglas demanded to know.

'As sergeant? '09. Yours?'

''09. Month?'

'April. You?'

'April.'

The tension was unbearable.

'The first!' Blevvins yelled.

A smile of pure relief brightened Douglas's face. 'The eight-eenth,' he said. 'Shall I hold your bowler, Mr Blevvins, sir?'

Blevvins snarled something decidedly uncomradely and squared his shoulders. 'Firearms,' he hissed over his shoulder.

The stairs were now thronged with a silent coven of constables, watching, waiting, wondering what Blevvins would do.

'We've got no authorization,' Douglas complained.

'Look!' Blevvins rounded on him. 'I'm going out there in a minute. Just me against upwards of a thousand bloody women. Do you know what they can do with a hat-pin? Do you? Do you?' He shook his old oppo till his teeth rattled. 'It makes them Chinese Boxers look like a Methodist Tea Party, I can tell you. Now, you crack open that case of Webleys in the basement, Eth, and you do it now.'

He caught sight of the men on the stairs. 'Any of you had firearms training?'

'No, Sarge!' they assured him to a man. Their choral speaking was good, but he wasn't sure he needed that just now.

'Oh, bloody marvellous. All right, Eth. You get yourself one. You, what's your name?' He jabbed a finger at the coated constable.

'Um . . . er . . .'

'Get a grip on yourself, man.' Blevvins slapped him around the head and the flour floated wide.

'Pentridge, sir.'

'Right, Pentridge. You get one, too. Sergeant Douglas will show you which way to hold it. You lot!' he barked to the boys on the staircase. 'Baton charge. I presume you can all handle a truncheon?'

'Yes, Sarge!'

Blevvins liked the solidarity of that answer.

'On the count of three!' They heard the war cry through the window.

'All right, all right!' Blevvins roared back. 'Keep your petticoat on, you old bat! Please,' he muttered. 'At all costs, keep your petticoat on.'

He looked at Douglas, peering anxiously through the fog. At young Pentridge, having had his baptism of fire already. At the lads on the stairs, cradling their weapons in nervous fingers. What would Lestrade do, he asked himself as he crossed to the door. Trip over the step, probably.

'One!' The harridan had started.

'Christ!' Douglas dashed back and made for the stairs to the basement, fumbling with his keys for the one that opened the firearms cupboard.

All the faces vanished from the windows. Men threw over furniture, crouched behind filing cabinets, gathered armfuls of shoeboxes and generally panicked.

'Two!'

'Yes!' Blevvins was suddenly out there with them, the only man in front of a river of women. His five foot nine looked surprisingly small as the line shifted, still silent. He heard muffled feet to his right and his left, but his eyes were still fixed on the cold muzzle of the Howitzer which always seemed to be pointing curiously at him.

'*You* are the senior man?' the harridan asked, now that her eyes were on a level with him.

'Detective Sergeant Blevvins,' Blevvins confessed.

'Chauvinist lackey of an uncaring chauvinist state!' someone screamed.

'Well.' The harridan smiled. 'You'll have to do.' And the next thing Blevvins knew is that he was assailed from all sides simultaneously, losing his balance in the press. He fought and kicked and gouged, but in the end he was a squad of one and the sheer weight of numbers prevailed.

Douglas and Pentridge stood with their faces to the window, drawing beads on the battling throng before them.

'I suppose me saying "Fire at will" wouldn't do any good, would it, lad?'

'More a case of "Fire at Wilhelmina", ain't it, Sarge?' The floury boy tried to make light of it.

'The trouble is, of course,' Douglas said, closing one eye to take careful aim, 'your Webley is a man-stopping weapon, certainly, but what about a woman? I'm not sure anyone's used one on a woman – not deliberately, anyway. Besides, if I killed one of them, I'd probably lose my stripes.'

'But that's one of our blokes, Sarge,' Pentridge whispered, his hand wobbling on the Webley.

They watched as Blevvins was thrown around like a rag-doll in a mob of crazed terriers. Then he disappeared.

'You're right.' Douglas eased off the cocked hammer of his pistol. 'But it's only Ned Blevvins. Nothing to die in a ditch for. Put the gun down, lad, there's a good constable. Before it goes off.'

And Pentridge did.

'Right, lads!' Douglas bellowed to the watchers on the stairs. 'There's one of our lads in difficulty out there. What do we do?'

The lads on the stairs looked at each other, not seeming to know.

'We charge the enemy, lads!' Douglas's voice was like a clarion call and it was drowned by the clatter of hob-nailed size elevens. They thundered through the door, across the pavement, fanning out in line abreast, before dovetailing again with their biggest bugger at their head – a tight, arrowhead formation designed to slice through the feathered phalanx that held the Embankment.

55

But the phalanx had gone. Vanished in the morning mist. The biggest bugger at the arrowhead's tip crashed into the granite wall, his truncheon slashing thin air. All they saw was the fog-shrouded river and all they heard was the angry bay of klaxons as the London traffic struggled to get back to normal.

'Bloody traffic's unbelievable this morning!' Lestrade growled, tossing his bowler to Constable Tait. The boy looked pale. And old. Constable Lyall didn't look any too chipper either. Lestrade flashed a scowl from one to the other. Surreptitiously, he checked his flies. No. All was well.

'Don't tell me they've made Ramsay Macdonald Home Secretary,' he quipped and turned to face the stern, moustachioed face of Sir Edward Henry, the policeman's policeman, Assistant Commissioner of Scotland Yard. 'Sir?' was the best the Superintendent could manage. He had *never*, in all his long and illustrious career, seen an Assistant Commissioner on *this* floor. In *his* office.

'Out!' Henry growled.

All three coppers turned to go. 'Not you, Lestrade,' Henry called him back. He waited until the door had clicked behind Tait. 'You've heard of course.'

'Er . . . ?'

'About Blevvins.'

'Er . . . ?'

Henry twirled to the window, the one with the imposing view of the wall opposite. He let his eyes wander downwards and there, scrawled in chalk on the lower brickwork, was a comment on the likely legitimacy of the Assistant Commissioner, signed in perfect copperplate by the Women's Social and Political Union. Henry twirled back. 'They've got him,' he said, fighting to keep his emotions in check.

'They?' Lestrade repeated. 'Him?'

'For God's sake, Lestrade!' Henry slammed his fist down on the Superintendent's plate of morning Peek Freans, shattering them in all directions. 'Must you sound like a bloody parrot on a wax cylinder? The Women's Social and Political Union have kidnapped Sergeant Blevvins.'

'Good God!' Lestrade sat down.

Henry sighed. 'Have you got a drink? My nerves are in shreds.'

Lestrade fumbled in a filing cabinet. 'Not very good brandy, I'm afraid, sir. I keep it for distraught witnesses.'

'Yes, well, it'll do for distraught Assistant Commissioners. Never mind a glass. Bottles were made before glasses – weren't

56

they?' He flicked his fingers, threw himself down in Lestrade's one half-way decent chair. He caught the bottle expertly and proceeded to swig its contents. 'Here,' he said. 'You'd better have a look at this. It arrived less than twenty minutes ago.'

Lestrade took the telegram that Henry had thrown in undisguised contempt on to the desk.

'We have your man Blevvins. Stop. Not much of a man. Stop. But will be less of one by twelve midday. Stop. Only way to prevent loss of wedding tackle is to send Lestrade. Stop. An unmarked cab will arrive at the Yard at eleven. Stop. Lestrade is to be on it. Stop. No tail. Stop. Or Blevvins gets it. Stop.'

It was addressed to Sir Edward Henry and was signed 'Boadicea'.

'Boadicea, sir?' Lestrade's eyes narrowed.

'She was a Queen of the Ancient Britons, Lestrade. You've walked past her statue thousands of times out there at the corner of Westminster Bridge. Her chariot had knives on its wheels. And she wore an iron corset.'

'Mrs Pankhurst?'

Henry shook his head. 'You know this woman, I understand?'

'We've met.' Lestrade nodded.

'Does this telegram sound like her?'

Lestrade looked at it again. 'It sounds a little rougher than I remember her,' he commented.

'Perhaps.' Henry nodded in turn. 'But the whole movement is desperate. What with Asquith's Cat and Mouse Bill and that stupid woman at the Derby . . . There was talk they'd have to have the jockey destroyed, you know. Luckily, he's making a full recovery. Of course, he'll never be able to join the Grenadiers, but there it is. Are you up for it?'

Lestrade looked at his superior. He'd saved the man's life once. Now he was being asked to save the life of another. And the irony was, it wasn't another man. It was Ned Blevvins.

'Do we know what she wants, sir?' Lestrade asked. 'This Boadicea?'

Edward Henry leaned back in Lestrade's chair and shook his head. 'Yes, Lestrade,' he said ominously. 'She wants you.'

5

The grim black stallion waited at the side entrance to the Yard. Cunning, thought Lestrade, of this Boadicea. No motor car. No registration plate. And he noticed too that the hansom's number was illegible, caked in mud. And it was difficult to find much mud in the middle of London, especially now the fog had cleared and the streets were bright in the sharp sunshine.

'Mr Lestrade?' The cabbie touched his hat.

The Superintendent looked up, shielding his eyes against the glare of the sky. If the cabbie was a woman, it was a brilliant disguise.

'Who are you working for?' Lestrade asked him, having no time to stand on ceremony.

'Myself,' the cabbie told him. 'Are you goin' to get in?'

It was probably one of the last horse-cabs in London and Lestrade clambered into it. He wouldn't be sorry to see these go. They were draughty and the leather squeaked. Above all, they were anathema to anyone with a penchant for *mal de mer*. Or even formaldehyde.

On the seat next to him was an envelope, marked clearly with his name. The cabbie whipped on the horse and the animal swung left into the Embankment traffic, honking and belching its way through the late morning. He ripped open the envelope, and read the letter – 'Dear Mr Lestrade, By the time you have read this, Sergeant Blevvins will be secured in a secret place with a stick of dynamite tied to his unmentionables. The cabbie will take you to Birdcage Walk. At Wellington Barracks you will alight. Another cab will take you on the next nether limb of your journey. At twelve o'clock precisely, Boadicea's henchwoman will light Sgt Blevvins's fuse. It will not be a pretty sight.'

Lestrade didn't doubt it. He stuck his head out of the window. 'Why have you gone this way, you idiot?' he yelled. The cab was rattling down the Mall, Buckingham Palace, grey and resplendent, ahead.

'I thought you'd appreciate the view,' the cabbie shouted back.

'Cut across the grass,' Lestrade ordered.

'I can't do that,' the cabbie told him. 'I'd lose my licence.'

'If you don't,' Lestrade snarled, 'that's nothing to what a colleague of mine is going to lose. Do it!'

The cabbie hauled the reins to the left, muttering about the shocking state of fares, and the hansom hurtled off towards the lake, ducks flying skywards at its approach. Startled strollers looked up, nannies swerved their perambulators and a Park policeman blew his whistle before giving chase.

In an unmarked motor car behind, Constable Tait saw it happen. 'Has the guv'nor gone mad?' he asked Lyall, gripping the seat next to him.

'Full throttle, Arnold,' Lyall shouted above the engine's roar. 'Mr Henry's orders were explicit. Stay with him at all costs.'

'But we'll be arrested!' Tait pointed out.

'All in a day's work,' Lyall barked. 'Put your foot down.'

'It's on the bloody grass, now!' Tait shouted and the Darracq screamed as its front wheels bounced across country. 'I thought we were supposed to be subtle about this. Mr Henry said "Softlee, softlee".'

'Yes, he did, didn't he,' Lyall screamed as Tait yanked his way through the gears at random, coughing and jerking. The car sounded rather rough too. 'I didn't really know what he was talking about, did you? Hello, he's stopped.'

The cab had. At Birdcage Walk, Lestrade leapt out of one hansom and into another. Passers-by could not have been aware of the miracle they were witnessing – Sholto Lestrade paying his own cab fare. The second cabbie had his orders and he rattled off through Buckingham Court and Grosvenor Place into leafy Belgravia, Tait and Lyall now maintaining a more sedate pace behind him.

'He's going right, into Hobart Place.' Lyall pointed. 'Right. Go right!'

'Who's driving this bloody thing? We've already drawn attention to ourselves. Look at all those bloody women.' Tait gestured wildly at the pedestrians on the pavement. 'Any one of them could be working under cover for the WSPU. Act casual.'

At Eaton Square, the cab lurched to a halt. Lestrade's feet no sooner hit the pavement than he had sprung into a third vehicle. Unfortunately, the door was shut and he bounced off it, before catching his breath and the handle and landing on yet another letter. The cab jerked forwards, swinging wildly around the Square before doubling back into Eaton Mews.

'Where'd he go?' Tait's head was twisting in all directions.

'Damn and buggeration!' Lyall slapped the dashboard. 'Lost him.'

Tait wrenched at the handbrake and sat cradling the wheel. 'Are you going to tell Mr Henry, or am I?'

Lyall stepped out of the motor. 'Feet were made before these things, Arnold; I have it on good authority. I'll go this way. You go that. House to house.'

'And if a woman answers?'

'Hang up!' Lyall said and dashed off along the cobbled surface of the Mews. There was no cab. Not even any horse droppings. Sholto Lestrade had vanished from the face of the earth.

Ned Blevvins appeared to be doing his Samson impression in the basement of the large house that backed on to Eaton Square. His arms were outstretched and his hands rested on two marble pillars to which he was chained. His legs were spread wide too and strapped to his left was a tourniquet into which a thoughtful member of the WSPU had tied with a pink ribbon a single, rather tasteful stick of dynamite.

Lestrade had been been whisked up the side steps, blindfolded quickly and led through the corridors of no power by unseen hands. He knew he was being taken down and he felt the chill and damp of a basement around his ears. As the blindfold was whipped off and his eyes became accustomed to the dark, he made out Ned Blevvins standing like a lamb for the slaughter, tethered like a goat.

'Blevvins?' His voice was oddly distorted in the empty, low-vaulted room.

'We'll ask the questions,' a voice interrupted from the darkness.

Lestrade turned to face the apparition who stood framed in a doorway to his left. A woman rather smaller than the late Queen stood dwarfed by a magnificent pair of Amazons. Lestrade remembered reading about these at school. If what he had read was right, these two could only muster a pair of breasts between them.

'You will release this man now,' Lestrade said levelly.

The diminutive woman emerged into a pool of light. She was fair-haired, nodding in the direction of middle age and had a slight stoop. 'Esmerelda,' she said softly. 'The light.'

Courtesy of Mr Edison, the basement room lit up. A naked bulb hung like a dead man from the off-white ceiling. Blevvins was not only bound, he was gagged. Only his eyes, rolling in his head, conveyed any message. It was, as usual, gibberish.

'Thank you for coming, Superintendent,' the little woman said. 'Won't you sit down?' She gestured to a chair.

'I didn't exactly have a choice,' Lestrade told her. 'And if you don't mind, I'll stand. Bearing in mind my colleague's predicament, I think I'll give chairs a wide berth at the moment.'

'Typical man's comment,' one of the Amazons sneered. 'They can talk about birth, but they don't go through it. Oh, dear me, no.'

'Thank you, Godiva,' the little woman said sharply. 'We aren't here to engage in semantics.'

Lestrade was glad to hear it. He'd had enough trouble with women, let alone Jewish ones. 'You are . . . ?' he asked the tiny one.

'Let's just say I am called Boadicea,' she said. 'Esmerelda and Godiva are not these ladies' real names either. All three of our *noms de plume* were wronged, in history and fiction, by men. *Semper eadem*, you might say.'

Lestrade might, if only he knew what it meant. 'Kidnapping is an extremely serious offence,' he said. 'Not to mention pointing a Howitzer at the Headquarters of the Metropolitan Police. Where did you get it, by the way? Not off the peg at Liberty's, I shouldn't think.'

'We have our methods, Mr Lestrade,' Boadicea said, lifting a hefty Havana from a box on a table beside her. 'Let it go at that.'

'What do you want?'

The Amazons' eyes flickered to their mistress. 'Your help,' she said.

'My help?' Lestrade repeated. There was a muffled moan from the corner. 'Shut up, Blevvins. I'm not even considering what to do with you yet, but I guarantee it will make your eyes water. My help with what?'

'With the death of Emily Davison.'

'Who?' Lestrade asked.

There was an inrush of air from the Amazons. As one woman

they took a pace forward, but Boadicea's bony fingers held them back. 'I will assume', she said, through pursed lips, 'that that question was designed to needle? Emily Wilding Davison died eight days ago under the hoofs of the king's horse at the Derby.'

'I do read the papers.' Lestrade nodded. 'It was tragic.'

'More than that, Mr Lestrade,' Boadicea said. 'It was murder.'

The silence was tangible until Lestrade destroyed it by sliding back the chair. He risked a booby trap and inched his way into it. All was well. 'Murder?' he repeated.

'I understand from Emmeline Pankhurst that you are familiar with the crime.' Boadicea blew smoke rings to the ceiling.

'I have a nodding acquaintance with it,' he said. 'But I understood Miss Davison to have committed suicide.'

Boadicea glided forward further into the pool of light. She appeared to move on casters, for her head stayed absolutely level the whole time. She sat on the chair on the other side of the table from Lestrade.

'It was Lloyd George,' she said softly.

'Metaphysically speaking, you mean,' Lestrade said.

Boadicea frowned. 'No, I mean literally, Mr Lestrade. Oh, I don't suppose he was man enough to do his own dirty work. No, he would have sent some thug, a henchman, to Epsom.'

Lestrade blinked. 'The *Police Gazette* said . . .'

'The *Police Gazette* is written by a man, Mr Lestrade.'

'But the *Daily Mail* . . .'

'Alfred Harmsworth's chauvinist rag? You only have to listen to the paper's name to grasp its affinities.'

'So what did happen?'

'Emily went to the Derby with her sisters to fly the flag.' Boadicea produced another large cheroot and one of her henchwomen lit it, before standing back to attention behind her chair. 'There were four of them. The names of the others need not concern you. Emily was a short woman, not much taller than I and her view of the course was restricted. Someone suggested she climb on to the rail to see the approaching horses. She'd put a few bob down on Thanks for the Mammaries at 64 to 1. All for the Cause, of course.'

'Of course.' Lestrade nodded.

'As the King's horse, Anmer, came tight on the curve, someone pushed her. She hit the animal's chest and she lost her balance. There was blood gushing from her nose and mouth. The horse somersaulted right over her.'

'The jockey was badly hurt, I understand.'

'Herbert Jones? He shouldn't have been riding the King's horse, should he? He could have been marching shoulder to shoulder with our sisters at Hyde Park that very day. As for poor Emily, her skull was shattered. They got her into a motor car and she was taken to hospital.'

'Where?'

'Epsom Cottage.'

'Where she died some days later?'

Boadicea nodded, as her namesake probably did all those centuries ago when her blue-painted harridans had put the fear of the gods into the Roman legions.

'You were there?' Lestrade asked. 'At the Derby?'

'Personally, no. But I know a woman who was.'

'Who?'

Boadicea smiled. 'I'm not sure she'll speak to you.'

'That's not very helpful,' Lestrade commented. 'Either you want my help on this or . . .'

'Or Emily Davison will go down as a martyr to the Cause; yes, I know.'

'Tell me, why do you think Lloyd George is responsible? According to your movement, all men are beasts, aren't they? There must be thousands of us who'd happily push a woman under the king's horse. It happens every day of the week.'

'You're being flippant, Superintendent,' Boadicea said through pursed lips. 'In truth, I could expect no more.'

Lestrade flashed a glance at Blevvins, like little Jack Horner to the left of the low-vaulted, shadowed room.

'Do I understand', he asked, 'that you went to all this trouble, aiming a Howitzer at Scotland Yard, kidnapping one of its officers, *just* to enlist my help? Couldn't you simply have asked?'

A smile flitted briefly over Boadicea's lips. 'Would you have come?' she asked him.

'Probably not,' he admitted.

Boadicea adopted that face and that pose known to men the world over; the one women do so well. The one that says 'I told you so'.

'Let my man go,' Lestrade said softly. 'And I'll see what I can do.'

Boadicea shook her head slowly. 'That's somewhat akin to what Mr Lloyd George said back in 1910 and Mr Asquith in 1911 and Mr Churchill in 1912. It is wearing a little thin, Mr Lestrade.'

'You never told me why Lloyd George,' he said.

Boadicea stood up and looked down at him. 'Lloyd George because Emily Davison blew up his house at Walton Heath.'

Lestrade raised an eyebrow. The Special Branch had been

hunting high and low for that particular mad bomber since Easter. 'I see,' he said. 'That puts a rather different complexion on things.'

'It does?' Boadicea stopped in mid-turn.

Lestrade nodded. 'Let my man go,' he said, 'and I'll find out who killed your Emily Davison.'

Boadicea's eyes flicked across to Blevvins, then to Lestrade. She searched the sad, brown eyes for a moment, the sallow, rat-like face. Then she issued her commands. 'Godiva, release him.'

'But Boa . . .' the henchwoman burst out in disbelief.

'Do as I say,' the ancient Briton hissed. 'For God's sake, don't show any divisions in our ranks now. Not to him!' And she jerked her grey, tousled head in Lestrade's direction.

Godiva strode across to the helpless figure of Blevvins. Her Bowie knife flashed in the darkness and from the gagged squeal from Blevvins, it sounded as though she'd hacked off the unmentionables Boadicea spoke of in her letters. In fact, she had merely cut the dynamite stick from his legs.

'I'm going to cut your hands free now,' she growled, standing nose to nose with the detective-sergeant. 'One bit of nonsense from you, Sonny Jim, and I'll shove this up your arse.'

Even Blevvins blenched at the woman's lack of refinement. He'd already had ample opportunity to assess Godiva's biceps. If the Yard had been more enlightened, she'd be a natural for the tug-o'-war team. Blevvins nodded, anxious to be rid of the ropes, the gag, the whole desperate situation.

There was a rip and the sergeant's hands fell free from the pillars that held him. His ankles of course were still bound and his legs spread. And he didn't care at all for the glint in his gaoler's eyes.

'Don't tease the idiot,' Boadicea commanded. 'After all, he may have a mother somewhere.'

Lestrade didn't doubt it. But he was less sure of a father.

'Where will your inquiries begin?' Boadicea asked him as Blevvins gasped in relief when Godiva let slip his gag.

'The woman who was there,' Lestrade said. 'I'll start with her.'

Boadicea nodded and took a folded piece of paper from her cuff. 'She may not talk to you,' she said again.

Lestrade nodded. 'If she doesn't, I may never find your murderer.'

Boadicea smiled. 'If she doesn't,' she said, 'you will never find the murderer of your sergeant, either.'

And Blevvins was more than alarmed at the smile on the faces of both of them.

Most places have their ups and Downs. But Epsom had its salts too. While Ned Blevvins assured everybody at the Yard that he'd been held down all morning by upwards of thirty women and that if Lestrade hadn't arrived, he'd have given them all a good seeing-to – at least, the pretty ones – Tait and Lyall limped back to Headquarters.

They were most relieved to find the problem solved, but Edward Henry knew what the late edition of the *Standard* would be screaming and he turfed the rookies out again on a fruitless raid on the house at Eaton Mews. As everyone with a wit slightly higher than Blevvins had realized, the place was empty. The birds had flown. Not a single woman was helping police with their inquiries.

And Lestrade had gone South by electric railway.

Henry Wicker had been quietly grazing his cattle, minding his own business, back in 1618, when he'd accidentally discovered some mineral springs. Seventy years later, Epsom was a famous spa and polite society came out from Town to take the salts. The train wound its way past The Durdans, where the Roseberys lived in palatial seclusion and into the little station. Only the previous month, Lord Rosebery had told a delighted world that he might never make another speech. The cheering took several minutes to die down. At the station, the Superintendent caught a cab and rattled out in the June sunshine, up the High Street, with its clock tower, and on to the racecourse, all white rails and stands.

It was in the summer of 1778 that a riotous group of the Fancy had met at a Surrey country house and founded a race for three-year-old fillies. The house was called The Oaks and they named the race after it. Three years later a similar race, but this time for colts and fillies, was organized by the Earl of Derby, leading light of the Fancy in those days. And the Fancy had not missed a Derby Day since.

Tom Eldridge came up to Lestrade's shoulder, a whippet of a man with the bowed legs of his calling. But he was not a maker of Queen Anne cabinets; he was a jockey, a prince of the turf and he stood on the fatal corner now, in the rather vulgar pink of Lady Cartland, nodding wisely as the Superintendent inspected the ground.

'The going was hard,' Eldridge remembered.

'What were you riding?' Lestrade asked.

It seemed an odd question, but perhaps the Yard man had led a sheltered life. 'A horse,' the jockey was able to assure him.

'I mean.' Lestrade straightened. 'What was it called?'

'Oh, Slasher Mary,' Eldridge said. 'By Crikey, out of Kilter. Sweet filly. Goes like a train.'

'Where were you in the field?'

'Twenty-eighth,' Eldridge told him.

'Out of how many?'

'Twenty-nine. But it was early days. It's no good rushin' 'em, y'see.' Eldridge tugged off his racing cap. 'They just can't be hurried. You've got to coax 'em, like.'

'And the king's horse?'

'Anmer? He was just ahead of me. Lucky start.'

'That was Herbert Jones?'

'That's right.' Eldridge draped his riding cap on the rails. 'It's a bleedin' shame 'bout poor old Herbie. Still, with a bit of luck, he'll ride again.'

'Did you see the woman?'

'Not until she fell.'

'She fell?'

'Francis!' the jockey suddenly yelled to a passing stableboy, even shorter than he was. 'What have I told you?' And he clipped the lad around the ear. 'You'll never get to be 'er Majesty's favourite jockey if you do that! Yeah, she fell alright.'

'Didn't jump, then?'

'Jump? Oh, a suicide, you mean? Pretty ropey way of doin' yerself in, ain't it? I mean, threshin' machine, ship's propellor, a little dither in the middle of Tower Bridge when it goes up – that I can understand. But jumpin' out in front of horses? What if she missed? She damned near did. Behind Anmer was me and behind me was sod all – at that precise moment in time, you understand. If she'd fallen a split second later, all she'd have got would be a muddy nose. As it is, well . . . utterly buggered the race for me, I can tell yer. They say 'is Majesty's none too happy.'

'Indeed they do. Tell me, Mr Eldridge, did you see anyone behind Miss Davison? To her left or right?'

The jockey thought for a moment. 'Nah.' He shrugged. 'You gotta remember, guv, I'm coming round the corner at the best part of thirty miles an hour. You ain't got time to take in the crowd. They're just a blur, whizzing past on the rails. Look at that!'

Lestrade did. The jockey was pointing to the lie of the land, where the green of the Epsom slope was criss-crossed with brown. 'What?' he asked.

'Bloody tyre tracks, that's what!' Eldridge spat volubly. 'Call me old-fashioned if you like, but if I remember my Bible, horses and beasts of the field were made before the motor car. Look at the bloody mess they make. If people want to bring their motors, they should go to bloody Brooklands.'

Her hair was the colour of fine-spun copper and candles danced and circled in her eyes. She wore a dress of claret laced with threads of silver and she held out her wrists to him as though for cuffs.

'I've been expecting you,' she said and the years fell away like a mirror, broken at a glance.

Emily Greenbush was wearing the same dress she'd worn when they'd met, all those years ago.

'You haven't changed,' he said.

'You have.' She let the wrists fall. 'You're married.'

He caught her looking at the gold band on his knuckle. 'You're still as sharp as ever,' he said.

She crossed the drawing-room and lit a lamp, for the evening dews and damps were closing in after the warm June day.

'You left Curzon Street,' he said.

'They're building a cinematograph palace there now,' she told him. 'I thought it was time to go. Do you still decline Scotch on duty?'

'Yes.' Lestrade smiled. 'And before you ask, it's Thursday. And I still don't wrestle with ladies on Thursdays.'

It was Emily's turn to smile. 'Who is she?' she asked, inviting Lestrade to sit on the sofa opposite her.

'Fanny,' he told her, placing the bowler hat beside him. 'I've known her for years. Her father was an old friend of mine.'

'Was?'

'He's dead,' Lestrade said. 'A shooting accident.'

'Do you have children?'

'With Fanny? No. Emma – my girl by my first wife – is quite a woman now. At Finishing School.'

'Well, well.' Emily Greenbush swept back the long, unbraided hair. 'I remember Christabel Pankhurst called you a chauvinist lackey when she met you. Sylvia thought you a despoiler of women.'

'And you?' he asked her. 'What did you think of me?'

'I loved you,' she said.

He chuckled. 'I thought you . . . annoying, irritating, silly. Oh, and I fell in love with you too.'

Her smile vanished. She felt an iron lump in her throat. 'Did you tell her?' she asked him. 'Did you tell your Emma about you? That you are her father, I mean?'

'Yes,' he said. 'Yes, I did. Boadicea didn't think you'd see me.'

'Neither did I,' she said, sighing suddenly to break the moment, wrenching free of those lingering ghosts that had haunted her down the years. 'Do you remember what I said?' she asked. 'The last time we met?'

'You said . . . you said, "One day, we'll meet in the polling station, my cross next to yours." '

'That's right.' She nodded. 'And it's no nearer now than it was ten years ago.'

'A lot of water under the bridge,' Lestrade said. 'A lot of blood.'

'Yes.' Her bright face fell. 'Emily.'

'Emily.' He nodded. 'Tell me about Emily, Emily.'

'I don't know what you want me to say. She was a sister.'

'And she's dead.' The words rang hollow. 'Boadicea seemed very intent to get me on this case. She went to quite extraordinary lengths. The least I can do is to earn her opinion of me. Everything. I need it all.'

'Very well.' Emily Greenbush took a deep breath. 'Emily Wilding Davison. She was forty-one. "On the shelf" to use a man's term. The WSPU prefer "Clean and ready for use". Let's see, she was the second of three children. Her father, Charles, was a businessman, but a failure. I think it was because of him she despised men so. She went to Kensington High School and Royal Holloway College, Esher.'

'Bless you,' said Lestrade.

'She took her degree in 1897. Another example of man's inhumanity to woman, Sholto. They gave her a degree and all she was allowed to do with it was become a governess.'

'It's a tough world,' Lestrade observed, not for the first time.

'She joined the WSPU in 1906. That's when I met her.'

'That's when we met her too,' Lestrade said. 'Her file at the Yard is three inches thick.'

'I'm sure.' Emily nodded.

'Eight imprisonments for stone throwing, post-box firing, window breaking. She was force fed over one hundred times.'

'They put a tube down your throat,' Emily said, her eyes wide with the memory of it. 'It looks small in the doctor's hand, but in your throat, it clogs and suffocates. You gag, but the tube is there, rammed back by the doctor. The warders have your arms and legs. You can't move. Your head is in a vice. The porridge is pumped into your mouth, your throat. You choke. You drown . . . I can't describe the pain.'

'She hid in a broom cupboard in the House of Commons.' Lestrade pretended he hadn't heard her, the woman he once had loved. Emily couldn't describe the pain. And Lestrade couldn't bear to hear it. All he heard in his head was a cold scream in a stone cell. All he felt was her terror. And her solitude.

'It was census night,' he went on. 'Two years ago.'

'She threw herself downstairs at Holloway,' Emily said.

'The college?'

'The prison. But she survived.'

'Is that what happened at the Derby?' Lestrade asked, leaning closer. 'Did she try to kill herself again?'

Emily shook her head. 'I don't know,' she said. 'Emily was unstable. If she went through that hell more than a hundred times, how could she be otherwise? She was carrying ribbons of our Order, the colours of purple, white and green. I thought she was going to pin one to Anmer's bridle.'

'At that speed?' Lestrade frowned. 'Impossible.'

'All I know,' Emily concentrated, shutting her eyes to remember, 'All I know is that she said she couldn't see. As the field came towards us, somebody, a man, said, "Let me help you." He grabbed her arms. She struggled. Oh, I'm sure he meant no harm, but can you imagine what that did to her? The feel of a man's hands on her shoulders, lifting her high? She was only a slip of a thing as you men say, light as a feather. Before I knew it, she was up on the rail, several hands holding her. I was pushed forward against the fence. Then . . . ' Emily shuddered. 'Then she fell, was pushed, I don't know. Her body hurtled past me. There was a sickening thud and the horse went down . . .'

She swallowed hard, fighting back the tears. In front of her was a man she'd loved, whose bed she'd shared. But he was right. Too much water. Too much blood. She'd cried in front of him before. She wouldn't do it again.

'What happened then?' he asked.

'Then?' Emily was lost, a little girl again in the horror of a memory. She saw Emily Davison somersault endlessly in the air, bounce off the racing horse like a rag-doll, sprawling on the grass, her face a mask of blood. 'Then, a doctor came from nowhere. I was glad. Funny that, isn't it? Glad that a man was on hand. A huge crowd gathered, threatening to tear down the rails. A man was helping Emily. I thought she was all right at first. She got up and walked unaided. Then this doctor arrived and she was carried to his motor car.'

'What did you do?'

'I tried to follow, but he said there was no room. My friends, my sisters and I, caught a carriage to the hospital. I couldn't believe Emily's wounds. When they finally let us see her, she was in a coma, her head swathed in bandages. We took turns to be with her.'

'Did she come to?'

Emily shook her head. 'No,' she said. 'She never spoke again.' She sighed. 'It was, I suppose, what she wanted.'

'To die?' Lestrade frowned.

'Yes.' Emily's face was tilted up to his, defiant again. 'To die for the Cause. Yes. She'd seen what I've seen, Sholto. Men with women's hair trailing from their jacket lapels. They're scalps, Sholto, like the savages in America wear on their lances. Trophies of their battles with us. I've seen Emily's dress white with spittle. I've seen her face black with bruises . . . I've seen her eyes closed in death. I don't think she wanted to live in a world like that.'

He reached for his bowler. 'This doctor,' he said, standing up. 'Is he from the hospital at Epsom?'

'I don't know.' She stood up with him. 'I didn't see him again.'

He crossed to the door. 'Thank you for seeing me, Emily Greenbush,' he said.

She turned to face him. ' "For it is the grandest movement" ', she whispered, ' "the world has ever seen, And we'll win the Vote for Women, wearing purple, white and green." '

He allowed himself a smile. 'Still fighting,' he said.

She nodded. And he missed the single tear that rolled down her cheek as he saw himself out.

The Press, of course, had a field day. 'Yard Caught Napping' bellowed the newsvendors as the City woke the next morning. 'Are Our Policemen Wonderful?' pondered the *Mail*. 'No, They're Not!' The *Mirror* was sure. Panic-stricken politicians looked frantically under their beds and gave their tweenies more careful scrutiny than usual. In Suffolk, the vicar of Stoke-by-Nayland was defrocked by a frenzied mob of female watercress pickers. And in Frensham, a small army of less-than-reputable ladies had turned their backs on a passing squadron of the Queen's Bays and pulled their dresses over their heads. The horses had stampeded in disgust. No one felt *safe* any more.

But Lestrade had no time to worry himself about the Suffragette marches in Hyde Park and the Pilgrimage from the North. He, Tait, Lyall and a rather chastened Blevvins were looking for needles in haystacks – two, to be precise. A medical student and a doctor. It was the old way – house to house, knocking on doors, whole herds of shoe leather. But by the middle of the month, it paid off. Andrew Salway sat in Lestrade's office drinking a cup of Constable Lyall's tea.

'Yes, she was incredibly lucky, really.'

'Lucky?' Lestrade's eyes narrowed, as he looked again at the fresh-faced blond young man, all teeth and stethoscope. 'She died.'

'Yes, I know,' Salway said. 'But that was the odd thing.'

'It was?'

The telephone didn't stop that morning. At a Suffragette rally on Clapham Common, a number of leading politicians' wives had been arrested. Mrs Lloyd George, Mrs Asquith, Mrs Churchill, Mrs Bonar Law. The Yard coped with those aliases stoically, although they all had to be checked. But when six women all insisted they were Queen Mary, a kind of hysteria set in and the Yard switchboard was jammed as operators hauled feverishly on wires and tubes.

'Well, yes.' Salway fished his last bit of collapsed Bath Oliver out of his tea. 'You see, she was dazed and had a nosebleed, but that was all. Concussed, clearly, but I would not have suspected a fracture of the skull. Obviously, I was wrong.'

'Did you accompany Miss Davison to the hospital?'

'No. Dr Cole said he could manage.'

'Did you know this Cole?'

'Never saw him before. But then, I don't have much to do with the Epsom hospital. I'm based at Tommy's.'

'Did you visit Miss Davison? In hospital, I mean?'

'No, I didn't, I'm afraid.'

'Would it surprise you, then,' Lestrade asked, 'to learn that she died after days in a coma, her face swollen and bloody?'

Salway blinked. 'Yes,' he said. 'Most assuredly it would. The patient had no facial injuries other than a nosebleed. There may have been internal bleeding, of course. Are you telling me she was bandaged?'

'Heavily across the head, yes. Tell me, Mr Salway, how far is the hospital from the racecourse? How long would it take by car?'

'By car?' The medical student screwed up his face in his calculations. 'Ooh, about ten minutes, I'd say.'

'Is the road through a built-up area?'

'No, most of it is across open country. Rather picturesque heathland as a matter of fact. Why?'

'Oh, nothing.' Lestrade smiled. 'Just leaving no stone unturned, as is our wont here at the Yard.'

6

The Turkey Trot was all the rage that season and Fanny Lestrade was determined to master it. More than that, she was determined that her husband should.

'No, Sholto,' she screamed as they pirouetted on the terrace. '*Left* foot. Always the left.'

'But I'm right-handed, Fanny,' was his only defence.

'I'm not asking you to dance on your hands, dearest!' she hissed and caught him a nasty one as their knees collided.

'How are you on feminism?' he asked as the gramophone, mercifully, began to slow down and he could slow down with it.

'What an odd question.' She whisked him to the left so that his neck clicked. 'And don't think I don't recognize a subject-change when I hear one. Right leg. Right leg. And . . . twist. Oh, wait a minute, I'll wind up the machine.'

He collapsed gratefully on to the bench while she swept through the french windows and grappled with the apparatus.

'I did read the other day', she called to him, 'that a woman was arrested for wearing a split skirt in Richmond. What I wasn't clear about was whether that was illegal or only illegal in Richmond.' She'd joined him again on the sunlit terrace. 'Up and out of it, Sholto Lestrade. They're playing our tune.'

They were. The needle was scratching out, for the umpteenth time that morning, the hit song 'Hello, Hello, Who's Your Lady Friend?' as Fanny twirled Lestrade up out of his seat and down towards the lily pond. 'Don't tell me you've fallen foul of Mrs Pankhurst again?'

'Worse.' Lestrade twirled sideways. 'A lady called Boadicea.'

Fanny looked at him. 'I thought she was dead.' She spun away from him and spun back.

'Wishful thinking,' he said. 'Look, who's leading?'

'You're supposed to be,' she told him. 'Do you want to sit this one out?'

Lestrade sighed in gratitude. 'I thought you'd never ask,' he said and sank on to a bench again as the strains of the melody lingered on.

'Lemonade, dear?' She lifted the jug.

'Couldn't make it a Scotch, could you?'

She tutted and tilted up a flower pot overturned on the table by her elbow to reveal a bottle of the amber nectar. 'The sun isn't over the bowsprit yet, let alone the yardarm. Ice?'

He looked horrified. 'Filistine!' he gasped and fanned himself with his boater. 'I ran into an old friend of mine the other day. Emily Greenbush.'

'How old?' She raised an inquisitorial eyebrow.

'Old enough!' he said. 'She was there when Emily Davison was hurt at the Derby. Cheers, my dear.'

'You know it's a mad, mad world, don't you?' Fanny asked him.

'It is.' He nodded. 'But why in particular?'

'I read in *The Times* yesterday – did you see it? A woman has been made a magistrate – the first in the country. Her name is Emily Dawson. Isn't that odd. One Emily is elevated by men, the other killed because of them. Insane.'

'That's always the way of it,' Lestrade said. 'Until January, I always thought that being there, being an eyewitness, would make all the difference – and yet Millicent Millichip died right in front of me and I saw nothing. Even so, I'd kill for a complete account of what happened at the Derby.'

'But there is one.' Fanny sipped her lemonade. 'I read it in the *Graphic* the other day. The race was filmed.'

'Filmed?' Lestrade sat bolt upright.

'Yes, by a foreigner. A Frenchman I think. Oh, I expect Madison's thrown the old papers out by now, but I'm sure you can find back copies at the *Graphic* offices.'

He kissed her suddenly, and as it turned out recklessly, on the lips, because she nipped his moustache with her teeth, open as they were to receive another slug of lemonade. 'I love you, Fanny Lestrade.' He winced through the pain.

'Well, that's all right, then, isn't it? Come on.' And she hauled him upright. 'This is a policeman's wife's excuse-me. *Right* foot.' She grabbed his hand and waist. '*You're* leading.'

'So you normally film races involving motor cars, Mr Lartique?'

'*Oui*, especially ze Gordon-Bennets and ze 'ill-climbs.'

'But on June 4th you decided to take moving pictures of the Derby?'

'*Oui*, and in a moment you will see just 'ow moving. If I can just . . .' He was wrestling with the juddering apparatus in the darkness of the bowels of Scotland Yard. ' . . . release zis sprocket from ze . . . ah, zat's it.'

A jerky grey blob appeared on the far wall, from which Constables Tait and Lyall had moved the lockers, sergeants, for the use of. The blob gave way to the image of a lady in an enormous feathered hat, grinning at the camera.

'Pardon,' apologized M. Lartique. 'Madame Lartique.' He banged his fist down on the apparatus and it jolted into motion. A young girl was cavorting with another by the seaside, their nipples surprisingly prominent under their striped swimsuits.

'*Merde*!' the projectionist growled and instantly shut the machine down. 'Film editors! Zey are ze pits. I have no idea who zose women are and I categorically deny zat I took ze footage.' He began to crank the thing on by hand. 'Ah.' He peered through the viewer. 'Zis is it. Zis is ze Derby.'

King George and Queen Mary tottered into view on the wall. Constable Lyall was crunching popcorn until a glance from the guv'nor made him put it away. Tait was sure that Her Majesty winked at him, but it must have been a trick of the light. The camera of M. Lartique panned along the excited crowds gathering on Epsom Downs, in a riot of feathers and shining black toppers. In an instant, Lartique's lens was down in the paddock, hobnobbing with the horse owners with large buttonholes, prodding jockeys in their jodhpurs, horses in their numnahs. At last the bobbing camera was still, pointing at the fatal bend.

'Now I was on top of a Darracq wiz my tripod,' the cameraman explained. 'Normally, of course, I take ze still pictures. Zis one is moving about.'

It was. The crowd moved as one, craning to see around the bend into the straight. The outsiders were visible first.

'Zere is Mister Major,' explained Lartique. 'Ze grey. And next to 'im is Zane, annuzer grey. Zat is . . .' But Lestrade wasn't watching the horses or listening to the Frenchman's running commentary. Instead, he was watching the crowd to the right of the rail, swaying, chattering. Here and there, binoculars came up or hats were thrown. Then he saw it. A woman was hoisted up on to the rail by male hands. She seemed to be holding something, fluttering, streaming out in the wind. Then she turned, twisting away, glancing down behind her, her fists in the air, her hat gone. She seemed to slip, thrown forward over the rail and the charging horse hit her as she fell. And as the animal's rump rose high in the air, Lestrade saw it. On the saddle cloth, where Herbert Jones's bum had been seconds before, Anmer's number. Fourteen. The same number printed on the red calling card that had killed Worsthorne Griffin two months before.

The wall went blank.

'Is that it?' shouted Lestrade.

'Of course.' The cameraman unshuttered his equipment and began to rewind the spool. 'At zat moment I stopped filming and rushed to do what I could.'

'Which was?' Lestrade asked.

'Nothing,' Lartique admitted.

Lestrade threw his hands in the air. It was rather a Gallic gesture for a man who had never been further East than Lowestoft.

'Did you see Miss Davison taken away?'

'*Oui.*'

'By a doctor, name of Cole.'

Lartique shrugged. 'I do not know 'is name. I only know 'e drove a Mephisto.'

'A what?'

'A Mephisto Fiat. One of ze finest racing cars in ze world, Monsieur Le Strade. I know. I 'ave driven one. She 'andles like a woman, soft, receptive, melting . . .'

A silence had descended on the basement and Lartique cleared his throat, slightly disconcerted by the look on the faces of Tait and Lyall.

'Of course,' he went on, 'in ze 'ands of Lancia 'imself, ze car is unbeatable.'

'And Miss Davison was driven off in this car?' Lestrade checked.

'*Oui.*'

'Mephisto,' Tait suddenly said. 'What does that mean, Mr Lartique?'

'Mean?' the Frenchman's voice echoed inside the tube of his cinematograph machine as he blew out the dust. 'It means ze devil, Constable. Mephistopheles is ze devil 'imself.'

The offices of Messrs Constable were in Orange Street, a few doors down from that little shop where Mr Churchill, the gun expert, sold twelve bores to the gentry, when he wasn't helping Scotland Yard with their inquiries.

An enchanting little filly sat at the counter on the morning Lestrade arrived. 'Mr Somerset Maugham?'

'No,' Lestrade told her. 'My name is Lestrade. I'm here to see Mr Allardyce.'

The enchanting filly rummaged through her desk diary. 'I'm sorry, sir,' she trilled. 'I don't appear to have you down. Was it *Crocheting for Profit and Pleasure* or *The Role of Wallpaper in Napoleon's Career* you submitted?'

'Neither, I'm afraid,' Lestrade said. 'I'm from Scotland Yard.'

'Ah.' The filly picked up the business end of a speaking tube. 'That'll be *I Caught Crippen*. You're using the pen name "Chief Inspector Dew". Crafty.'

Lestrade was about to protest that he'd never take Walter Dew's name in vain when the filly waved her hand and shouted into the tube, 'Mr Allardyce? Mr Dew is here for you, sir . . . Mr Dew . . . Chief Inspector . . . Scotland Yard.' She smiled at Lestrade, then half turned her back and spoke *sotto voce* into the mouthpiece. 'You know, that ghastly tosh about catching Crippen . . .'

But Lestrade had placed a hand over the tube. 'Which floor?' he asked.

The filly looked horrified. Obviously, she'd been less than discreet. 'Um . . . third . . .' she said. 'But you can't . . .'

But Lestrade had. He bounded up the stairs two at a time while in the filly's view, then slowed down to a more sedate one at a time on the turn of the stairs. Allardyce's office was straight ahead.

'On his way up?' he heard the editor say as the door crashed back. Allardyce stared at him, the mouthpiece still in his hand. He seemed to subside. 'Jessica, my pet,' he hissed into the tube. 'This is Superintendent Lestrade, not Chief Inspector Dew. Remind me to fire you at the next possible opportunity . . . What?' Lestrade saw a guilty smirk appear on Allardyce's face. 'Oh, all right, then. But don't forget the clotted cream.' And he put the tube down. 'Mr Lestrade.' He stood up and extended a hand. 'Good to see you again. Coffee?'

'Thank you, no.' Lestrade accepted the proffered chair.

'You don't mind if I do?' Allardyce busied himself with a steaming machine behind him that gurgled and gasped like a retired general. 'It's been a bitch of a morning, frankly. See that?'

He waved in the direction of a pile of papers on his desk. Lestrade saw it.

'Anthony Hope's latest. *Return to Zenda*, it's called. Well, it's not a patch on the first. Even *Rupert of Hentzau* was all right, but this one . . . Hope*less*, I'm afraid. But you didn't come to listen to the whinges of an editor, I feel sure.'

'The car,' Lestrade said. 'The car involved in the hit-and-run at Hyde Park Corner. I never asked you the make.'

'The make?' Allardyce frowned.

'Unless you don't know one car from another . . .'

'Oh, but I do. I even do a spot of driving myself. Drove at Brooklands, once . . .'

'Brooklands,' Lestrade repeated.

'It's a racecourse in Surrey,' Allardyce told him.

'I know,' Lestrade said. 'It's just that it's a name that's cropping up a lot lately.'

'Well, the car, I'm pretty sure, was a Mephisto. Quite an unusual one to find touring London in a pea-souper.'

'Why?' Lestrade asked.

'Well, it's a racing jalopy, Mr Lestrade. Designed by the Italians to cope with hill-climbs and hairpin bends. Do you know, it does nought to thirty in four point eight minutes?'

'Get away!' Lestrade was impressed. Many was the hour he'd had to coax his Lanchester out of the stable. Only the previous year he'd gone to his doctor with cranker's elbow.

'But all this is in the report I gave to the constable,' Allardyce told him, stretching out with his feet on the desk.

'Indeed.' Lestrade nodded. 'Tell me about the constable.'

'The constable? Well, let me see. He was . . . middle-aged. Standard height – for a policeman, I mean. Letter F on his collar. Took notes very fast, I remember. I was impressed.'

'Yes,' Lestrade said. 'Those letters on his collar bother me.'

'Oh?' Allardyce raised an eyebrow. 'Why?'

'F Division is in Paddington. Your constable was patrolling in A Division's manor.'

'Well, I didn't ask him what Division he was in. He was asking all the questions. He did tell me his name, though.'

'Really?'

'Yes. Smith. Alexander Smith. Tell me, Mr Lestrade, was there something odd about this policeman? Something I should know?'

'When I know it, Mr Allardyce,' the Superintendent said, 'rest assured I shall tell you . . .'

But Lestrade wasn't telling Allardyce anything. There *was* no Alexander Smith in F Division.

A shrill whistle shattered the morning. 'Yes, Jessica?' Allardyce had picked up the tube. 'When? Who? John Adams? Never heard of him. Oh, all right. Yes. Yes.' He reached across Hope's tome. 'Yes, here it is. When did he leave it? Well, he may have insisted, but you really mustn't let any Tom, Dick or Harry into my office, you know. Yes.' His sharp tone had left him. 'All right, yes. Thursday. Oh, and don't forget the fly whisk.' And he put the mouthpiece back.

He held up another pile of paper. 'Unsolicited,' he said. 'Yet again. I do wish these people wouldn't just leave things like this. What's wrong with a letter, a synopsis?'

Lestrade commiserated with the man. Even so, he thought an operation was going a bit far. He saw himself out and at the bottom of the stairs, Jessica was purring into the mouthpiece again, discussing all kinds of kitchen utensils and their uses.

The light burned blue late at the Yard that night. The glow of sunset had died away and Sholto Lestrade sat in his creaking office chair while detectives lit lamps around him and pens scratched on paper.

'They're tied up,' Lestrade said to Blevvins for the umpteenth time that night. 'Don't ask me how, but they're connected. Worsthorne Griffin dies of a heart attack after receiving a card with the number 14 on it – the same number as on the King's horse at the Derby. That horse killed Emily Davison. And the dying woman was carried away by a doctor in a Mephisto racing car, the same make of car that ploughed into Robert Peel at Hyde Park Corner. Are we chasing shadows, Sergeant?'

There was a snore from the corner. 'Blevvins!' Lestrade snapped.

'Uh? Oh, sorry, guv. Dozed off a bit there, I'm afraid. You were saying?'

Lestrade threw his cigar butt into his empty cup. 'I was saying, go home, Blevvins. And don't talk to any strange women.'

'Oh, righto, guv.' And Blevvins reached for his hat. He nearly collided on his way out of the office with a world-weary Inspector Kane, boater in hand, breath in fist. They mumbled to each other as implacable foes do and Kane plonked himself down on Lestrade's second-hand Chesterfield.

'Sorry, guv,' he said. 'You don't mind, do you? It's been a long day.'

'It has that, John,' the Superintendent agreed. 'Knocking off?'

'Well, I would,' the Inspector said. 'But something's come up.'

'Not your number, I hope.' Lestrade smiled. 'I'm chasing numbers myself at the moment.'

'Does the name Thomas Allardyce mean anything to you?'

'Allardyce? Yes. He's a witness to that hit-and-run back in the pea-souper in January. Why?'

'When did you see him last?'

'When?' Lestrade fished for his half-hunter. 'Er . . . twelve hours ago, give or take. Why do you ask?'

'He's in the London Free,' Kane told him. 'Acute poisoning.'

'What?' Lestrade sat upright, suddenly aware that John Kane was looking at him intently.

'Can you be exact, guv?' the Inspector asked him. 'About the time you left him, I mean?'

'Er . . . no.' Lestrade tried to think. 'No, not exactly. It was gone eleven, I think. I was with him . . . what . . . twenty minutes, I suppose. How did you get involved?'

'Call from C Division. Sam Weatherley.'

' "Buck-passer" Weatherley? Is he still trying it on?'

'Said he wasn't "up" on poisons. Wondered if HQ could help. He got through to the policeman's policeman, who got through to me.'

Lestrade shrugged. 'Yes, that's the chain of command, all right.' He nodded. 'So how is Allardyce?'

'Well, he's stable now, but it was touch and go this afternoon. Constable contacted us. A distraught woman on the other end of the line.'

'Jessica,' Lestrade said.

'That's the one.' Kane nodded. 'She seemed very solicitous. Nice to find such loyal employees.'

'Yes,' Lestrade said. 'Although I think you'll find she's at her most loyal on Thursdays in the company of clotted cream and a fly whisk.'

'Good God!' Kane said.

'I know.' Lestrade raised his hands in the air. 'I don't know what the world's coming to. Temptation is a wicked thing, isn't it? I'm just glad we haven't got any women on the staff here.'

'Ah, you haven't heard about Mrs Robley-Brown, then?' Kane looked almost apologetic.

'No.' Lestrade raised an eyebrow. 'But I've a feeling I'm going to.'

'She's one of a group of women raised by Miss Nina Boyle who seems convinced that girls crying "rape" are being mishandled by male officers.'

'I suspect what narks Miss Boyle', Lestrade observed, 'is that they are being handled at all.'

'Quite,' Kane agreed. 'Anyway, Mrs Robley-Brown patrols up and down Shaftesbury Avenue in a uniform of her own design.'

'Really?'

'Yes, it's pink. Lots of tulle.'

'Subtle, at least.' Lestrade nodded. 'Why is Shaftesbury Avenue so lucky?'

'Well, apparently, Mrs Robley-Brown takes luncheon at the Trocadero and tea at Pattinson's Patisserie. That sort of shapes her manor. And the length of her shift.'

'God save us!' Lestrade sighed. 'So the solicitous secretary called the law?'

'She did,' Kane said. 'As soon as Allardyce collapsed, she was on the blower.'

'You've talked to Allardyce?'

'He wasn't very coherent. Rambling a little. In and out, if you know what I mean.'

'What were his symptoms?'

'Stomach pains. Slow pulse, the doctor said.'

'Colour of vomit?'

'Green as grass,' Kane told him.

'Hmm.' Lestrade nodded. 'Digitalis would be my guess. The purple foxglove.'

'Well.' Kane sighed, rubbing his burning eyes. 'No shortage of that in Orange Street of a Tuesday morning.'

'Try the coffee,' Lestrade suggested.

'What?'

'You haven't been to his office?'

'Haven't had time.'

'Well, do it tomorrow, John, when you've had a few hours' kip. He's got one of these new Cona coffee machines. Give the glass bit to the boffins on the fourth floor. If it hasn't been washed out, I think you'll find the odd tincture of digitalis purpurea at the bottom.'

'So, what are we saying?' Kane asked his boss. 'That the coffee makers of Brazil are careless in their bean-picking?'

Lestrade thought for a moment. 'Tom Allardyce was a witness to a murder, John,' he said softly. 'I don't think Brazil has anything to do with it. Unless, of course, our man is mad.'

'Mad, guv?'

'Don't you know your *Charley's Aunt*? That's where the nuts come from.'

Mr Middlemass of Twinings was co-operation itself. By lunchtime the next day, John Kane knew all about the medicinal properties of coffee, vouchsafed by the great Arab physician Avicenna. He knew that Anthony Sherley introduced the drink to London and that beans cost £5 an ounce. And back in 1621, that was no trifling amount. John Evelyn, having little better to do at Oxford than write his diary, Volume One, met a Greek called Nathaniel Conopios who drank the stuff regularly. No, Mr Middlemass assured the Inspector, it never contained extract of foxglove and was utterly harmless. In fact, the caffeine that coffee contained was enervating and nourishing and, in Mr Middlemass's experience, did wonders for the cuticles. Messrs Twinings delivered coffee and tea to Messrs Constable on a regular basis and had never had any complaints. Mr Middlemass was certain that whatever had incommoded Mr Allardyce, it was not Twinings's coffee.

But it was. John Kane was a good copper. Years at the knees of Frank Froest and Fred Wensley and Sholto Lestrade – the big three as they were known in those days – had not been wasted. Kane leaned in the time-honoured tradition on the boffin on the fourth floor and he came up with the findings that Allardyce's coffee machine, lifted from Allardyce's office only that morning, did indeed contain traces of digitalis.

'Who made his coffee?' Kane's dark eyes burned intensely into the blank face of the poisoned man's secretary.

'I did,' she said, her moist lip quivering slightly.

'How?' Kane asked her.

'Well, I put the paper in and sprinkled the coffee on to it. Tom ... Mr Allardyce ... likes his coffee black, so I added another spoonful.'

'And this is how you always made it?'

'Yes. Ever since Mr Allardyce had the machine installed. It's an American idea. Apparently, it's all the rage in Chicago and on Wall Street.'

'Wall Street?' Kane repeated.

'That's in New York.' Jessica showed off her encyclopaedic knowledge of the Atlas. 'Littlejohn and Robin use it all the time.'

'They do?'

'Yes. They're our American outlet, experimenting with a floppy-covered book they call a paperback. It'll never catch on, of course.'

'Of course,' Kane agreed. 'What time did you make Mr Allardyce's coffee?'

'Ten o'clock,' Jessica remembered. 'As he arrived.'

'He arrived at ten every day?'

'Yes,' she said. 'Except Fridays.' And she blushed suddenly, crimson to her hair roots.

'You made the coffee as usual.' Kane ignored it. 'Nothing different?'

'No. I told you ...'

'I know you did. It's just that this time, Miss Fry, there were traces of digitalis in it. Poison.'

'Oh, no.' Her hand rose to her lips. 'That's not possible.'

'Really? You called the police. You must have had reason to suppose ...'

'I called everybody.' She sobbed quietly. 'The police, the ambulance, the fire brigade. I ... panicked, I'm afraid.' And the tears welled up and burst out into uncontrollable floods. John Kane, it has to be said, was a sucker for a pretty woman in trouble. He

81

whisked out his extra-large mansize hanky, the spotless one he kept just for such moments, and patted Jessica's shoulder while she blew into it with the volume and finesse of a Clyde tanker.

'I have a confession to make,' she sniffed.

'Oh?' Kane stopped his patting.

'Tom and I . . . well, we are something of an item,' she told him.

'Really?'

'Of course, only on Thursdays.'

'Of course.' He nodded. Such omniscient patience had he learned from the great Lestrade himself.

'Mrs Allardyce goes Quantity Surveying on Thursdays.'

'Quantity Surveying?' Kane's eyes narrowed.

'At the Polytechnic. That leaves Tom and me alone in Hammersmith.'

Which sounded like a fate worse than death to Kane, but he didn't like to say so. 'Do I assume that Mrs Allardyce is not aware of this situation?'

'Oh, God, no.' Jessica shuddered. 'She thinks Tom is in the local Cribbage Club. Oh, Inspector.' She leaned towards him. 'I'd never do anything to hurt dear Tom. He's the sole reason I came to work for Constable – apart from the fact that they're marvellous employers, of course. Until today, the future looked so bright; the future was Orange Street.'

'Until today . . .' Kane frowned. 'Mr Allardyce will be all right, Miss Fry,' he explained. 'Whoever laced his coffee didn't get the blend right. Now, tell me, who might have had a reason to want him dead?'

Jessica blew one last time and handed the soggy linen back. 'Well, it's a cut-throat business, modern publishing,' she said. 'I know he was about to turn down Mr Hope. The other day, he was less than enthusiastic about *People My Father Knew* by Megan Lloyd George.'

'Lloyd George?' Kane echoed.

'Yes.' Jessica sniffed. 'I believe he's the Chancellor of the Exchequer.'

'Yes.' The Inspector smiled. 'I have heard it said. So, do failed authors really kill their publishers?'

'A rejection slip is a terrible thing, Mr Kane. It's like the black spot. I've got a horrible feeling that Tom would have turned Mr Stevenson down, had the two of them met.'

'Yes.' Kane nodded. 'He should have stuck to railways, I think. Tell me, did anyone come to see Mr Allardyce that morning?'

'Er . . . yes. That nasty little man calling himself Chief Inspector Dew. Of course, that was peculiar.'

'What was?'

'Well.' She checked that they were alone in the chintz-laden reception room. 'His real name, it transpires, is Lestrade. And he's not a chief inspector at all; he's a superintendent. But you must know him, surely?'

'Oh, you know.' Kane grinned. 'Ships that pass in the night. Do you know why he came to see Mr Allardyce?'

'No. But he behaved very oddly. Giving a false name and shooting up the stairs without an appointment. Is that normal police procedure?'

'Normal, no,' Kane conceded. 'But it may well be police procedure. Was there anyone else?'

'Um . . . oh, yes, a Mr Adams called. John Adams. I told him Tom hadn't arrived – this was before ten – but he insisted he left a manuscript in his office.'

'And did he?'

'I don't know . . . wait. Yes, yes he did, because I rang Tom, while Mr Lestrade was there in fact, and told him Mr Adams had left the manuscript somewhere and Tom said he'd found it on his desk.'

'Did you know this Adams?'

'No.' Jessica shook her head. 'I didn't know him from Adam.'

'Would you know him again?'

Jessica frowned. 'I really don't know,' she said. 'I doubt it. He was middle-aged, dark hair, rather small eyes. Rather nondescript, really.'

'And he was alone in Mr Allardyce's office?'

'Yes, but only for a few seconds. It didn't take me long to haul up my skirts and hare after him. I was the Under Eighteens Uphill Sprint Champion at school, so he can't have had much time.'

'And you, at this stage, hadn't made the coffee?'

'No.'

'But when Mr Lestrade was there?'

'Tom was already drinking.'

'You don't know exactly when he took his first cup, I suppose?'

'No.'

'It's lucky he didn't have more than two. As it was, the stomach pump jammed.'

'Oh dear.' Jessica's lip quivered again. 'The poor darling.'

'I'd like to see Mr Allardyce's office, now.' Kane stood up. 'It's all right,' he said. 'I'd like to see it alone.'

A rather awful photograph of Mr de Vere Stacpoole grinned smugly from one wall and an even worse one of Miss Marie

Corelli from another. But it wasn't the décor Kane was interested in. One of Sam Weatherby's lads had already half-inched the coffee maker for forensic purposes, but this was the first time a detective had been in this room since the visit of Superintendent Lestrade. He was careful with his dabs, though from the state of the place, every copper, ambulance driver and fireman in London had already careered through it, several times. He mechanically checked Allardyce's drawers. Manuscripts spilled out in an untidy profusion; pens cluttered the desk furniture. He picked up a handwritten book – *Return to Zenda* – and read the opening paragraph – 'I wonder when in the world you're going to do anything, Rudolf?' said my brother's wife.

'My dear Rose,' I answered, laying down my egg-spoon. 'Why in the world should I do anything? I've already impersonated my distant cousin King Rudolph the Fifth and had all those rattling adventures with Sapt and von Tarlenheim . . . ' and if he hadn't still been standing up, Kane would probably have fallen asleep. He dropped the manuscript as Tom Allardyce had already done and picked up another. It was called *I Caught Crippen* and was written by Chief Inspector Walter Dew on an upright Remington of the type they used at the Yard. But it was a third manuscript that caught Kane's eye. It was called *Thirty-five Years at the Yard* and the author's name was Sholto Joseph Lestrade. What caught Kane's eye even more was the line scrawled across it in what seemed, from other examples lying around, to be Tom Allardyce's handwriting. 'What appalling rubbish. Tell this idiot he's wasting his time. T. A.'

Well, well, well, Kane mused. His old guv'nor had literary ambitions he hadn't dreamed of. And these literary ambitions lay rejected on the desk of a man visited only yesterday by that same old guv'nor; on the desk of a man who had narrowly missed death by digitalis poisoning.

Lestrade should have taken a holiday that July, but what with the time he'd lost through his fall from the *Titanic*, he thought it only right to soldier on, his shoulder to the wheel, his nose to the crimestone. The truth was, it was as though the murk and silence of the pea-souper had never left him. Everywhere he turned, he faced brick walls, wreathed in fog, an intangible something just out of his reach. And if that wasn't bad enough, he had a visit, at the Yard, from Alaric Bligh.

'Mr Lestrade, I'm not one to carp,' the managing director said. 'But you did intimate, nearly three months ago now, that poor old Worsthorne Griffin was done to death, did you not?'

'It is my belief, sir, yes. Would you like a Peek Frean?'

'No, sir!' Bligh bellowed. 'I would like a few answers. How are your inquiries going? Why, after your initial sortie, have you not questioned my staff? What about the other houses in the City? And have you considered Morant?'

'Morant?'

Alaric Bligh sat back in his chair. 'I won't have it said that I'm a vindictive man,' he said. 'But Charles Morant is the one man on the Stock Exchange I'd not turn my back on.'

'Tell me more,' said Lestrade.

'He's known as "Broker" Morant in the City,' Bligh told him. 'Made his first million before he was twenty-four. A child prodigy, Lestrade, and clever with it. Mind like a razor.'

'What makes you suspect him?' Lestrade asked.

'He'd sell his own granny down the river. Back in '95 that was. He did it for a bet. Made a few hundred that day, I believe. Of course, the old girl was frightfully upset, not being terribly dapper on the tiller.'

'She was in a boat?' Lestrade checked.

'Lord, no, tied blindfold to a raft. The bet was, would she make it to Teddington before a lighter got her. There was hell to pay with the Port authorities. Of course, Broker's father thrashed him to within an inch of his life.'

'The old girl was his mother?' Lestrade asked.

'No, the raft was an heirloom the elder Morant's grandfather had built. Could have been damaged. That's the sort of people they are, Lestrade. Scum of the earth, in fact.'

'Indeed,' Lestrade concurred. 'But what is the link with Mr Griffin?'

'Well.' Bligh leaned forward confidentially. 'That's just it. Morant is with Dewsman Porter, Lombard Street. They're renowned for insider dealing – handled the Marconi business.'

'Indeed?' Lestrade said again, this time in the form of a question.

'But that isn't all.'

'It isn't?'

'No. You remember that peculiar calling card you showed me? The one with the Devil's head on it?'

'And the number 14 on the back? Yes, I do.'

'Well, you asked me at the time if it meant anything to me and I said it didn't.'

'And?'

'And . . . ' Bligh looked carefully around him, as though the wastepaper baskets and shoe-boxes had ears. 'I've been unable to get that devil's face out of my head since. And suddenly, just yesterday it came to me. Broker Morant has a racehorse. It ran in the Derby last month.'

'Did it now?' Lestrade sat up.

'Know what its name was, Lestrade?' the stockman asked.

The Superintendent shook his head.

'El Diablo,' said Bligh, the silence after he spoke sending little shivers up the spine of Sholto Lestrade. 'That's Spanish for the devil.'

7

His Imperial Majesty Napoleon III always had a thing for England. The house in Leamington Spa where he stayed as a young man still stands and to the end of his colourful life, he contined to cherish the hardwood tipstaff they gave him when he was sworn in as Special Constable to thump the Chartists on Kennington Common. And when the end of that colourful life did come, they buried him in the unpretentious acres of the mausoleum at Farnborough and with him, his wife Eugénie, who had lived out her years at Farnborough Hill.

But something else had happened at Farnborough. A man had been killed. It was a sign of the times perhaps that he died two days after a delegation had gone to see the Prime Minister, demanding he consider a tunnel under the Channel. That was how mad the world was in the year of our Lord 1913.

If Sam Cody was honest with himself, which he hardly ever was, he'd have had to admit that he was a little narked that J. T. C. Moore-Brabazon had carried out the first *officially* observed flight at Stepney five years before; that Charlie Rolls had whizzed backwards and forwards like some blasted flying shuttle across the Channel and back; and that T. O. M. Sopwith had reached Belgium on a wing and a prayer. And yes, it *did* rankle that his name was not among the first eight who were to aviate under the auspices of the Royal Aero Club. What really got his goat, however (the animal was very loyal, for a pet) was that B. C. Hucks had looped the loop and flown upside down without falling out two years before. Cody did try to console himself with commenting to all and sundry that all one could do with a loop was loop it, but it didn't really convince anybody.

So here he was, on that gorgeous August day, striding manfully to the controls of his Codified Deperdussin, gleaming and shining in the sunshine. As usual, he was alone. It was still early. In the meadows he saw old Hatfield driving his cows slowly o'er the lea for milking, his dog a black-and-white speck, harrying and chasing at their cloven heels, adding to the dust and noise of their progress.

He patted the crate's fuselage. Funny how these old totems clung. He was nearly fifty-two years of age, too old, too slow, too heavy. And above all, too mononumular. Everybody else in the flying business seemed to have a double-barrelled name; Moore-Brabazon, Santos-Dumont, Graham-White, Mortimer-Sizer, even Rolls-Royce. Never mind, he'd show them. He'd show them all. He clambered into the cockpit, fitting the leather driving helmet under his chin and hauled on the gauntlets. Should be bliss up there today. Wind from the south-west, no sign of thorms. He'd be up there with the swallows in a jiffy. He waved to Murchison on the ground and the funny little mechanic who was his facto-tum raised his thumb and leapt up to catch the propellor shaft. Cody's thumb hit the joystick button and it coughed once, twice, then belched into action, shuddering like some juggernaut. The wheels of the old perambulator slid forward over the yellow grass of summer and the dust flew out behind him as he hauled on the controls and swung to his left.

His rudder flapped in vague accordance with his efforts and he just had time to see the red calling card jammed in his dashboard before he was careering on to the long runway, Murchison disap-pearing in a cloud of dust. He paused before he pulled his goggles down and pulled the card out of its jam. A face, was it? It was jiggling around as the throttle eased forward and he couldn't focus properly. Yes, a face. A devil's face. Leering. Evil. He knew that face. He'd seen it before. He flipped the card over and just as the wind took it and ripped it out of his grasp and up under the upper wing, where it caught in the struts, he made out the number '14'.

Now the great hangars tilted as the plane gathered momentum. Grass flitches flew skywards as the pram wheels cut and gouged into hard earth. Cody braced himself, trying to ignore the old trouble in his back as the wind whipped like rawhide and he felt his stomach bounce off his chin and he was in the air.

There was turbulence at thirty feet, calm once he'd cleared the cedars. Now the rush of air was sweet and good and he was at one with the morning. He saw the runway below like a silver pencil on a parchment table-cloth and the yellow fields waiting for the harvest in still patience. He checked that he had the necessaries between his legs – Fry's chocolate and the ingredients for making soup. This was Hampshire – it paid to take precautions. He saw the Whitewater like a glittering ribbon in the distance and the cluster of houses around the great squares and barracks at Alder-shot. By his own reckoning now he was travelling south-east, over Dogmersfield towards Long Sutton, at about two thousand feet.

Above him was all azure and silence, flecked with the tails of the racing mares, chequered with the spluttering roar of his own engines. How marvellous it would be, he thought, tilting back his goggles, to switch off that damned Antoinette for a moment and just drift. What a silence that would be. Gliding like an eagle on the currents, like a leaf on the stream.

And Sam Cody, too old, too slow, too heavy, was still thinking that when it happened. The unthinkable. The impossible. The Antoinette coughed, spluttered like a consumptive with ruptured lungs and died. But Cody heard no silence. He heard the pounding of his heart, smashing in his ears, drumming in his head. He tugged off the helmet so that his wild hair blew free. His thumb pumped the button. He twisted this way and that, wrestling with the joystick, fighting the plane and the air together.

He knew of course that there was no danger. André Jacques Garnerin had leapt out of a balloon at 3,000 feet up over London as long ago as 1802. He was sick of course, but that may have been to do with his landing in St Pancras. And an American chappie, Captain Albert Berry, had hopped out of his Benoist over Jefferson Barracks, Missouri, only two years ago. He'd hit the ground running and reported at once to his commanding officer. Even a woman had done it, for God's sake, albeit an American, only two months ago over Griffith Park, Los Angeles. There was absolutely no problem. Except one, of course. The one that mattered. Sam Cody didn't have a parachute.

He fought those controls all the way down. Keep away from that church, from those children on their way to the harvest fields, from that haywain and those plodding horses. The Deperdussin slid like a blasted bird, hanging and dead, past the cedars that ringed the lake. If only he could reach the water, all would be well. Keep her nose up. Up. That's it. That's the way. Ease to starboard. More. More.

There was no more. Only the sickening crash as the aircraft tore through the beeches, ploughing into the copse like a bullet through butter. The propellor bent, the fuselage disintegrated. Pram wheels spun off in all directions like King Richard's crown at Bosworth Field, to lie neglected in the shrubbery yards away. Sam Cody's neck snapped at the fourth vertebra, as surely and cleanly as if John Ellis, the hangman, had come to call. They heard it in Aldershot. They saw the smoke in Basingstoke. They felt it most keenly in the Aero Club. For Sam Cody never knew how much they all thought of him – J. T. C. Moore-Brabazon and the others. Only that morning, among his effects back at the airfield, the police found a letter he'd never opened, inviting him to join.

'Samuel Cody,' John Kane said, stroking the granite chin that was already marking him out as a manhunter of the Yard under the big three. The pieces of paper plastered over his office wall were beginning to multiply. The plump corpse of Millicent Millichip looked up at him from her photo on the slab, the dead eyes still open, taunting him, mocking him. 'Come on,' they seemed to say. 'It's been eight months. What have you been doing?' His eyes flickered to the photograph of a wrecked plane, its fuselage twisted like chicken wire in the spinney into which it had ploughed. 'Samuel Cody,' he said again.

It had reached him, the short straw. The Millichip case was dying and Edward Henry, the policeman's policeman, couldn't keep men on cases like that for ever. He'd transferred eight of Kane's lads to traffic, now that someone had decided that buses were dangerous. Time to descale the operation. Take stock. Move over. Move over to Samuel Cody.

'This looks familiar.' Kane turned at the sound of the old voice.

'Guv.' He'd been startled none the less. 'I was miles away.'

'Farnborough, by the looks of it.' Lestrade recognized the smashed plane.

'Samuel Cody.' Kane nodded.

'No relation to . . . ?' Lestrade suggested.

'No.' Kane shook his head. 'Mere coincidence.'

'You've been there?' Lestrade asked.

Kane nodded. 'There was hardly one bone left in place,' he said. 'I wouldn't want to go that way.' He sighed, straightening his tortured back. 'I wouldn't really want to go at all, but I certainly wouldn't want to go that way.'

'Perhaps he did.' Lestrade perched on the corner of Kane's desk, scattering a stand of pens as he did so. He tried to catch them and knocked over an inkpot. 'Oh, bugger. Sorry, John.'

'What? Suicide, you mean?'

'It's a thought.'

'No.' Kane shook his head. 'Know what this is?' He passed a piece of fractured metal to Lestrade while mopping up the flow with his tea-towel, inspectors for the use of.

'Not part of Ned Kelly's armour, is it? I know old Waverley in the Black Museum's been after that for quite a while.'

'It's a fuel pipe,' Kane told him. 'Off the plane Cody was flying when he crashed.' He stood up and placed the wet blue cloth into the hands of a passing constable. 'What do you make of that?'

Lestrade peered at the copper tube. 'It's been cut,' he said. 'Jewel saw, I'd say.'

'So would I, guv. Now why would a man who wanted to kill himself bother to saw through his own fuel pipe? All he need have done, if he had to do it in a plane, was to pull the joystick. Or push it. Whatever you do.'

'Point taken,' Lestrade agreed. 'So somebody wanted Mr Cody dead.'

Kane nodded, still staring at the wall. 'They did,' he said. 'And you'll never guess what my lads have come up with – the three Mr Henry's left me, anyway.'

'Go on,' Lestrade said. 'I could do with a chuckle about now.'

'Samuel Cody and Millicent Millichip knew each other.'

'Go on,' said Lestrade again, this time with a different emphasis. 'In what way?'

'She did for him.'

'Don't be silly, John,' Lestrade said after the enormity of Kane's statement had sunk in. 'She's been dead for . . . oh, I see. She was his cleaner.'

'At his house in Mortlake. Some years ago, of course.'

'She ran a pub, didn't she?' Lestrade had had his hands full since Millicent Millichip had collapsed into his arms in the pea-souper. Details whirled in his head like dervishes.

'Came into some money, I've discovered.'

'Ah,' Lestrade said. 'A rich uncle?'

'A benefactor of sorts,' Kane told him. 'But I'm damned if I know who at the moment. And that isn't all. Seen this before?'

He passed the battered red card to Lestrade.

'We found it in the wrecked plane,' Kane said.

'The devil's calling card,' Lestrade muttered.

'Can I help you, by the way?' Kane asked.

'Hmm?' Lestrade was staring at Mrs Millichip now too, and at the calling card. 'I thought you wanted to see me, John.'

'Did I? Oh.' Kane slapped his forehead. 'I'm sorry,' he said. 'It's been one of those days. Did you ever find your chiv? The one with the brass knuckles?'

'No.' Lestrade shook his head. 'Oh, it'll turn up. I do feel lostish without it, though. We've been together through some scrapes, those knuckles and I. Why do you ask?'

'Oh, no reason. Does this look familiar to you?'

Kane flicked open a ledger on his desk and handed Lestrade another scarlet card with a devil's face.

'My God,' Lestrade said. 'Are you printing these, John? Where did you get this one?'

'Between the floorboards at the Phlebotomist's Arms. I had my lads tear the place apart, in some desperation, I might add. Didn't please the old girl's clientele one little bit, all that hammering and sawing. Put a hell of a froth on the beer, though. And that isn't all we found.'

'Oh?'

Kane crossed to a filing cabinet, scarred with years of policemen's finger-nails and policemen's feet. He hauled out three canvas sacks from the bowels of a drawer.

'Cash?' Lestrade's eyebrows rose.

'Nearly three thousand pounds in used notes.'

'Three thousand?' Lestrade whistled through his teeth. 'Plenty of money in the brewing trade, then.'

'Too much, in my opinion,' Kane said. 'I talked to Millicent's paramours, George Potter, Arthur Weston, Archie Emblin. They were all very fond of the old girl, but they don't remember her coming into money or flashing it about.'

'Perhaps she was just mean.' Lestrade shrugged. 'And didn't want the banks to have it. Or the Chancellor of the Exchequer. Some people are like that.'

'No, they're not.' Kane chuckled. 'No one's like the Chancellor of the Exchequer! Now, about that card . . .'

'Aha!' Lestrade wagged a finger. 'So that's it. Here you are, inviting me round for tea and Peek Freans . . .' He coughed at this point to help the penny to drop.

'Oh, God, yes. Sorry, guv. Dangerfield!'

'Sir?' A fresh-faced copper shoved his head around the door.

'Tea and biscuits. Make them snappy!' Kane ordered.

'I'll do my best, sir,' the lad said.

'. . . tea and Peek Freans,' Lestrade continued, with a wistful smile on his face. 'And all the time, you're picking my brains and pinching my cases. Well, I tell you, John.' The guv'nor slid into Kane's best chair. 'You can have 'em. All of 'em. I'm getting too old for the murder game, I can assure you.'

'Nonsense, guv.' Kane chuckled. 'You'll go on for ever. Now . . .'

'I know, I know, the card.' Lestrade picked it up. 'Mine had a "14" on the back.'

'Yours?'

'The one somebody sent to old Worsthorne Griffin, of Raleigh Harman in the City. I think it was designed to kill him.'

'Kill him?' Kane's ears pricked up. 'Bit hit and miss, wasn't it?'

'Hit and miss?' Lestrade repeated.

'Well, yes. Sorry to teach my Superintendent to suck eggs, guv, but . . . well, a knife, a gun, a blunt instrument, any of that lot will do nicely, but a calling card . . . ' Kane picked it up. 'All right, it's horrible, I'll grant you. But I doubt it would frighten my Michael and he's only eight – not that many people know that, of course.'

'Hmm,' Lestrade said. 'But it's the connaughtations, isn't it? An old man, dicky ticker, never the same since his son died, sees something that reminds him of something. Wallop! Zing go the strings of his heart.'

'All right,' Kane said. 'But where does that leave Mrs Millichip?'

'Chiswick Crematorium, if I remember aright,' Lestrade said, straight-faced. 'She'll be coming up roses this month, I shouldn't wonder.'

'Your tea, guv'nors.' The fresh-faced bobby was back. 'Oh, and . . . er . . . Mr Lestrade, sir?'

'Yes?'

'May I have your autograph, sir? Oh, it's not for me, you understand, it's for my young lady friend.'

Lestrade frowned. 'What's this, Inspector?' he growled. 'You allow your officers to have lady friends?'

Kane smirked at him.

'It wouldn't have done in my day.' And he scribbled his signature on the boy's extended pocketbook. 'There,' he said. 'And think yourself thankful that I'm not your guv'nor. Was she sent it, d'you think?' Lestrade was back to the red card, to the job in hand.

'I don't know,' Kane admitted. 'Perhaps she was the sender.'

'Perhaps she was.' Lestrade nodded while Kane was mother. 'It's food for thought, anyway. And when I've demolished this food for flesh, I'll see if there's a connection between old Griffin and the dear-departed publican. And then, of course, we need to know who sent the card to Samuel Cody.'

'Guv,' Kane said, his face stern in the glint of the afternoon sun. 'I must admit I wouldn't object to a little help on this one. I've got dead publicans, dead aviators. The only thing that isn't dead around here is a certainty.'

'Ah, yes.' Lestrade nodded. 'And we mustn't forget Miss Emily Davison and how she fits in to this little devil's triangle, must we?'

The Lanchester was coughing a little these days. It had been eleven years since His Late Majesty, Edward VII, by the Grace of God, had given it to the then Chief Inspector Lestrade as a mark of his affection and gratitude. After all, the Chief Inspector as was *had* just saved the king's life.

People said to Lestrade, 'Why don't you trade it in, Sholto? A Darracq perhaps, or a Hispano-Suiza? After all, you're comfortably off now, married a rich woman and so on. You can't be short of a bob or two.' No, he wasn't. And yes, he'd married a rich woman, but the Lanchester's seat fitted his bum pretty well and she usually started first crank in the morning.

So Elsa coughed her way up the gravel drive that sun-gilded evening. They had company. Fanny was sitting on the terrace with a woman in a monstrous feathered hat. Old Glich stood by the cedar of Lebanon looking as if he was rooted to the spot.

'Evening, Glich!' Lestrade called, as he always did when he saw the old boy anywhere in the grounds. But for once, old Glich didn't respond. Usually, he'd doff his cap in mock deference. Mock, because Lestrade happened to know that he was a fully paid-up member of the Gardeners' and Odd-Jobbers' Union, Surrey Branch and was in regular correspondence with a Russian named Trotsky. This time, however, the old Socialist stood to attention, with nary a flicker on his weather-beaten old features.

As he rounded the corner, the sun was full in Lestrade's eyes and he grabbed the brake. Elsa slewed sideways, her rear wheels spinning in a dust cloud, which, when it cleared, revealed Madison, Fanny's man, standing, as he normally did, with Lestrade's brandy glinting in his hand.

'What's the matter with old Glich, Madison?' Lestrade clambered out of his motor. 'Standing there as if he's got a shotgun up his arse?'

He did a double take as he realized that Madison had adopted the same pose, with a frozen grin etched on his narrow face. Lestrade took the glass from him and passed him his bowler, as was their custom. A daycap for a nightcap, Lestrade called it when the dark drew in.

'Madison?' Lestrade said. 'Are you all right?'

'Mr Madison has had rather a shock,' a female voice rang out. 'Your entire male household has.'

Lestrade shielded his eyes from the sun. Standing by the ivy trellis at the corner of the house was a little woman Lestrade had met before. 'Boadicea,' he growled. He glanced at her motor, shimmering in black, half-hidden in the shrubbery. To his surprise, it had no knives on the wheels.

'It's a Bugatti "Black Bess",' she told him. 'More souped-up than cock-a-leekie. It's for fast getaways.'

Lestrade glanced back. An Amazon he recognized as Godiva was removing a twelve bore from the smock old Glich habitually wore and she pushed him ahead of her up the drive. Esmerelda slid noiselessly from the rhododendrons, a brace of hatpins in her hand.

'Miss Esmerelda was entertaining us earlier', Madison said, rather shakily, 'to a darts contest. I used my red-and-white feathered jobs, she just used her hatpins. I thought I'd better just stand here, after that, like she said.'

Realization dawned on the Superintendent. His house had been occupied by the enemy. 'Fanny!' he roared and was about to dummy past Boadicea when the wife of the same name strolled around the greenhouse with her guest in the feathered hat.

'Sholto, whatever is all the noise? I believe you know Mrs Pankhurst.'

Lestrade did. Their paths had crossed on two occasions. He had hoped never to meet her again. But the Gorgon, She-Who-Must-Be-Arrested, looked old and tired and ill. She'd lost weight on her prison fare and the hunger strike hadn't helped.

'Mrs Pankhurst,' he said. 'It's been a while.'

'Indeed it has, Mr Lestrade,' she said, her grey eyes still sparkling, her smile still winning, unlike her Cause. 'My ladies were just admiring your lovely house. Godiva was discussing tradescantia with your groundsman. Esmerelda has been playing darts with your valet.'

'So I understand,' Lestrade said.

'Delilah is seated near the telephone in case it rings – I would have hated my conversation with your charming wife to have been interrupted.'

'Oh, really, Emmeline.' Fanny chuckled. 'There was no need for that.'

'Oh, but there was.' Mrs Pankhurst beamed. 'Wasn't there, Mr Lestrade?'

The years had hardened Emmeline Pankhurst. At first, it was a novelty, a lark even. Throw flour at an MP, knock off a policeman's helmet. But now, they forced rubber tubes down women's throats, they cut off women's hair and wore it like battle honours on their lapels. Now, a woman was dead. It wasn't a game any more. It was real.

'Yes.' He nodded. 'Fanny, we're under siege here. Have they hurt you?'

Fanny Lestrade looked at her husband. She was always afraid of this moment. Her uncle Wilfred had gone the same way. He was last seen wandering along the Great North Road muttering 'Beecham's Powders, Beecham's Powders'. The problem was, he was a High Court Judge. 'Sholto . . .' she said.

'Shall we go inside?' Emmeline suggested. It seemed a reasonable idea. Lestrade knew that the neighbours to their left were deaf anyway. And to the right was Virginia Water Cemetery. Anyone there with twenty-twenty hearing would not be of much use to Lestrade tonight.

He filed into the drawing-room, past the terrace, gently prodding Fanny ahead of him. A woman sat by the phone, knitting like some old crone at the foot of the guillotine. He continued into his study where another old besom sat copying out addresses from Lestrade's address book.

'If you can read that,' he said, leaning over her, 'thank a man.'

'Shall we?' Emmeline spread her satin skirts and invited the Lestrades to join her. The copyist closed the book, and stood sentinel on the door. Boadicea stood beside her, twirling a .38 slowly around her index finger.

'Emmeline . . .' Fanny was now beginning to wonder whether there wasn't something in her husband's fears after all.

'Emily Wilding Davison,' Emmeline said suddenly, ignoring her hostess. 'What progress has there been?'

'You could have come to the Yard,' said Lestrade. He reached inside his jacket for a cigar, but Boadicea's pistol whirled into action and he heard the click of the hammer as she extended her arm.

'There's no safety catch on a Mark IV Webley, Mr Lestrade,' she said.

Fanny started, but Lestrade's glance quieted her. 'So I believe,' he said. 'Cigar, Mrs Boadicea?'

'Thank you, no,' she said.

'It's a disgusting male habit.' Emmeline nodded.

'It is,' Fanny agreed, gliding across to her husband. She slipped a hand inside his jacket. 'I keep telling him, but will he listen.' He felt her pull out the Havanas. He also felt something heavy drop into his inside pocket. His brass knuckles. His companion of a mile. She'd found them. She winked at him and turned away, tutting. 'Now, don't you get those out again, Sholto Lestrade; not unless you really have to.'

'So,' said Emmeline. 'Emily Davison.'

'Emily Davison,' Lestrade repeated, wondering which would be faster, his knuckles or Boadicea's bullet. 'I've seen the moving pictures.'

'Moving pictures?' Emmeline and Boadicea chorused.

'Taken by a man,' Lestrade said triumphantly. 'I'd tell you his name, but you'd only invade his house, threaten his staff and otherwise outrage common decency.'

The Ladies of the Hat Pin ignored him. 'What does it show?' Emmeline asked. 'This moving picture?'

'It shows Miss Davison on the rails. Then it shows her off the rails.'

'Is this a conundrum, Mr Lestrade?' Emmeline asked.

Lestrade looked at her. 'I believe they call it a tantalus,' he said, nodding at the locked decanters by the Suffragette's elbow.

'What else did the moving picture show?' Her voice was deeper than his.

'A man's hands,' he said. 'Clearly placing Miss Davison on the rails; I would say against her will.'

'Could you see the man's face?' Boadicea asked.

Lestrade shook his head. 'No,' he told her.

'You're sure?' Emmeline asked.

'As God is my witness,' Lestrade said.

'And She is not mocked,' Emmeline assured him. And if anyone should have known that, it was Emmeline Pankhurst. 'After such a tragic life.' She sighed. 'Born on the site of the great feudal uprising in 1381.'

Lestrade remembered that from his days at Mr Poulson's Academy. Funny how those little things stay in your mind. It had happened under the school's foundations on the bare uplands of Blackheath. And if Lestrade remembered it aright, the Peasants' Revolt had been largely, if not exclusively, carried out by men.

'Wattie Tyler,' Mrs Pankhurst reminisced, as though she'd been there. Looking at her in the gathering dusk, she might have been. 'A woman of the plough,' she mused. 'Salt of the earth, soul of iron. Yes. Emily was born to a proud heritage.'

'What did her father do?' Lestrade asked.

'Her father', Emmeline scowled, 'was a failure. Charles Davison. A businessman of sorts. Flutterings in the City, I believe. He was "hammered" in 1893 and died soon after. He didn't live to see his little Emily get her degree, God Bless Her. Not that he'd have approved, I don't suppose. So . . . whom do you suspect?'

'A woman,' Lestrade said.

Fanny wondered inwardly whether that was wise.

'A woman?' Emmeline Pankhurst was barely audible and Boadicea's pistol was steady as a rock in her tiny fist.

'It wouldn't surprise me. Either of your ladies outside could pass muster. Godiva or Esmerelda. Put a false moustache and a Homburg on either of them and I'll stand next to them in any urinal in the land.'

All the Suffragettes shuddered and closed their eyes.

'It would be very easy for either of them to haul Miss Davison up on to the rail. Perhaps they taunted her, shouted something daft like, "Why not be a martyr and throw yourself under the king's horse?" Perhaps she didn't cotton to the idea, was a little reticulated about it. So one or both of them gave her a helping hand. Let's have a big hand for the little fanatic from Blackheath!' And he began clapping slowly, ironically, mocking the fanatics sitting before him.

Unnerved, Boadicea glanced at Emmeline. This was Lestrade's moment. Looking back in later years, Fanny remembered it as one of pure poetry. Lestrade's brass knuckles flew across the room, clashing on Boadicea's Webley which exploded, shattering the tantalus by Emmeline's elbow. As the woman by the door shrieked and rushed forward, Fanny Lestrade's foot came up and the Amazon stretched her length on the goatskin rug.

When the hysteria had died down, Lestrade had Boadicea's head tucked gently but firmly under his arm, like something out of the Bloody Tower.

'Now,' he said, having picked up the Webley with a deftness surprising for one of his vintage and juxtaposition. 'When I have any news on the murder of Emily Davison, rest assured I shall be in touch with her family in Northwood. Until then, I'd be grateful if you people gathered up your skirts and left.'

Fanny removed her boot from the Amazon's neck. The door crashed back and Emmeline's seconds now stood there, panting in their exertions to restrain Madison and old Glich on hearing the shot.

'Ah, ladies.' Lestrade smiled. 'It *has* been fun. But', and the grin vanished from his face, 'if you so much as put one of your size tens on my gravel again, I'll have you inside so fast, your heads'll spin.' And he pushed little Boadicea gently so that her ladies caught and steadied her.

'Emmeline,' said Fanny, 'I'm not one to bear a grudge. I welcomed you to my home in all good faith earlier today. I should, of course, have known better. You see, I am on something of a pedestal in this house, not because I am a woman, but because I am loved by a man. That might be something you ladies might like to try one day. But in the meantime, please accept this little memento of your visit.' And she caught Emmeline Pankhurst a beauty with her right cross.

Mrs Allardyce was a mousy little woman to whom the years had not been kind. She peered around the front door as one used to dealing with Jehovah's Witnesses and door-to-door lavatory cleansing salesmen.

'Yes?'

Inspector Kane flashed his warrant card. 'John Kane, Scotland Yard,' he said. 'This is Detective-Constable Jenkins.'

Abel Jenkins flashed his warrant card too.

'May we see your husband?'

'He isn't well, you know,' she told them, the door remaining to the same degree of ajar that it had been since she opened it.

'Indeed, madam,' said Kane. 'That is why we are here.'

'Well, just for a moment, then. He's still on the beef tea.'

He was. Tom Allardyce lay like Marley's ghost, pallid and worn out on a pile of pillows. The blinds were drawn at the house in Watling Park and a glass of water gleamed beside his bed.

'Mr Allardyce, we have to ask some questions, I'm afraid.'

'Not long, Bayard,' Mrs Allardyce said with a voice that could have etched glass. 'I have told these gentlemen not long.'

She had. All the way up the stairs, past the floral wallpaper and the Chinese dado, along the landing festooned with engravings of the widows of Ashur, being extraordinarily loud in their wail, she had lectured them. 'He's not well, you know. Don't keep him long. He needs his rest.'

'Thank you, dearest.' Allardyce's voice was still weak.

She sat down with a satin sibilance. The men looked at her.

'I wonder, Mrs Allardyce,' Kane ventured, 'if we might talk to your husband alone?'

'Alone?' She bridled like a scold. 'Why?'

Kane looked at Abel. 'It is customary police procedure, Madam,' he said. 'Detective-Constable Jenkins will be asking you some questions too – perhaps in the drawing-room?'

Mrs Allardyce clutched her bombazine throat. 'I'm not sure that's correct,' she said. 'I understand the Women's Social and Political Union is insisting that any woman interrogated by the police should have a second woman present. Not that I'm a feminist, you understand . . . It's just a little . . . ' She looked Jenkins up and down. 'Well, unseemly, that's all.'

'I'm sure Constable Jenkins doesn't bite, my dear,' Allardyce croaked.

Mrs Allardyce sat up sharply. 'Don't be vulgar, Bayard. I won't have such vulgarities in the house!'

'Edith . . . ' But the man was no longer master here, even if he ever had been.

'It would be of inestimable help to us, Mrs Allardyce,' Kane insisted as gently as he could. 'I can assure you that Detective-Constable Jenkins is the very model of delicacy. Happily married. A lay-reader at his church, I understand . . . '

Jenkins was none of these things, but he was quick on the

uptake. 'Amen. Bendigedyg,' he intoned with as much Evangel-istic fervour as he could manage for a man who had never been nearer to Wales than Swindon.

'Very well,' Mrs Allardyce said, after a moment's wrestle with her conscience. 'But I warn you, Inspector.' She stood up. 'One hint of impropriety, the slightest suggestion of a liberty being taken, one unbridled glance at my nether limbs, however casual it may seem, and I shall be taking legal advice.'

'Absolutely,' Kane assured her, standing up with Jenkins and ushering them both to the door. The Inspector allowed himself a glance at the Constable's flies, just to check he had adjusted his dress since the detour to the urinals in Wimpole Street. All was well. And he saw them out.

'Now, then, Mr Allardyce.' He turned back to the invalid. 'Bay-ard, isn't it?'

'No, it bloody isn't!' The impatient patient hauled himself up-right. 'It's Tom. Inspector, make a dying man happy, will you? Over there, third drawer down. You'll find a Bible.'

'A Bible?'

'Yes, you know. The good book. Not something I've seen much of recently. Is it me, or is the standard of literature dropping to an all-time low?'

Kane found the volume. Large, brass-bound. Hollow. He passed it to Allardyce, who flicked it open to Leviticus and flicked out the little flask of brandy secreted there. His head flopped back grate-fully as the amber nectar hit his tonsils.

'My wife, Inspector, as you may have gathered, is not as other women. In fact, she's a religious maniac with a suspicious mind. Pass me a Mint Imperial, will you? Second drawer. I'd get it myself, but she'd hear the bed squeak downstairs and know I'd got up.'

'Would that distress her?' Kane asked, finding the sweets and passing them to the patient.

'Oh yes.' Allardyce sucked on a lozenge. 'You see, it's Tuesday. If I can get out of bed, then I can be back at work on Thursday.'

'Thursday?' Kane played dumb.

Allardyce scowled and handed him the brandy flask to conceal again in its holy hiding place. 'Come off it, Inspector, you and I are men of the world. You've talked to Jessica.' His voice fell to a whisper. 'You know where I go every Thursday night. Edith thinks I play cribbage. My one fear is that she'll send a telegram tomorrow telling them I won't be playing. And they'll send one back saying it doesn't matter because I haven't played since 1910 and they've cancelled my subscription.'

100

'You lead something of a double life, Mr Allardyce,' Kane was bound to comment as he replaced the Bible and the Mint Imperials.

'You don't know the half of it,' Allardyce moaned.

'Tell me,' Kane said. 'Does your wife ever visit you at the office?'

'At Constable? Good Lord, no, we print books on themes other than religion,' he said. 'Edith had a strict Baptist upbringing. She doesn't approve.'

'How long have you and Miss Fry . . . ?'

'Been having an affair?' Allardyce *sotto voced* the rest of Kane's sentence for him. 'Nearly four years. It has been something of a strain. Sometimes I ask myself, why do I stay with Edith? Do you know, I have never seen my wife naked, Inspector. Her body from neck to knee is a mystery to me. Certainly better than most of the mysteries I'm asked to read these days. I had some tosh from Arthur Conan Doyle the other day. Worse, if that's possible, than his Sherlock Holmes drivel.'

'Does your wife know, Mr Allardyce?' Kane asked. 'About you and your secretary, I mean?'

'Edith?' Allardyce had gone pale again. 'God, no. If she had so much as an inkling, I'd be out on my ear. The house, the car, the life insurance, the various endowment policies, they're all hers. *That's* why I stay with her, Mr Kane. Pathetic, isn't it? Pathetic and predictable.'

'So, in the poisoning department.' Kane wanted clarification. 'You don't think that your wife . . . ?'

'Edith?' The thought had obviously not occurred to Allardyce. 'Well, now you come to mention it. There was some rather dubious blancmange she made last year . . . but surely, if Edith wanted to kill me, she'd do it here, at home, wouldn't she?'

'Not if she wanted to allay suspicion, no,' Kane told him. 'Here, she'd be in the frame. The first person we'd talk to. At the office, the world is wide. *Anybody* could have slipped in and doctored your coffee.'

'I had two visitors that morning,' Allardyce remembered. 'A Mr Adams, whom I missed, and your Superintendent Lestrade.'

'Why did he come to see you?' Kane pondered.

'Following up the hit-and-run I saw back in the January peasouper. Wanted to know what sort of car it was.'

'What sort was it?'

'A Fiat Mephisto, like Fryer's.'

'Fryer?'

'I do a bit of driving in my spare time, Inspector,' Allardyce told him. 'Whenever Edith lets me out.'

'Never on Thursdays, presumably?'

'Cribbage!' Allardyce winked at him. 'I've never been known to miss a match. I occasionally drive at Brooklands. I'm not bad, either. But I can't beat Fryer. Nobody can. Drives like the devil, he does.'

'And he drives a Fiat Mephisto?'

'Yes.'

'I didn't know', Kane tried to be casual, 'that Mr Lestrade had literary pretensions?'

'What?'

'The book he left with you – *Thirty-five Years at the Yard*. I gather you didn't like it.'

'Didn't like it? I've never heard of it. What are you talking about, Inspector?'

Kane blinked. 'There was a manuscript on your desk, Mr Allardyce,' he said. 'With Lestrade's name on it. You had rejected it. There was a line written on it in your handwriting.'

'*My* handwriting?' Allardyce repeated. 'Not possible. I'd be delighted to publish anything written by the great Superintendent Lestrade. In fact, on Thursday . . . no, let's make it Friday, shall we? I'll be on the telephone to him. There could well be a book in it.'

Downstairs in the drawing-room, as icy as its owner, despite the heat of the August day, Edith Allardyce made sure that Detective-Constable Jenkins wrote down the name clearly, sitting as he was at the opposite end of the room from her. 'Fry.' She pursed her lips around the word with some distaste. 'Jessica Fry. My husband has been touching this woman's private parts for the past four years, mostly on a Thursday evening when he purports to be playing cribbage. He does this presumably because he has the appalling basic instincts of a man and because there is insufficient privacy in the premises at Orange Street. Take my word for it, Detective-Constable, my husband is an animal with unnatural appetites. I am his wife. I allowed him access to me in the March of 1911. What more can any normal man ask? And I'll tell you something else – write it down – my husband poisoned himself.'

Jenkins paused in mid-sentence, looking at the woman in disbelief.

'That's right,' she said. 'Poisoned himself. How is obvious. Why is still a mystery. But that's the job of you Scotland Yard chappies, isn't it? What are you waiting for?'

To get a word in edgeways, Detective-Constable Jenkins was tempted to say. But he didn't have the nerve.

8

Emma Bandicoot-Lestrade came home that month from M. Le Petomaine's Finishing School in Geneva. She was nineteen years old and mercifully had inherited her mother's looks. There was none of the sallow face and parchment skin about Emma. Her eyes were clear grey and her hair a soft gold and many were the young men whose eyes swivelled right and left as she glided up the theatre stairs with Fanny, who was quietly hoping, as more mature women will, that they might be taken for sisters.

Lestrade was not with them. He was at his second home, on the second floor of Scotland Yard, where he had often slept jammed between the shoe-boxes and the filing cabinet. It was for that reason, among others, that all those years ago, when little Emma was just a babe in arms, he had taken her by the Great Western with its newly standardized gauge, to Huish Episcopi and to Bandicoot Hall. There would be nights, he knew, and days, when he would never see his little girl at all. So he had given her to his old friends Harry and Letitia Bandicoot, who had all the time and all the money and all the love in the world.

That was a long time ago, Lestrade mused as he met his golden girl at the station and she flew into his arms. He was glad he had given her to the Bandicoots and that that gift had turned out to be a loan; because here she was, home now and his, full of stories of what an old duffer Le Petomaine was and this or that ski-instructor. He held her to him for a moment, taking in her fragrance. Then she was gone, laughing with Fanny and tickling Madison's bald head as she always had.

'See you later,' Lestrade said and whistled up a cab. He'd forgotten his wallet. Emma had lent him five bob.

'It's a thriller, dear,' Fanny said. 'I thought we'd have a spot of dinner at the Trocadero afterwards, but your father has rather put the kibosh on that, I'm afraid.'

103

'Why?' Emma slipped her stage binoculars out of their natty bag.

'Well, even with Mrs Pankhurst and Co., ladies don't dine in the West End unaccompanied.'

Emma had already caught the eye of the handsome naval officer in the box opposite. She had a bit of a thing for uniforms. He had a bit of a thing for gorgeous girls with upswept gold curls. It was the way the world turned in the year of their Lord 1913. 'I think we'll be all right.' She smiled, suddenly fluttering her fan in his direction. 'Anyway, by comparison with Switzerland, England is the most enlightened country in the world. It's my guess women won't get the vote there until 1971.'

'Huh!' snorted Fanny. 'Your father might have retired by then.'

'Now, Fanny, dearest.' Emma patted her stepmother's hand. 'You mustn't be cross with him.'

'But on your first night home . . .' She tutted.

'Ever since I can remember, this is how it's been,' Emma said, listening to the orchestra tune up. 'First, when I knew him as Uncle Sholto, then when he told me who he really was. It's a policeman's lot, Fanny. You know that. You've been where I am.'

She had. Fanny was a policeman's daughter and a policeman's wife. But her father had not retired. Her father had gone down to a murderous shotgun blast on the lawns beyond the pond at home where she still lived. There was no marker, just grass where the leaves whirled wild in autumn and the crocuses nodded in spring. She didn't go there any more.

The strains of the National Anthem struck up.

'They're playing the King's tune,' Emma whispered and Fanny giggled. 'By the way, do you Turkey Trot?'

'Like a gobbler.' Fanny beamed. 'I think your father's version's already trussed and stuffed for the oven!'

The young naval officer in the box opposite stood with the straight hand salute peculiar to his service. None of the audience, nor the orchestra, nor most of the cast waiting in the wings saw him do it, but Dick Auger, the Properties Manager at His Majesty's, carefully loaded the Smith and Wesson .32 safety revolver and passed it to Anton Le Grand who nodded, slicked down an errant eyebrow hair and took his place behind the side curtain. Across the sulphur-lit stage he saw his target, Herbert Wilson, checking his make-up in a mirror. Bit late for that, heart, Le Grand thought to himself. Not really worth it for a walk-on part, is it?

The orchestra had stopped and a single violin's strains filled the theatre. The curtains slid apart and the floodlights came up. True to the tradition of West End audiences, they applauded the drawing-room set that was unveiled before them. Hector McGrègor, the set designer, sitting in the third row, stood up and took a bow. No one knew who he was and there were loud hisses for him to sit down.

'Darling!' Effie Howard ran across the stage in a frothy creation in nectarine, like a hippopotamus tangled in a clothesline.

'Divine dress,' Emma commented to Fanny. 'And so much of it.'

'Darling, are you there?' The actress scurried backwards and forwards. 'Darling, please say you are.' She peered into the wings. Where *was* the idiot?

'Darling!' Herbert Wilson's voice boomed behind her. The scene-stealing buffoon had crept in through the french windows. The audience burst into rapturous applause. He acknowledged it with a flourish taught to him by Beerbohm Tree, thereby destroying all dramatic illusion, and resumed his place behind the sofa.

'Patrick. Is it you?' Effie felt she ought to check.

'Bernice.' He held out his arms. 'It is I.'

God, thought Emma, who wrote this tosh? It made M. Le Peto-maine's Academy for Nearly Finished Ladies in Geneva's produc-tion of *Paradise Lost* look quite polished.

'Oh, Patrick.' She melted into his arms, dipping her head to avoid the devastating effects of his breath. 'It's been so long.'

Hmphh! Le Grand snorted. Boasting again! He checked the pistol in his pocket, winding the white scarf around his neck and reaching for the silk topper.

'Your husband?' Wilson asked her, holding her at arm's length. God, he thought, just as well the audience couldn't see what he could. Under the five and nine, the years had not been kind to Effie Howard. She had more tucks than a Robin Hood story.

'He's away, my darling,' she said, twirling away from him and sliding on to the sofa. 'Sit beside me, light of my life.'

'Is this a comedy?' Emma asked Fanny.

The older woman shrugged. 'I'm beginning to understand why Sholto had to be elsewhere,' she whispered.

Emma let her binoculars wander to the naval officer. He had let his do the same and for a while, their lenses locked in that first heart-thumping moment when all else stands still and the world is as a dream, a vision of no consequence.

'So!!' Her attention was drawn to the stage again at the stentorian tones of Anton Le Grand, entering stage right, as though from a night at the theatre. Damn! he thought. No applause. For a moment, he toyed with coming on again, but this wasn't the Music Hall, it was legitimate theatre. Except for Wilson, of course – he was illegitimate.

The actors on the sofa sprang apart and one of the springs gave a loud twang of relief. The third violin sniggered.

'Darling!' Effie shrieked.

'George!' Wilson shouted.

'What is the meaning of this?' Le Grand wanted to know.

'I . . . We . . .' Effie was lost for words.

'No, darling.' Wilson came centre stage, deftly flicking the corner of the carpet out of the way. 'It's no good.'

'Darling?' Le Grand repeated. 'Whom are you addressing?'

Not you, grandad, Wilson thought, but trouper that he was, he crossed to Effie and attempted to get his arm round her ample shoulders. In the end, he settled for one of them.

'Darling,' he said to her. 'We must face this together. Roger . . .'

'George!' bellowed Le Grand. What an amateur!

'George,' Wilson corrected himself. 'For nearly a year now, Bernice and I have been . . . lovers.'

There was an inrush of air from the audience. Torrid stuff, this, for 1913.

'Lovers?' Le Grand took several paces backwards. Not content with that reaction, he turned to face the audience to let them have the full frontal effect of his emotions. It didn't take long. 'My God!'

'Don't blame yourself, darling,' Effie said, crossing to him, flicking the other corner of the carpet out of the way. 'We didn't mean it to happen, but you were always away. The Amazon expedition. The mountaineering. The war.'

'Exactly.' Le Grand threw back his cape to reveal a row of glittering medals. 'While I was serving King and Country, you and this . . . this philanderer . . .'

'Philanderer?' Wilson boomed, moving Effie aside. 'You'll take that back!'

'Never!' Le Grand insisted and whipped the pistol from his pocket.

In the orchestra pit, the tympanist waited, drumstick at the ready in case of a misfire. On two out of the eight nights of the run so far, there had been a dismal click. On the third night, the damn thing had gone off in Le Grand's pocket and the audience assumed he'd shot himself in order to give his wife and her lover the chance of a real life together.

'Put that down, you fool!' Wilson shouted.

Effie shrieked so that the chandelier tinkled.

'Dally with my wife, would you?' Le Grand took a pace forward.

'Put it down, I say. Face me like a man.' And Wilson raised his fists, looking more like a ballerina than a prize fighter. Le Grand turned to the audience again, then he turned back to let them see

106

his fine profile and the ridge of his jaw flexing with fury. He clicked back the hammer.

'Don't!' Effie screamed, but her word was drowned by the crash of the revolver. The tympanist sighed with relief and put down his drumstick.

In the next minute and a half, Herbert Wilson gave the best performance of his life. He flew backwards, somersaulting over the settee, the carpet slipping under his feet. He had the most appalling pain in his chest and the front of his dickie was darkening with a spreading scarlet stain. Effie looked aghast. Le Grand frowned. He couldn't see at first through the smoke, but that wasn't supposed to happen. What was Wilson playing at, upstaging everyone again? He slipped the revolver back into his pocket and turned to the audience. 'Oh, my God, what have I done?'

'You bastard,' Wilson croaked.

The audience's inrush of breath was even more audible. A retired colonel from Tunbridge Wells in the eighth row determined to write to *The Times* there and then, except that he had no paper and couldn't see in the dark.

Wilson lay at an awkward angle with his left leg bent uncomfortably beneath him. 'You stupid, careless bastard!'

The third inrush of the evening brought mutterings. This theatre was a little too verité for the West End.

'How do they do that?' Emma asked Fanny. But Fanny wasn't listening. Her own father had died like that, his chest shattered by a gun. Something was wrong. Something awful.

'We must call the police,' she said. 'Call your father.'

And Herbert Wilson did something that Anton Le Grand said he did every night – he died on stage. His hands fluttered convulsively, daubed with scarlet as they were, and his head flopped back. In the seconds of indecision, Le Grand tried desperately to remember his next line and couldn't. Effie slumped to her knees, unable to speak, scarcely able to breathe, staring at her dead co-star with the blood seeping on to the carpet.

The conductor rapped his baton so hard that it snapped, but the bewildered orchestra broke into 'They're Moving Father's Grave' – hardly the most appropriate in the circumstances – and the curtain came down.

'Better than a play,' Emma murmured numbly. Suddenly, the handsome young naval officer was the furthest thing from her mind.

Lestrade had trod the boards before, but never at His Majesty's. There was an opulence about the gilded boxes, the velvet fittings, the embroidered tabs. Four burly lads from C Division had lifted the corpse of Herbert Wilson and carried him downstairs into a basement room where he lay on the trapeze thingummy the theatre used for the traditional Christmas pantomime *Mother Goose and Dick Whittington in the Wood.*

The Superintendent inserted the blade of his brass-knuckled knife, the one Fanny had lost and found for him, gingerly into the dead man's wound. He could feel the bullet nudging against the blade's tip. Ironic, really. An inch or two to the left and Herbert Wilson would have lived. He couldn't fault Anton Le Grand's aim. He'd paced out the stage, tripping over the corner of the carpet, and he'd counted twenty-one paces. He didn't need expert ballistic help on this one. Mr Churchill could sleep on over his shop in Orange Street. The gun lay in the palm of his hand now as he put the knuckles down and clicked back the secret blade. It was a small pistol, blue steel with a black Bakelite grip. The hammer was shrouded in the steel shoulders and Lestrade broke the gun to inspect the chamber. Five bullets still lay in their grooves, the sixth had left them behind, spinning at an impossible speed through the lights and powder of a stage set to thump and bury itself in the chest of an unsuspecting victim. A heavier weapon would have fired .44 ammunition and would have taken a large lump of Wilson's back with it.

Inspector Day from Dabs had flicked the weapon with his brushes and gone away to the Yard to do the paperwork. There wasn't much doubt about it, though. Over four hundred people had seen Anton Le Grand murder Herbert Wilson. What else could it be but an open-and-shut case? Lestrade clicked the barrel up into place and put the gun down beside its victim. Then he turned out the light and left.

The papers, of course, were full of it next day. There were suggestions of a blue plaque on the wall of the rather awful digs Herbert Wilson lived in. Thespians past and present bewailed such a sad loss to their profession. Sir Johnston Forbes-Robertson set up a fund in his memory, to be called Wilson-Aid.

Effie Howard was distraught. When an insistent Superintendent Lestrade found her, she was draped elegantly on her *chaise longue*, a black veil over her face.

'Mrs Entwhistle?'

She sat bolt upright in the darkened room, the veil falling as she did so.

'Mrs Agnes Entwhistle?'

'Who's there?' she asked with a crystal voice.

'My name is Superintendent Lestrade from Scotland Yard. I fear I must ask you some questions. Could we have some light, I wonder, only Detective-Constable Lyall here isn't very good at writing notes in the dark, are you, Constable?'

'Positively average, sir,' Lyall had to concede.

'I'll light the lamp.' She sniffed. 'I'd raise the blinds, only I couldn't bear to see the day.'

'It must be a shock for you. May we sit down?'

She fumbled with the matches, but her hands shook, so Constable Lyall took over and the room was bathed in light. Lestrade saw what Herbert Wilson had seen on the last night of his life – the less than pretty sight of Effie Howard at close quarters. She slumped on to the furniture again.

'Your maid showed us up,' Lestrade explained. 'Believe me, if there was any other way . . .'

'No, no.' She wafted a handkerchief dowsed in smelling salts under her nose as Lyall sat poised with pen and notebook. 'I appreciate that you have a job to do.'

'Perhaps you'd care for Mr Entwhistle to be present?' Lestrade thought it helpful to suggest.

'I last saw Alf Entwhistle on a pigeon-fanciers outing to Barnsley', she growled in something less than her West End stage delivery, 'sixteen years ago. Of course.' The incisive diction had returned. 'I was very young. Very, very young in fact. I knew little of the ways of the world.' And she fluttered her eyelashes at the very, very young constable, who squirmed with embarrassment, turning puce in the oil-lamp's flare.

'Tell me about Herbert Wilson,' Lestrade said, trying to find somewhere among the theatrical debris to put his bowler.

'Darling, darling Herbert.' Effie sniffed. 'Such a professional. So supportive.'

'A married man?'

'No, no. Oh, there were admirers, of course. We in the profession have this cross to bear. Why, I myself have scores of proposals of marriage every year.'

'Scores?' Lyall had misheard.

'Yes,' she snarled in her native Yorkshire. 'Scores. No, like many of us, Herbert was a trouper to his fingertips. He had no time for affairs of the heart. The theatre was his only true love. When I starred with dear old Sir Henry Irving . . . of course, I was very, very young then, I remember Henry saying to me, "How should I play that line, my dear? I'm having difficulty with it." And I said to him . . .'

'Did Mr Wilson have any enemies, Mrs Entwhistle?' Lestrade asked.

'Howard,' the actress insisted. 'I only use the name Howard these days, Superintendent, if you don't mind. No, Herbert didn't have an enemy in the world . . . Except Anton, of course.'

'Anton Le Grand?'

Effie snorted. 'Not his real name, of course. The nearest he's been to France is Ramsgate. He played the summer season there, oh, Lord, I don't know how many years ago, but I do know Lord Beaconsfield was Prime Minister.'

'He and Mr Wilson didn't get on?'

'Anton is that most tragic of characters, Mr Lestrade,' the actress said. 'The actor who is past his prime. Not that his prime was very good. No. His timing was off, his diction dire. He insisted on playing the handsome young lead, when he was neither handsome nor young, nor equipped for the lead part. I understand he had a following among the lower orders, the sort who breed whippets and eat saveloys wrapped in newspaper.'

'You talk of Mr Le Grand as if he were dead, Miss Howard,' Lestrade said.

'Well, isn't he?' she asked. 'The man is guilty of murder, Superintendent. We do still hang murderers in this country, don't we? And even if, by some miracle, he gets off, his career is in tatters. He won't even be able to play the Rochdale Hippodrome after this.'

'He has assured investigating officers that he thought the gun was loaded with blanks,' Lestrade said.

'Well.' She bridled. 'He would say that, wouldn't he? I believe the man had some experience of active service against one of our colonial enemies . . .'

'The Boers?'

Effie frowned. 'You mustn't be taken in by his appearance, Superintendent,' she said. 'It's all clever make-up, you know. No, I think you'll find it was the Sikhs.'

Constable Lyall had won the History prize at school and quietly refused to write that down. He knew a piece of untethered bitchery when he heard one. He also knew that we'd last fought the Sikhs in 1849. Since then, the beturbaned chaps had been utterly loyal.

'Whoever it was, he ought to know a live round from a blank one. No doubt he's passed the buck to Dickie Auger.'

'Auger?' Lestrade checked.

'The Props man. Dear, dear Dickie. Such a poppet. And an enormous fan of mine, of course.'

Constable Lyall realized that Miss Howard would *need* an enormous fan, but it wasn't his place to say so.

'Augur loaded the gun?'

'Probably. Although it would have been perfectly simple for Anton to reload at his convenience. Quite clever, isn't it, to carry out so foul an act in public?'

'You mean the double bluff?' Lestrade said.

'Exactly.' The actress nodded. 'If he did it in an alleyway, in the dark, as in fact befits his cowardly nature, there was the risk he'd be seen, or leave behind some vital clue, such as his false teeth. By doing it in broad stagelight, people would say "Oh, he couldn't have known. Someone must have doctored the gun".' Her face darkened again and the Yorkshire lass reared her ugly head. 'The devious bastard!'

'You didn't explain his motive, Miss Howard,' Lestrade said. 'Why should Mr Le Grand want Mr Wilson dead?'

'Simple,' she trilled à la the West End. 'Pure old-fashioned professional jealousy. Le Grand was over the hill, in fact he was a long way down the other side. Herbert, dear Herbert . . . ' And she paused with immaculate timing to wipe away a tear. ' . . . was coming to the pinnacle of his career. There'd be bevies of luscious young ladies at the stage door every night. Of course, he only had eyes for me.'

'Of course.' Lestrade smiled. 'There must be a lot of up-and-coming young actors threatening Mr Le Grand's position.'

'Hundreds,' she agreed. 'I'm surprised he didn't bring a Hotchkiss on stage. That way, he could have mown down the lot of 'em.'

Dickie Augur was a prey to nervous disorders. Even before the tragic incident that had ended the West End run of *The Wife, Her Lover, Their Chauffeur and the Rest of the Domestics* and had temporarily closed down His Majesty's, he was renowned for his backstage jitters. Obsessed by the roar of the grease-paint, Augur had longed to be an actor, but the number of roles available to a man with a cleft palate was surprisingly limited in the Edwardian theatre and he'd ducked backstage where his impediment was less of an impediment. Here, he proceeded to make everyone's life a misery, clucking like a mother hen, bustling about with books and crockery, furniture and cigar boxes, getting in everyone's way.

Even now, in the locked theatre, he was sweeping up.

'Of cour'e,' he said in that harsh delivery that skated over consonants. 'I don't usually do thi'.'

'What?' asked Lestrade.

''weep up.'

'Quite. Tell me about the gun.'

'Gun?' Augur put the broom down and lit a nervous cigarette with trembling fingers. 'It' been lyin' about here for years,' he said. 'I remember we u'ed it in Ib'en's *The Ma'ter Builder* – the alternative version. And again in *Henry the Fif'*. Pi'tol carried it. Or wa' that *Henry the Four'* Part Two? Anyhow, it' never killed anybody before.'

'These are the blanks you loaded?' Lestrade held the tin in his hand.

'Ye'.' Augur drew deeply on the cigarette. 'I u'ed to roll my own, y'know, but I can't do it any more.'

Looking at the wreck of a man, Lestrade could believe that.

'Who else had access to them?'

'Anyone,' Augur said.

'Where were they, on the night in question?'

'In the Prop' cupboard until half pa' 'ix. Then I loaded the revolver and put the tin back.'

'And you gave the gun to Le Grand?'

'Ye'.'

'Did you see what he did with it?'

'Ye'. He put it in hi' pocket.'

'That's all?'

'That' all I 'aw. I didn't have time to 'tand around. I had to get Mi' Howard' wrap for the 'econd 'ene.'

'Quite,' Lestrade realized. 'Well, thank you, Mr Augur, for your inestimable help.'

'That' all right.' And the Properties man threw back a couple of pills to steady what was left of his nerves.

Anton Le Grand's room at the Scrubs was scarcely what he was used to, but actors who stood accused of murder couldn't afford to be choosy and bail had been denied. He spent most of his day, when he wasn't walking around in a pointless and ever-decreasing circle in the exercise yard, watching the cockroaches playing hopscotch on the floor of his cell. Any spare time he had after that was fully taken up with scratching. They'd taken away his belt, his shoe-laces and that rather vicious-looking wig, in case he did, in prison officers' parlance, 'something stupid'.

'This is outrageous,' he told Lestrade.

The Superintendent nodded. It had been a long day and he was worried about Fanny. The demise of Herbert Wilson had brought it all flooding back, the death of her father, Lestrade's old friend, Tom Berkeley. True, Emma was with her, but it wasn't the same. In the long watches of the night, she'd need him there.

'Why did you kill Herbert Wilson?' Lestrade asked.

'For God's Sake!' Le Grand thumped his mattress and the bugs jumped. 'Why is every policeman in London asking me that question?' His voice was as booming in his cosy little six by nine as it was on the stage of His Majesty's. 'Anyway, I didn't. Oh, I did technically, dear boy, but only because the script called for it.'

'The script?' Lestrade repeated.

'Yes.' Le Grand sighed as though talking to the village idiot. 'That's the stuff we actors have to learn to tell the story.'

'And the story was?' Lestrade had long ago learned not to be needled by alleged criminals, especially alleged criminals facing the gallows.

'Oh, some slight tosh about a pair of adulterers. I played the husband – a national hero betrayed by his wife. Not a bad part, although of course I had to rise above some balefully banal banter.'

'Of course,' Lestrade commented. 'Go on.'

'Well, the play opens with me finding my wife, played with abysmal timing by Effie Howard, as you know, in the arms of Patrick Wiley, played, if that word is remotely relevant, by Herbert Wilson.'

'And you shoot him.'

'Yes. Well, not really, of course.'

'Of course,' Lestrade said again. It was that sort of conversation and that sort of crime. 'And then what?'

'Well, the rest of it is hushing the murder up. The wife is in an agony of despair and there's a weekend house party coming up, with guests traipsing all over the place, sitting on the very trunk and so on where the body is temporarily stashed.'

'So it's a comedy?'

'Well, no, it isn't apparently. That's what I thought when I first read it, but the author, whoever he is – I think he was introduced to me once – seemed to believe it was saying something profound about Asquith's England. Couldn't see it, myself.'

'Tell me about the night in question,' Lestrade said.

'Not much to tell,' Le Grand said, suddenly aware that his armpit had a visitor. 'I went on as usual. That idiot Wilson had come on from the wrong place again and Effie was of course totally thrown by it.'

'She struck me as being rather professional,' Lestrade said.

'Huh!' Le Grand grunted. 'About as professional as something

113

you pick up on the Haymarket of an evening. No, take my word for it, on that stage, I was an eagle surrounded by turkeys, a lion among hyenas and any other metaphor the world of nature has to offer. I delivered my lines with the suave bravado my vast public has come to expect and shot him. Funny, the thing sounded different.'

'Live rounds do.' Lestrade nodded. 'But then, you'd know that.'

'Know what?'

'About live rounds. What with your war record.'

'My . . . er . . . ' Le Grand looked a little more discomfited than the fleas would merit.

'Your war record. Miss Howard's told us all about it.'

'Ah, yes, well.' The actor looked a little sheepish. 'Just a bit of living up to my curriculum vitae there. No, actually, I did volunteer, but was posted to Catterick.'

'Hmm,' mused Lestrade. 'That is a shade nearer than Pretoria.'

'Not my fault, I assure you,' Le Grand was anxious to confirm. 'Fortunes of War. So you see, I've never actually fired a shot in anger.'

'But . . . at Catterick,' Lestrade ventured. 'The ranges.'

'I did concerts for the troops about to embark,' Le Grand admitted. 'I'm not sure anyone below the commissioned ranks understood my soliloquies, of course, but there it is. I blame Haldane.'

'You do?'

'Well, of course. Territorial Army, indeed. Travesty. Utter travesty.'

'Who loaded the gun?'

'What? Well, Augur, I suppose. Dickie Augur, the Props man, perfect pest in performance.'

'You had ample time to switch bullets.'

'What?' Le Grand stared at him. 'Are you mad? I told you, Lestrade, I've never fired a real gun before in my life, not with real ammunition, anyway.'

'Your aim wasn't at all bad. You fired from . . . what . . . twenty-one paces away. Drilled his heart. That's quite impressive.'

'Lucky.' Le Grange shrugged.

'Lucky?' Lestrade repeated.

'Well, no,' Le Grange fluffed. 'Not lucky, exactly. Downright unlucky, come to think of it, but . . . well, there it is.'

'I understand there was no love lost between you and Mr Wilson,' the Superintendent said.

'I wouldn't put it as strongly as that,' the actor demurred. 'No, I barely considered him, really. I mean, he came to me for advice constantly during rehearsals. It was very much a case of patron and protégé.'

That was another play Lestrade had never heard of, so he let it go. 'You weren't jealous of him, then, of his rising star, his success with women?'

'Succ . . . ' Le Grand laughed aloud, not so odd a sound in Wormwood Scrubs where one or two men died laughing. 'You jest.'

'I do?' Lestrade was prepared to go as far as a smile.

'Well, of course. Rising star! The man had only ever done Panto. That and the Essex Working Men's Club, Colchester. *The Wife, Her Lover, Their Chauffeur* was his big break. Had rather less than his hour upon the stage, as it transpired. And as for women, I find it rather apt that his last production was *Poof in Boots.*'

'You mean . . . ?'

'Well,' scoffed Le Grand. 'You only had to look at him, ever checking himself in the mirror, squeezing past the set changers when there was plenty of room to go round. There's a lot of it in my profession, Lestrade, as I'm sure there is in yours.'

'Well, I . . .'

'And, of course, inept financially.'

'Really?'

'Oh, yes. We all of us, we actors, have a bit stashed away for a rainy day. Mine's in gilts.'

That figures, thought Lestrade, bearing in mind the man's present predicament.

'That was something else Wilson came to me for advice on, as well as timing, voice projection and stage falls. He said he had some money, oh, a trifling amount I'm sure and would I tell him where to invest it.'

'And did you?'

'Certainly not. I wasn't sharing my nest-egg with Mr Amateur Actor of 1913. He said his money was in Krugerands. I advised him to leave it there.'

'And he seemed happy with that?'

'I told you. He was inept. If I'd told him to buy green cheese, he'd have done it. What an amateur!'

'Mr Le Grand.' Lestrade scraped back the metal-framed chair. 'I cannot disguise from you the fact that things look gloomy for you. You've talked to a lawyer?'

'Interminably. He's very optimistic.'

'Really? Who is he?'

'Walter Spratchett of Spratchett, Letterman and Spratchett.'

'Ah.' Lestrade's face fell. 'Well, I'll see myself out.'

He hadn't the heart to tell the condemned man that Walter Spratchett hadn't won a case since 1893.

Lestrade held Fanny close to him that night. And as he knew she would, she sobbed quietly into his wincyette.

'I'm sorry, Sholto,' she said. 'At the theatre last night, it was like . . . just like . . . ' But the words wouldn't come.

'I know.' He smoothed her hair and kissed her forehead. She was warm and soft, like the little girl he'd known all those years ago. 'I know.'

'What possessed him to do it?' she asked, soothed by her husband's kisses, the strength of his arms.

'He didn't,' Lestrade said. 'Somebody switched bullets on Augur, who it's my guess wouldn't know a live round from a dead square. The man is so nervous, he'd have picked up the shells and loaded them without looking. His attention would have been anywhere, everywhere else.'

'So Augur didn't do it, either?'

'No. The ammunition in the tin was live, all of it. A guilty man would have replaced the live rounds with blanks, adverting suspicion from him to the firer of the shot. No, whoever did this got into the theatre at some time that day I'd say and switched tins. He'd seen the play before, so he knew when the shots were to be fired. Of course . . . '

'What?' She looked up at him, resting her head on his shoulder.

'Chummie *might* have been there the previous night. Depending on who he or she is, he could have found some excuse to go backstage, perhaps to deliver flowers or congratulations, and done the switch then. All Augur would have done would be to check that the tin was in place. Why should he look inside? And anyway, as I've said, he'd be none the wiser if he did.'

'Oh, Sholto.' She squeezed his arm. 'You're so clever.'

'Am I?' he said, looking down at her.

'You are.' She snuggled closer. 'That must be why you're still wearing your bowler!'

Sholto Lestrade didn't give many pats on the back. Especially to rookies. Yet one exception was to Detective-Constable Nathan Tait, whose eagle-eyed search of the late Herbert Wilson's dressing-room had come up trumps. Someone had indeed visited backstage the previous night and had delivered a bouquet to Herbert Wilson. Except that it was rather reminiscent of the one the Marquess of Queensbury had sent to the late Oscar Wilde. It consisted of a pile of not terribly fresh cauliflowers, the florets very past their best. It was not that that caught Tait's eye, however. It was the card that accompanied them. It was scarlet and bore the devil's face. And when Lestrade counted the cauliflowers, he was astounded. It must have taken a handcart to deliver. There were fourteen of them.

9

'Charles Trevelyan Morant,' Sergeant Ned Blevvins said. 'Ana Broker Morant. Blimey! This bloke's seriously rich, guv.'

'Yes, I thought he would be. All right, lads. Get me a cab. We'll dispense with the Maria today. It's a bit heavy for a friendly chat.'

'On my way, guv.' Blevvins reached for his hat.

'Not you, Blevvins,' Lestrade checked him. 'I haven't forgotten the Russian connection yet. Tait, Lyall, hop to it. The sergeant here has to continue to plough his laborious way through the ticket stubs at His Majesty's for the night before last yet. Cheer up, Blevvins,' he said as the sergeant subsided again. 'That's what real police work is all about. Lyall, your turn for the sandwiches.'

Broker Morant was a stone left unturned, a lead not followed up, a report unwritten. It was a madhouse on the floor of the Silent Call-room of the Stock Exchange. Banned by law from entering the Exchange itself, Lestrade and his lads had to use the complicated telephone system next door. Tait was the flavour of the month, so Tait had the honour of slipping into the glass-doored box like some furtive Catholic and dialled the number he'd been given.

Above the hubbub of the jobbers, scurrying like ants beyond the great glass windows, they heard the commissionaire bellow through the brass trumpet, 'Paging Mr Morant. Paging Mr Morant.' Men were dashing in all directions, waving pieces of paper, screaming at each other as though the end of the world was nigh. But no individual came to the Silent Call-room.

'You're wasting your time, I'm afraid,' a voice said. Lestrade peered up to stare into the impassive face of Alaric Bligh, the man who *was* Raleigh Harman. 'Broker is playing soldiers at the moment. You'll find him on Hounslow Heath. He's a Major in the Inns of Court Regiment. All stuff and nonsense of course.'

'Of course.'

'But,' Bligh put his arm across Lestrade's shoulder and led him away from the rookies, along the line of telephone booths where hatless walk clerks dealt away small fortunes. 'I'm very glad you're following up my little suggestion. Broker is quite a slippery customer, believe me.'

'And I'm glad I happened to run into you, Mr Bligh,' Lestrade said.

'Really? Why is that?'

'It's a little murder case I'm working on at the moment which I have reason to believe is connected with the death of your Mr Griffin.'

'Old Worsthorne?' Bligh's eyes widened. 'Really? Headway at last?'

'Possibly,' Lestrade said. 'This man has killed at least three people, Mr Bligh, and I'm trying to establish links between them. Does your firm ever deal in Krugerands?'

'Krugerands? Never. Not since the war. Bloody Boers! I wouldn't cross the street, I can tell you. I haven't forgotten Spion Kop, even if the rest of the world has. Morant's company does, though. Dewsman Porter.'

'Does it?'

'Look, what's this about, Lestrade? What's this got to do with Griffin?'

'I'll let you know, sir,' Lestrade promised, clicking his fingers to summon his lads. 'Hounslow Heath, I think you said.'

Lestrade dithered at first. Manoeuvres were likely to be sweaty, weren't they, at the height of the summer? And he'd done that once, a long time ago, with the Yorkshire Hussars, when they'd given him a homicidal horse to ride. Yet Morant, with his Diablo racehorse, was a character Lestrade was anxious to meet. In the end, he tossed a coin to see whether they'd go to Hounslow or not – one of Lyall's because he had forgotten his wallet – and he won. Or was it lost?

Anyway, the upshot was that the Yard men rattled West out of the City, on the District Line to Hounslow. In the High Street, they caught a cab and trotted, cheek by jowl, out on to the open plain that was the Eastern Command's Headquarters. They heard the firing long before the growler stopped.

'Are we there?' Lestrade stuck his bowlered head out of the window.

'*I* am,' the cabbie assured him.

'What?'

He waved his whip ahead. 'Look. The red flag's up. That means they're using live ammunition.' He turned on his perch. 'That means real bullets to you blokes. Besides, there's more mares out there than I've had hot dinners. Norman's pricking his ears and other parts of 'isself up as we speak. Got nostrils like a bat's ears has Norman. Sniff a mare a mile off. I swear I'll have to start spelling the word before too long.'

To Lestrade the animal in the traces looked dead, but he assumed the cabbie knew his horseflesh and alighted.

'Where will we find the Inns of Court Regiment?' Lestrade asked.

'Bloody 'ell, squire.' The cabbie held out his hand for the fare. 'Seen one bloody soljer, seen 'em all. They all bloody wear kacky these days.'

'Thanks.' Lestrade grimaced at him and grunted to his subordinates to pay the man.

The road effectively ended at that point, disappearing in a cloud of dust and short-cropped yellow grass. Wagon tracks had ploughed their tell-tale signs in the soft mud of the spring and the sun of summer had baked them iron-hard. The firing was random and far away as the dauntless three trudged on towards a hedge that ran away into the distance.

Suddenly, there was a shellburst to their left and the ground thundered. Lestrade had never been knocked off his feet by an explosion before. When the Fenians had let off a big one under the Yard back in 1886, young Inspector Lestrade had been out to lunch. Now, he was lying upside down in a trench, a bunch of creeping buttercup where his fob watch used to be.

'Bloody hellfire!' a voice wheezed beside him. It was Constable Tait, his face blacker than a nigger minstrel's.

'Are you all right, lad?' Lestrade asked.

'I think so, sir.' Tait knocked the clod of earth out of his ear.

'Where's Lyall?'

'Gregory?' Tait called. 'Gregory, where are you?'

There was a short-lived whine that whipped somewhere near his head and a cloud of dust flew up past his left ear. He felt himself being dragged downwards by his guv'nor. 'Keep your head down, lad. It's the only one you've got.'

'This is a bloody war,' Tait observed.

'And a sickly season, I shouldn't wonder. And I thought they only used live ammunition on the stage. Lyall?'

'Over here, guv,' a voice called back. 'Across the road.'

The Superintendent and the Constable were a little more wary this time and they peered over the earth parapet where the sedge had withered. A similar hatless head and pair of ears appeared out of the trench at the other side.

'Are you all right?' Lestrade asked.

'I think so.'

'How many fingers am I holding up?' Tait asked. Immediately his guv'nor knocked them down.

'Three more than you're going to be able to in a minute,' he hissed. 'Lyall, can you see anybody? On the road, I mean?'

'No, guv, I . . . Wait a minute. Bloody hell!'

Lestrade and Tait looked at each other, then slid their backs upwards against the trench wall until they could look out. A party of cyclists was winding its way in a wobbly fashion towards them, in field-grey uniforms with knapsacks on their backs.

The policemen climbed cautiously out of their shell holes and stood bedraggled as the leading rider braked his Raleigh.

'Hello, are you Press?' he asked, tilting back his field cap.

'No, we're the police,' Lestrade said, a little less than enchanted by this fellow's bonhomie.

'Oh, well, it's all right. We've got permission and all that. This *is* War Office land, you know.'

'I think we'd gathered that. We're looking for the Inns of Court lot.'

'Oh, the Devil's Own. God knows where they are. You might try towards Stanwell. The A Team are pretty strung out, I think.'

'What did you say?' Lestrade stared at the man.

'I said "The A Team . . ." '

'No, no, not that. About the Devil's Own.'

'Oh, yes. That's the nickname of the Inns of Court Rifles. The Devil's Own. They've even got Old Nick portrayed on their buttons. They're all lawyers, you see. Unlike the Artists' Rifles – they're all artists, obviously.'

'Who are you?' Lestrade asked, bewildered.

'Oh, sorry. Devonshire.' He tugged off his glove.

'You're a long way from home.' Lestrade wiped whatever it was from his fingers on his trousers and gripped the man's hand.

'Hmm? Oh.' The officer chuckled. 'I see. No. My name is Devonshire. Bruce Devonshire. Second Lieutenant, Cyclist Corps.'

'We run errands,' a burly sergeant lolling over his handlebars behind the officer said in a Scots accent more dour than a house.

'Yes. Thank you, Sergeant.'

'Like a bunch of cissy post office boys,' the sergeant muttered.

'Yes, thank you. Thank you, Sergeant.'

'I ask ye,' the man went on. 'What a bloody namby pamby way to run a war, eh?'

'Thank you, Sergeant!' Devonshire screamed and he leaned closer to Lestrade. 'Turned down by the London Scottish. Hadn't got the legs for the kilt. Never got over it.'

Lestrade tutted and shook his head. The sergeant spat copiously on to Hounslow Heath. Funny the little things that will derange a man.

'Now,' said the Superintendent. 'The Inns of Court Rifles . . .'

'Right, now then.' Devonshire straightened across his crossbar and pulled a map out of his saddlebag. 'Now, we're here, aren't we, Sergeant?'

'Dinna ask me,' the man grunted. 'I've just been riding around all morning like a poxy butcher's boy, I have.'

'Yes. Quite. Well, somebody's got to do it. Yes, here we are. The Press ought to be around somewhere, which is why I thought you were they. We're the B Team. Our task is to . . . Aha, no.' He grinned. 'Can't be too careful. Last year the blighters used spies in mufti. Over a casual pint and pasty at the Volunteer's Arms one lunch-time, the entire South Staffordshires were surrounded. Anyway, I've no idea of deployment of their fellows.'

'He's no bloody idea of the deployment of our fellows, either,' the thick-set sergeant commented. 'Come to think of it, he's no bloody idea at all.'

Devonshire scowled at him and glanced back at Lestrade. 'Got to make allowances,' he said. 'Father was a docker.'

'Tsk, tsk.' Lestrade shook his head.

'Look, if you follow this hedge and then cut right across that field, the one with the bullocks, you ought to reach the North Somerset Yeomanry.'

'The North Somerset are here?' Lestrade asked.

'Yes, they're with us. The A Team have got the Notts Hussars, worse luck for us. They've won the regimental polo three years running now.'

'Aye,' snarled the sergeant. 'Typical bloody ponces.'

Devonshire cleared his throat. 'Well, we can't dally on the way.' And he slipped the map back.

'Wait a minute,' Lestrade said. 'What if the shooting starts again?'

Devonshire consulted his hunter. 'Oh, it won't. That last salvo marks the end of the morning's sortie. It's off to the Gentleman in Khaki now for a noggin. Care to join us?'

Lestrade took another look at the sergeant. Deciding that he made Ned Blevvins look like a choirboy, he declined.

'Corps, mount!' the Lieutenant ordered and saluting Lestrade, the officer pedalled off down the road, his sergeant swearing and cursing in his wake. 'Hope you find your man!' Devonshire called.

'So do I,' Lestrade shouted back. He looked at his black-faced, begrimed constables. 'Come on, lads. Let's go and say hello to an old friend of mine in the North Somerset Yeomanry. And don't worry, they don't let the Yeomanry have swords any more. Or anything sharp, come to that. They've just got Lee-Enfield rifles. We'll be all right.'

Constable Lyall had won the History prize at school. Now that was a blessing for his proud mum and dad, but it was a curse that sweltering August day in the noonday heat for Constable Lyall. As he slogged up to the North Somerset Yeomanry's position without rifle or pack, all those murderous hills in history came flooding into his mind – Senlac, Bunker, Majuba, Graham and Jimmy. That cluster of trees seemed an awfully long way away, but his guv'nor kept on walking, his boots crunching on the flinty hillside, then padding on the pock-marked grass. The sun blazed off the black of the Superintendent's bowler and Nathan Tait looked across at him. Tait hadn't won any prizes at school, but his terror at that long stretch of open country lying ahead was none the less than Lyall's.

'Halt!' There was a rattle of musketry, a snicker of bolts. 'Who goes?'

'Police officers,' said Lestrade.

A khaki-clad Yeoman in brown leather bandolier poked his head out of a bush. Then another.

'D'you think they're Press, Grenville?' he asked in broad Somerset.

'Could be, Tarleton.' The other one adjusted the peak of his cap. 'Could well be.'

'We're not the Press,' Lestrade assured them. 'We're the police.' And he reached for his warrant card. The two rifles came up to the level and two detective-constables hit the dirt. Lestrade just stood there in the dust cloud they'd kicked up.

'They could be zpies, Grenville,' Tarleton suggested, closing one eye, then the other as his sights settled on the bridge of Lestrade's nose. 'From the A Team, eh?'

'They could well be, Tarleton,' Grenville agreed.

'Do you have a Harry Bandicoot with your lot?' Lestrade asked.

The Yeomen looked at each other. 'Bloody gert well-informed zpies, Grenville,' Tarleton said.

'Oh, I've had enough of this.' Lestrade took his hands off his hips and marched straight forward. As he reached the business ends of the two Lee-Enfields, he shoved his index fingers into both muzzles. 'Would you like to get up?' he barked at his constables. 'And would you like to blow us to merry Hell, or are you going to take us to Harry Bandicoot?'

The Yeomen, Grenville and Tarleton, dithered as the rookies recovered themselves with what dignity they could. Then, as one, the men of Somerset shouldered their weapons, saluted and escorted the policemen up the hill and through their lines. The clumps of elder and gorse came alive around them as the bushes turned magically into men. At the top of the ridge, sitting in immaculately cut khaki on a fallen log, smiled Lestrade's old friend, Harry Bandicoot.

'Harry!' Lestrade held out his hand. 'Thank God. I expected you to be hiding in a tree, not sitting on one.'

'Sholto.' The blond giant gripped the man's shoulders. 'You got my telegram, then?'

'No,' said Lestrade. 'I'm here on the job. Oh, these are my constables, Tait and Lyall.'

'Gentlemen.' Bandicoot saluted.

'He may look like a Field Marshal now, boys.' Lestrade smiled. 'But not long ago, this whippersnapper was standing where you are.'

Lyall shook his left foot free of a cowpat.

'Well, perhaps not quite where you are,' the Superintendent observed. 'How's Letitia?'

'She's well. That's what my telegram said. She's joining us at the Grand on Saturday. End of manoeuvres bash. Is Emma home?'

'She is and as gorgeous as ever.'

'Excellent.'

'Major Bandicoot, zir . . .' Grenville saluted. 'We found these men wandering below the lines, zir. We have reazon to believe they are the Press.'

'Or zpies, zir.' Tarleton saluted. 'They could always be zpies.'

'Tell me, Major.' Lestrade brushed a speck of dust off the embroidered crown on Harry's cuff. 'Do you have sufficient authority to have your privates shot?'

'Please, Sholto.' Harry winced. 'Don't even joke about it. We've been given new War Office directives about how to wear our Sam Browne holsters. Shooting our privates is now a distinct possibility, believe me! Bring your chappies and have some champagne. I don't think my brother officers have *quite* cleared the Fortnum's hamper yet.'

Lestrade felt quite mellow after a few flutes of bubbly. He, Tait and Lyall had cleaned themselves up courtesy of the slop buckets of the North Somerset Yeomanry and the peppered ham and partridges were divine. They were a genial bunch of chaps, Harry's brother officers. Lestrade had met a couple of them before when he had stayed at Bandicoot Hall.

Now, after luncheon and before the red flag went up for the afternoon's assault, he shared a cigar with the galloping Major under the cooling boughs of a mighty oak.

'So you're looking for the Devil's Own,' Bandicoot said, blowing rings to the leafy canopy.

'Why is it that everybody but me knows that nickname?' Lestrade asked.

'Is it important?'

'It might be. There again, it could be coincidence. Actually, I'm looking for one man – Broker Morant.'

'Morant?'

'Do you know him?'

'I know of him. His little brother was in my House at Eton. Bit of a duffer if I remember rightly. "Moronic" Morant we called him. Broker is altogether a different kettle of fish, if half of what I read in the *Financial Times* is correct.'

'Of course, you've got a few bob here and there, haven't you? In stocks, I mean.'

'Oh, small potatoes, Sholto. I'm not in Broker's league. I remember the family had estates in Haiti. None of us at school knew where it was, so we asked old Attenborough, our geography master. He didn't know either.'

'Ah, that's the way of geography masters,' Lestrade remembered. 'Ours couldn't find the staffroom by himself. By the way, Harry, what are you driving now?'

'A Panhard. Oh, I've still got the Silver Ghost of course. Can't bear to part with that. Ivo's got a Mephisto.'

Lestrade's cigar nearly fell out of his mouth. 'A Fiat Mephisto?' he asked.

'Yes. It's a bit racy for a boy, but I mustn't say that. He's twenty-one at Christmas. You and Fanny are invited by the way. Christmas at Bandicoot Hall and that's an order.' He flashed him the rather lazy cavalry salute. 'And tell Edward Henry, if there are any problems with that, to come and see me. Or rather, I'll come and see him.'

Lestrade laughed. 'You know, I half expected to find Ivo here with you today,' he said.

'In the Yeomanry?' Bandicoot smiled. 'Not Ivo. Oh, he's a first-class horseman, you know that, but well, he's very enamoured of Corpus Christi. Stayed up at Cambridge all summer, as a matter of fact.'

'Ah, the dreaming spires.'

Harry laughed. 'It's not so much the spires he's dreaming about, Sholto, as a pretty little lass at Girton. Letitia isn't sure of course . . . Not since Rupert went . . .'

'Harry.' Lestrade's smile vanished. 'I wanted to ask. I just wasn't quite sure how. It's been over two years now.'

Harry nodded. 'Two years, three weeks. Oh, Ivo's a brick. He lives for both and of course, we've still got Emma from time to time.'

'You have,' Lestrade assured him. 'In fact, only yesterday she was saying she intends to spend the second half of her holiday with you. I said she ought to ask first.'

'Nonsense.' Bandicoot slapped his boot. 'She's as welcome as blueberry pie,' he said. A bugle call shattered the afternoon. 'That's it, Sholto. Boots and saddles. Listen, you'd better move with us. There'll be no shelling of the high ground this afternoon and as long as you wear one of these.' And he handed Lestrade a scarlet armband. 'You'll be taken for one of the Provost-Marshal's men and not only will you not be shot at, but people in all shades of khaki will be saluting you.'

'That's kind, Harry.' Lestrade got up with him. 'But you know me and horses.'

'Don't worry. We've got a hospital wagon through those trees. You and your lads can hitch a ride. The Sirdar's coming down at tea-time for a bit of an inspection. It'll be something to tell your children. Well, come to think of it, I can't see Emma being very interested in a boring old fart like Kitchener. She can tell her children. Sarnt-Major!' And he was gone in a blur of khaki and leather.

It may have been his age. It may have been the heat. It may have been the champagne. Whatever the reason, Sholto Lestrade dozed off that afternoon under the cool canvas of the hospital wagon, parked once again in the trees. He gave Tait and Lyall strict instructions to spell each other and to take turns with their borrowed field-glasses to watch out for the Devil's Own. Harry had described their uniform – field-grey for the rifles. Their cavalry unit had green facings and shoulder chains in full dress, but they weren't there that day. Tait and Lyall wished they had been – at least the sun sparkled on shoulder chains over a distance. It did nothing whatever to highlight grey. Neither of them could believe that the guv'nor had slept right through a full-pitched cavalry skirmish, but he had.

On the tilt of the slope, the North Somerset Yeomanry had caught the flankers of the Nottinghamshire Hussars napping.

'Permission to try a charge, sir?' Harry had asked the Colonel. Old 'Goofy' Glyn was too long in the tooth for this *Boy's Own* stuff, but he admired guts in his junior officers.

'Go for it, my boy!' The old man had beamed. 'And the devil take the hindmost.'

The hindmost were Privates Grenville Nadger and Tarleton Ogg, although they were doing their best. Harry's squadron sliced through the Hussars like a knife through butter, everybody with strict instructions of course not to hurt anybody else. And to be fair, no one was too rough. Harry kept his sword sheathed, as did all the officers. And if there was a bit of gouging and kneeing at close quarters, well, this *was* supposed to be practice for the real thing.

The bugle for tiffin sounded prompt at four thirty and everything stopped for tea. Lestrade was roused from his slumbers in time to see the Sirdar arrive. Lestrade had met a few great men in his time, but Horatio Herbert Kitchener, whose parents clearly couldn't decide whether he should be an admiral or a cook, had always passed him by. This was largely because Kitchener had spent most of his serving career abroad. And also because, unlike every other man in the Empire, Lestrade refused to be cowed by Kitchener's extraordinary moustache. Even from this distance, Lestrade could see the man's cheeks burning vividly under the white of his peaked cap. He looked like a Christmas pudding.

Around him fluttered the plumed hats of his staff, their owners in scarlet and gold lace, their glossy horses groomed to within an inch of their grooms' lives. Fighting was over for the day and the entire B Team, a thousand men strong, was assembled in hollow square, Kitchener at their centre.

There were barked orders, carried and distorted on the rising wind from where the Yard men watched. A rumbling of drums, a shrill of bugles and the thud and rattle of a thousand men coming to attention. The sun kissed the blades of Harry's brother officers as they saluted the Sirdar with their swords.

It may have been Lyall who saw it first. Arguably it was Tait. But it was Lestrade who reacted faster. 'There!' he shouted. 'A gunman on the grassy knoll.'

But his words did not carry to the hollow square, and even before he'd said them and started hurtling at a crazy pace down the slope, the smoke appeared and the crash rang out. There was confusion around Kitchener, the Sirdar reeling in the saddle and the horses, shifting, whinnying as they barged into each other. The tightness of the square loosened, its corners crumbling, its edges rolling outwards.

'Kitchener's dead!' Lestrade heard the cry as he raced for the mêlée, running through them now, batting aside bewildered, tired soldiers, who had been looking forward to a few words of praise and an early tea.

'The Sirdar's down. He's killed,' was all he heard on every side, as he fought his way through the surging square and at last, into its centre. One of the first men he recognized was Harry Bandicoot, his sword on the ground, his cap gone, kneeling in the dust. And next to him the Sirdar, his face a livid purple, his eyes rolling, his moustache a clarion call to the Empire. The left sleeve of his blue Field Marshal's tunic was wet with the blood that dripped on to his buff gauntlets. But Kitchener wasn't dead. Kitchener wasn't even hurt. He was cradling in his arms a young man who couldn't have been more than twenty-five. The boy wore the scarlet uniform of an ADC and he was shaking, crying, trying not to show the men that he was afraid.

The sky was black with armed men around the Sirdar. No one would have a second chance that day. And as Kitchener held him, the boy coughed blood once, twice. And he died.

There was a hush in the camp that night. Somewhere out towards Stanwell twinkled the fires of the A Team. The news had spread. Flags hung at half mast in the warm August darkness, that curious darkness that was half light. Ordinarily, it would have been beer and tall tales and relief that the Mrs wasn't there. But tonight was the night after a battle, the 1913 equivalent of *Te Deum* and *Non Nobis*.

Kitchener sat in his folding camp chair, still in his field service blues as he had not expected to be there so long. He'd had a telegram sent to His Majesty explaining the situation and apologizing for his absence. The King had boys. He'd understand. The hero of Khartoum and Suakin and Dongola and Khartoum again sat with his Engineer's sword still buckled about him, his left sleeve stiff with the blood of the boy.

'I don't understand.' General Lovell was shaking his head. The General was several years Kitchener's senior and had had the honour of having his head patted by Wellington as a small boy. Since then, it had been downhill all the way. The General had a veritable hedge of a beard, of pepper and salt tones. He was known in Eastern Command as 'The Lavatory Brush'. 'I just don't understand. No one's been killed on manoeuvres here since 1881 when some chappie in the Old 69th fell off an ammunition mule.'

'I won't ask', Kitchener said flatly, 'what he was doing on an ammunition mule in the first place.'

'I should think not,' the Brush ventured. 'Nothing odd about the Old 69th, y'know. Have the boy's family been told?'

'I sent one of my staff,' Kitchener told him. 'Better that than a curt telegram. "Killed in action" has a hollow ring, doesn't it, Brush, when there's no action going on?'

'Who's this police chappie?' the Brush wanted to know. 'Awful dress sense. Needs a day or two on double drill and no canteen.'

'Superintendent Lestrade,' Kitchener told him. 'From Scotland Yard. A good fellow, from what I've heard. Knows his job.'

'Look here, Kitch – you don't mind if I call you Kitch, do you, after all these years?'

'Not a bit of it, Brush. Fire away.'

'Well.' The old man dug deep into his jodhpur pockets for his pipe and matches. 'There's a rumour going round that the assassin was one of my chaps, from the A Team, I mean.'

'Stuff and nonsense, Brush! No disrespect to your people, but they're Territorials, aren't they? Most of 'em couldn't hit a barn door at a hundred paces. No, this is political.'

'Is it?' The very mention of the word bewildered Lovell. The introduction of the secret ballot in 1872 had so confused him, what with the element of choice and having to make your mark (something he'd never done) that he hadn't voted since. Democracy was as a closed book to him. 'Well, I'm glad. Er . . . I mean, that you don't think one of my chaps was responsible. We did get a thorough licking today, as it happened, but that's war, isn't it? I mean, when you were at Pretoria, you didn't get all peevish after Spion Kop and start rounding up women and children or anything, did you? And putting them in camps, and so on?'

'Er . . . well . . .'

'Well, of course not.' His brush lit up in the match's glare and for an unseasonal moment he looked like Father Christmas. Then the match died and he looked like a lavatory brush again. 'Ah, here's that police chappie.'

It was indeed. Lestrade made his way from the tent where the dead man lay, a soldier at each corner with his head bowed and his hands clasped on his rifle butt. He sat down on the canvas chair, next to Kitchener.

'Well?' the Sirdar said. 'Here. Noggin?'

It was the most welcome brandy Lestrade had seen in a long

time. He took the proffered hip-flask. 'Thank you, sir. Your continuing good health.'

'What news?'

'The coroner says it's a Lee-Enfield bullet,' the Yard man told him. 'Apparently, he served with you, sir, at Paardeburg and saw plenty of them.'

'Hah.' Kitchener lit a cheroot of vast proportions. 'I'm sure he did. Well, well, Paardeburg.'

'Have you any idea how many Lee-Enfields were in use today?'

'Brush?' Kitchener turned to the Head of Eastern Command. It was a bit like turning in your sleep.

'Well, now you've asked me,' Lovell realized. 'Haven't a clue, Kitch. Quite a few, I suppose. There's a quartermaster here somewhere, but I'm not sure I'd recognize him in the dark.'

'It doesn't really matter,' Lestrade said.

'Oh?' said Kitchener. 'Why?'

'Because our man isn't a soldier. Oh, he may have dressed as one today. He'd be a fool not to. My lads and I have stood out like sore thumbs all day. But this murder attempt has nothing to do with these manoeuvres. It was simple importunism.'

'Was it?' Kitchener asked.

'The grassy knoll was a perfect place. High ground surrounded by trees. You, a sitting target. All eyes turned towards you, away from him. It was only the merest chance that I spotted him. And that did no good.'

'Don't reproach yourself, my dear fellow,' Kitchener said. 'The pair of legs aren't made that can beat a bullet. You did your best. I feel for young Danby, of course, but we must be grateful that chummie wasn't much of a shot. What did you see, exactly? Anything you'd recognize again?'

Lestrade shook his head. 'I caught the flash of the sun on the rifle barrel and the blur of a head beyond it. I couldn't even swear it was a man.'

'That's it.' Lovell snapped his fingers. 'A woman. Your would-be assassin's a female, Kitch, one of those Suffragette people. What are they after? The vote, isn't it? Can't understand it myself. They can have mine any day.'

'Field Marshal?' Lestrade asked.

'Lord, I don't know,' he said. 'What are you asking me? Who'd want to see me dead? Well, where do you want to start? A few thousand Boer, perhaps, or the Fuzzy-Wuzzy followers of the mad Mahdi. And that's before I get to the bleeding hearts over whom I've been promoted. Socialists who resent my Viscountcy and various government grants for being such a thundering good hero. Photographers because I don't like my picture being taken. Artists because I refuse to appear on any poster whatsoever. Masters of Ceremonies because I loathe public dinners. I've been getting some pretty funny looks from Winston Churchill lately, too. I tell you, Lestrade, the list's as long as your arm – except that no one has an arm long enough.'

'There are officers ringing the camp, sir,' Lestrade assured him. 'Half the Middlesex Constabulary are out there.'

'Thank you for that,' Kitchener said. 'But Allah created the English mad as Mr Kipling tells us. I don't think chummie waited around for a second shot.'

'He got away from the Yeomanry, then?' Lovell checked.

'They gave chase as soon as we realized what was happening,' Lestrade said. 'Nothing. He'd just vanished into the Middlesex countryside.'

'It does that, country,' Kitchener observed. 'It's worse on the Veldt. Flat as a pancake and nary a tree for miles. You'd think you'd spot a Boer a mile away, but not a bit of it. The buggers blend like margarine. You could be staring one right in the eye and you wouldn't see him. Uncanny.'

'Think this chappie's a Boer then, Kitch?' Lovell asked.

'It's possible, Brush.' Kitchener sighed. 'Anything's possible. Paul Kruger's a bit of a bad loser between you and me. I wouldn't put it past him to send out some sharp-shooting reprobate.'

'The dead officer,' Lestrade said. 'Er . . . Lieutenant Withers?'

'Danby, yes. Eighteen last month. Deuced unfair him stopping that bullet for me. Deuced unfair. His family will be heartbroken.'

'An army family?'

'Lord, no. Something in the City, I believe. They made a killing in Krugerands before the war. Had something on Cecil Rhodes, I think.'

'Did they now?' Lestrade's eyes narrowed. Robert Peel worked in the City. So did Worsthorne Griffin. And Herbert Wilson had shares in Krugerands. Somewhere, somehow, there was a rattling in Lestrade's tired brain. Pieces were beginning to fall into place.

'I don't know you very well, Lestrade,' Kitchener said. 'But I'll say that's an inscrutable look that's just come over your face. I said he was good, Brush, didn't I? Are you deducing or whatever you chappies do?'

Lestrade smiled. 'Well, sir, it is only an idea at this stage, but . . .'

'Yes, man,' Kitchener said, twirling the vast moustache above the huge cheroot. 'Out with it.'

'Well, what if our man was a better marksman than we think?'

'Eh?' Lovell was lost.

'What if you, sir, weren't the real target at all, but that the murderer found his real target?'

'Young Danby?' Kitchener frowned. 'Surely not.'

'Lad's barely finished shitting yellow,' Lovell commented.

'Oh, I don't pretend to understand it yet,' Lestrade said. 'But let me do some digging. There's a pattern to all this – a pattern of evil. If I come up with something, *anything* – then it means, Field Marshal, that your life is not in danger after all.'

'Haha, Lestrade, Lestrade.' Kitchener laughed. 'My life has always been in danger. It always will be. But I'm not quite ready for my coffin yet. Dig and be damned.'

10

Lestrade wasn't sure what surprised him more – the black Delaunay-Belleville or the black driving it. The man looked like a tar-baby, with huge white eyes rolling behind the goggles and tightly curled hair compressed under the leather cap, with the peak on backwards. What had *actually* surprised Lestrade *most* was the roar of the motor's klaxon as it rounded the bend and slewed across the road to scream to a halt just short of the pond.

'I was looking for Major Morant,' the Superintendent said. 'Of the Devil's Own.'

The negro rested an arm on the Delaunay's door and poked his head out of the open canopy. 'Someone had to fight de Debbil,' he crooned. 'Sound upon Gabriel's horn . . .'

Just what Lestrade needed when up to his neck in murder – a nigger minstrel. 'Do you happen to know where I can find him?'

A white face popped up out of the open back of the car, moustachioed, wearing a khaki peaked cap. 'Right here,' the passenger said. 'I'm Charles Morant. Who are you?'

'Superintendent Lestrade,' Lestrade said. 'Scotland Yard.' And flashed his warrant card.

'Toussaint.' Morant nudged the negro. 'Have you been over-zealous on the clutch again?'

'I swear, massa.' The chauffeur tilted back his goggles, shaking his head vigorously. 'I ain't never done mo' than fifty-five in an area what's built up.'

Morant slapped the man's huge biceps. 'Stout fellow. Was there anything else, Superintendent? Only my regiment's moved up somewhat since breakfast. I feel I ought to put in a show.'

'It's not about speeding, sir,' Lestrade told him. 'It's about your regiment – and a racehorse.'

'Well, well.' Morant beamed. 'A conundrum. How exciting. Look, step in, would you? I don't believe in marching when I can ride. Toussaint, I think the champagne's sufficiently chilled now.' He checked his hunter. 'It's a *little* early, but I'm not one to stand on ceremony.'

The negro alighted and held the door open for Lestrade. As soon as the Yard man was inside, the chauffeur unstrapped an ice-box on the running board and popped the cork with an explosion that probably worried the Honourable Artillery Company, reconnoitring to the South.

'Oh, lordy, lordy!' Toussaint said, catching most of the froth in the twin champagne flutes he'd liberated from the Fortnum's hamper strapped to the Delaunay's rear.

'Listen to him.' Morant chuckled. 'You wouldn't think he was Harrow and Brasenose, would you? Not bad for a Haitian.'

Lestrade knew little about these things, but he knew it was unusual to find anyone from Haisia in England at all, whatever his features. 'This is a remarkable vehicle, Mr Morant,' Lestrade said, leaning back in the soft, black leather. Morant seemed yards away.

'Oh, this old thing?' Morant laughed. 'Only a four-litre six-cylinder engine with side valves. The cane panels are quite fetching, I suppose. It's all right as a runabout. I'd personally settle for my Siddeley-Deary Two, wouldn't you?'

'Absolutely,' enthused Lestrade as Toussaint cranked the engine and hopped behind the wheel.

'What do you drive, Mr Lestrade?' Morant asked.

'A Lanchester.' The Superintendent beamed.

'Oh.' Morant's face fell. 'Well, now, to this conundrum of yours. My regiment and a racehorse, I think you said.'

'I think I should tell you, sir,' Lestrade said as Toussaint applied the accelerator, 'that I am conducting a murder inquiry.'

'Really?' Morant sat up, tightening the straps of his Stowhasser gaiters. 'How riveting. Whose?'

'Danby Withers's for one,' Lestrade said.

'Withers?' Morant looked vague. 'Oh, yes. Of course. But that was a near-miss, surely. Blighter aimed for Kitchener and muffed it.'

'That might be the case, sir,' Lestrade said.

'Well, chin chin.' Morant clicked his flute with Lestrade's. It was a *little* early for the Superintendent and didn't, to be honest, sit too well with the sausages roasted on an open fire he'd put away not an hour since, as the sun climbed over the horse-chestnuts and he swigged the indescribable coffee of Kitchener's camp.

'Did you know the dead man?' Lestrade asked.

'Danby? I think I pushed him on a swing once when he was still in knickerbockers. Old Withers will take it hard.'

'His father?'

'Grandfather. His father, poor fellow, was beaten to death in a

134

riot at Gordon's school in Khartoum. Rather unfortunate, really. He'd been invited out there by the Chairman of the Governors to talk to the boys on the importance of commerce in the Empire and they rather took against him. Some chance remark, a slur on their honour – you know what pubescent boys are like, Superintendent.'

The Superintendent didn't.

'Anyway.' Morant poured his second glass. 'There was a bit of an argy-bargy and "Googie" bought it. Tragic really.'

'So Danby . . .'

'Was brought up by his grandfather, yes. Oh, Googie saw him all right, though. Had a few Krugerands stashed away. Had something on Cecil Rhodes, I understand.'

Lestrade understood that, too.

'But all this is by-the-by, Mr Lestrade,' Morant assured him. 'No, Kitchener was the target. As soon as the galloper from B Team arrived last night, I said to Toussaint – the chaps in the D. O. – that's it, I said, old Kruger's got him at last. Or near as dammit. It's been a long time coming.'

'You don't like Field Marshal Kitchener, sir?'

Morant looked as if he'd swallowed a torque-wrench. 'Like? Kitchener? My dear fellow, that's a contradiction in terms. You might as well like a rattlesnake or a dose of the pox. The man's a first-class boundah. How he got where he is today, I'll never know. No, no.' Morant tested the flying air with an upraised finger. 'I tell a lie, I *do* know. It's in his eyes. Vicious, triangular things they are. Triangular eyes means ruthlessness. It's one of the secrets of the face. And Kitchener is so ruthless, he's positively isosceles.'

Lestrade knew nothing of Kitchener's religion, so he let the matter drop. 'Your regiment,' he said.

'Ah, the D. O., yes, yes. Idiots.'

'Idiots?' Lestrade was confused.

'Well, yes, they're mostly lawyers, aren't they? You show me a bright lawyer and I'll show you a good time. We all absolutely refused to join the 27th London back in '08. So we became an Officer Training Unit. Well, somebody's got to do it, Lestrade, or, come the next war, our army will be led by donkeys.'

Toussaint hit the klaxon, but was forced to slow for a wandering flock of sheep behind which a minuscule man was wandering, every now and then tapping one of them with a fly swat.

'I'm sorry,' Lestrade said. 'I just automatically assumed that you were here for your King and Country.'

'That poppy-eyed buffoon with the appalling wife? Good Lord, no. It's a tax dodge, Superintendent. Expenses. I have to pay Toussaint here, buy field cars, horses, uniforms – I've even got a sword somewhere.' He suddenly winced. 'Ooh, yes, there it is.' And adjusted his clothing. 'I can set it all against tax. Then, there are the mess bills, the port, the cigars. Oh, it's a marvellous life in the new irregular Territorials.'

'What made you join the Inns of Court?'

'My dear man.' Morant chuckled. 'You don't *join* the D. O. Not as an officer, anyway. No, you have to be put up, like a club, which is what it is. They're very choosy. Various chaps have been blackballed – oh, sorry, Toussaint – just for dropping their aitches. They had no aspirations, of course.'

'You don't *have* to be a lawyer, then?'

'For the 14th Middlesex Rifle Volunteer Corps? Not a bit of it. Oh, they used to be, yes. All Bar and Silk and such nonsense, but they long ago realized – as all lawyers have – that money talks. So chaps like me, who own much of Knightsbridge and a sizeable chunk of Swaziland – we're accepted with open arms. Connections, you see. That's what oils the wheels of finance, Mr Lestrade, connections. I'm sure it's the same in your line.'

'Indeed.' Lestrade nodded. 'So your regiment's number is 14.'

'That's right. What about it?'

'Tell me, Mr Morant, do you have a calling card?'

Morant looked aghast.

'Is the Pope Pius X?'

Lestrade had no idea, but it sounded feasible. 'May I see it?'

'Be my guest. Left, here, Toussaint. Billy Devereux will have followed the river – it leads to the King's Arms.' And he fished out his calling card. It was white with 'Charles Morant. Honest Broker' embossed on it in a sophisticated grey. 'You seem disappointed.' The motoring Major refilled their glasses.

'I was hoping it would be red,' the Superintendent confessed.

'Sorry if it offends your artistic sensibilities.'

Lestrade checked the back. No number '14'. No devil's face. 'This is the only one you have?'

'Lord no, I've got thousands of them – oh, I see what you mean. Yes. That's the only design I use.'

'Tell me about El Diablo,' Lestrade said, watching the hedge-rows skimming by. His third flute was beginning to cause him problems. Either that or Toussaint's driving was getting more erratic.

'Three-year-old filly, by Thunder, out of Order. Goes like a train – or is that Mrs de Vere? I bought her last year – Diablo, that is, not Mrs de Vere.'

'It ran in the Derby?'

'Yes. Not very convincingly, I'm afraid. Although my jockey assures me that he was idling at the back, lulling the others into a false sense of security and was just about to make his move, when that wretched woman got in Anmer's way.'

'Did you know Miss Davison, Mr Morant?'

'Know her? Good Lord, no, and thankfully not in the Biblical sense, having seen the photos. Knew her dad, though – again, not in the Biblical sense.'

'Really?'

'Yes. Old Charlie "Jangers" Davison. Oh, he died years ago. Rumour was he topped himself.'

'Really?' Lestrade had been this way before.

'Well, that's how it is in finance, Mr Lestrade. My office told me yesterday there was a hiccough in Icelandic haddock and something of a blip in Anglo-Zanzibarian cowrie shells.'

'Much call, is there?' Lestrade found himself wondering aloud. 'For Anglo-Zanzibarian cowrie shells?'

'Well.' Morant drained his glass. 'Not to my taste personally, but the horse-furniture of the 10th Hussars is festooned with them. No, the point I was endeavouring to make is, by this morning, the window ledges of Lombard Street will be littered with jumpers.'

'Is that some sort of token?' Lestrade asked. 'Hanging clothing out of windows?'

Morant gave him an old-fashioned look. 'I'm talking about suicides, Lestrade,' he said. 'People who jump.'

'Ah. And Mr Davison jumped?'

'From the Clifton Suspension Bridge. I noticed people who disliked him had the good grace not to refer to him as an old stick-in-the-mud after that.'

'Oh, good,' Lestrade said. 'Thoughtful.'

'Look, Lestrade.' Morant leaned towards the Superintendent. 'I appreciate that it's your job to ask questions, but why me in particular?'

'Oh, it's routine, sir, I assure you,' Lestrade lied. 'Sort of tying up loose ends, you know.'

'One of those ends wouldn't be Alaric Bligh, would it?' Morant asked.

'Bligh?' Lestrade played it nonchalant. 'Why?'

Toussaint snatched at the handbrake and stopped the Delaunay. Below them, a whole vista had opened, like a painting of a battle. The London Scottish, led by a huge piper in French grey, were plodding across the heath, ultra-mindful as only men who wear kilts can be, of the gorse. Away to their left, hidden behind a double hedgerow, a skirmishing party of the London Irish were creeping into position.

'Oh, nothing.' Morant tapped his chauffeur on the shoulder. 'Dynamite, Toussaint, please. One stick should be enough. Bally stuff costs an arm and a leg. Do you have a light, Lestrade?'

'Er . . .' It was with some alarm that Lestrade found himself reaching for the Swan Vestas. Morant held out the lethal weapon to him.

'Would you be so kind? Oh, I've no time for the London Scottish personally, but, well, play the white man – oh, sorry, Toussaint – they are on our team – aren't they, Toussaint?'

'Yes, massa,' the negro assured him. 'They sure are.'

'Umm . . .' Lestrade thought he ought to comment.

But in a sense it was too late. He'd mechanically struck the match and Morant had lit the fuse. Now he sat there with the thing fizzing and hissing in his hand. 'No,' he said, calmly watching the manoeuvres below the ridge. 'This has all the hallmarks of Alaric Bligh.'

'It does?' Lestrade found himself squirming, just a little.

'Yes. You see, I should explain, Lestrade, that Alaric and I go back a long way.'

'You do?' Funny, isn't it, how your collar seems much too tight in the presence of dynamite?

'Yes. Comrades, I suppose you'd call us.'

'He . . . er . . . he's in the Devil's Own?'

'Bligh? Good Lord, no. Too busy making money. Or attempting to. No, no, that's unfair.'

'Is it? Look, Mr Morant. Shouldn't you do something with that?'

'What? Oh, this.' Morant chuckled. 'Yes, of course, when the time is right.'

The fuse had burned half-way down. 'In the rightness of time stakes' – Lestrade felt his voice rising – 'I'd say this is it.'

'No, never underestimate Bligh. He'd cut your throat for a penny.'

'That's . . . er . . . that's more or less what he said about you.'

'Yes.' Morant smiled. 'I guessed it would be. So he sent you here, did he?'

'I really think . . .' Lestrade began to wonder what sort of madhouse he'd stumbled into. The huge black chauffeur didn't move, just stared ahead watching the unfolding battle. There were bugle calls away to the North, Harry's North Somerset on the move again. But the only sound Lestrade could hear was the hiss of the dynamite fuse. And soon, even that was drowned out by the rising thunder of his own heart.

'Another bottle, I think, Toussaint.' Morant yawned. 'The Special Reserve.'

'Yes, massa.' The negro smiled, his teeth like piano keys and he solemnly trudged to the back to open the hamper again.

'Mr Morant . . .' Lestrade was shrieking now, unsure whether to grab the dynamite or leap out of the car or both. Morant suddenly stood up and hurled the stick. It tumbled through the clear cobalt of the sky, trailing smoke and sparks. Lestrade doubled up, no mean feat for a man who had already stared sixty in the face, and his moustache said hello again to his knees, his hands wrapped over his head. There was an almighty explosion and the Delaunay rocked.

'Man, that's mighty strong stuff!' Toussaint stood there with champagne froth trickling over his fingers, the cork lost in the Middlesex heathland. A shower of dust settled over them all, but the day had been saved. The London Scottish broke and ran for cover and the London Irish, alarmed by the noise, fired wildly in all directions. Lestrade had never seen so many Irishmen exposing themselves simultaneously before.

'A result, I think.' Morant beamed and raised the glass Toussaint had poured. 'Back to HQ, please, Toussaint. It wouldn't do to achieve more than one military miracle in one day. Your very good health, Mr Lestrade.'

And Lestrade downed the champagne in one.

Sholto Lestrade had never had a dream like it. It seemed as though he was in the centre of wildly flickering candles and writhing black bodies gyrated past him to the frenzied beat of tom-toms. Eyes rolled, teeth gnashed and a naked girl, her breasts slippery with oil or sweat, lowered herself on to him. He was getting too old for dreams like that.

All the more alarming, then, that when he woke up, it was to stare into the face of one of the oddest-looking men he'd ever seen. The features were flat and broad, the eyes large and compelling. The hair was centre-parted and curled up over the ears like the devil's horns. But the devil wore his collar back to front.

'Aarghh!' Lestrade realized it was his voice shrieking.

'It's all right, it's all right.' The priest's hands were holding him by the shoulders. 'You've had rather a nasty experience.'

'Have I?' Lestrade wondered. The face and the room were swimming and blurring in front of him. He was in his underwear, lying on a couch.

'You're safe,' the priest said. 'Do you know who you are?'

Lestrade blinked. What a bloody silly question. 'Of course. I'm Superintendent Sholto Lestrade of Scotland Yard.'

'Thank the Lord.' The priest sighed. 'Then we're not too late.'

'Too late for what?' Lestrade tried to sit up, but his head rebelled and the room reeled.

'Take this.' The priest was pressing a steaming cup into Lestrade's hand.

'What is it?'

'Never mind,' his nurse told him. 'It will do you good.'

'Look, Mr . . . er . . . oh, my God!' Lestrade had never tasted anything so foul in his life.

'Summers,' the priest said. 'Montague Alphonsus Joseph-Mary Augustus. But you can call me Monty.'

'Oh, good,' Lestrade gasped. 'What *is* that?'

'Better you don't know,' Summers assured him, putting the cup with its steaming green contents aside. 'Now, tell me, Superintendent Sholto Lestrade, the last thing you remember.'

'Look, Mr Summers . . .'

'Monty . . .'

'Monty. Do you mind telling me where I am?'

'The Retreat,' Summers said, leaning back in his chair and cradling an upraised knee (his own).

'The Retreat?'

'Well, it is a *little* pretentious, isn't it? Actually, it's Thirty-one Whimbrill Avenue, Stanmore, but we Anglo-Catholics do like our little bit of mystique.'

'How did I get here?'

'Ah, now that's quite interesting. I found you wandering.'

'Wandering?'

'Stark naked except for your necessaries and your bowler hat.'

'My knuckles?' Lestrade said suddenly.

'They're fine.' Summers patted both the patient's hands.

'No, not *those* knuckles. My brass knuckles.'

'Ah, yes. I found those. And your warrant card. I doubt you'll get your clothes back, though.'

'I don't understand . . .'

'Focus,' Summers said patiently, clasping Lestrade's hands between his. 'Concentrate. Now, what is the last thing you remember?'

Lestrade frowned. His brain felt like scrambled egg, though after Summers's concoction, his stomach didn't. 'I was in a motor car.'

'Good.' Summers nodded. 'Do you know what type?'

'Er . . . it was black.'

'Right. That's good. That's very good. Tell me, was there a black person in this car?'

'Yes.' The scramble was reconstituting itself. 'Yes, there was. A black driver. Called Toussaint.'

'Toussaint!' Summers's eyes were bright. 'All the Saints. That's excellent. Was his second name Patrick?'

'I don't know,' Lestrade said. 'I wasn't told his second name.'

'All right. Go on.'

'Morant was there.'

'Morant?'

'Charles Morant. He's a stockbroker.'

Summers was suddenly writing things down in a little book.

'We were on Hounslow Heath. He had some dynamite. God, I thought he'd never get rid of it.'

'Was there . . . now, think carefully . . . was there a snake?'

'A snake?' Lestrade was lost. 'No, I don't think so.'

'A cockerel? Was there a white cockerel?'

'Er . . . no. Look, Mr . . . Monty. What is all this about?'

Summers sighed and closed the little book. He got up and began pacing the room. As he did so, Lestrade started to take it in. It was a study, oak-panelled and lined with row upon row of leather-bound volumes. The strange-looking priest leaned against the leaded window, his squat outline black against the sunlit acacia trees outside.

'Mr Lestrade, let me explain. I found you wandering in the early hours of this morning in just your underwear and bowler hat.'

'Yes.' Lestrade already knew that.

'Your warrant card, brass knuckleduster and what I suppose are your house keys were strewn at some distance from you. Your eyes were rolling as though you were suffering from *grand mal* and you were foaming at the mouth.'

'My God!' Lestrade sat bolt upright, whatever the cost to his throbbing head. 'Rabies!'

'No, no. Nothing so permanent, thank God. The effects were caused by a certain chemical compound. What you have just drunk – what I have been giving you to drink ever since I found you, every hour, on the hour – will have neutralized all that. But you were lucky. I have known total paralysis to ensue, even death.'

'Then it seems I owe you my life,' Lestrade said.

'Well, I don't want to over-dramatize,' said Summers, 'but, in essence, yes. What is perhaps more important is that I've saved your soul.'

'You have?' Lestrade wondered whether all this ballyhoo wasn't the Anglo-Catholic equivalent of the Sally Army's bowl of soup, tambourine and 'Halleluya, brother!'

'Does the name Celestina mean anything to you?'

Lestrade thought for a moment. 'No, I don't think so.'

'Baron Samedi, Baron Cemeterre, Baron Crois?'

'No.'

'What about Damballah Ouedo?'

Lestrade shook his head.

'Aida Ouedo?'

'Look, Mr Summers, I'm afraid I haven't the faintest idea what you're talking about.'

'Haiti, Mr Lestrade,' Summers told him. 'I'm talking about the island of Haiti and the hateful, nay, abominable practices that go on there. It makes transubstantiation look pretty tame, I can tell you.'

'I'm all ears,' Lestrade said.

Summers didn't doubt it. 'Voodoo, Mr Lestrade. Black magic. It's here in the heartland of Middlesex. In sleepy middle England. You, I believe, had a brush with it last night. Let me shake your hand.'

'What? Er . . . oh, all right.' And he felt Summers's thumb slide between his thumb and index finger.

'Does that feel familiar?'

'Well, it's similar to the Grand Lodge handshake,' Lestrade told him. 'Several of my colleagues . . . but you don't want to know about that.'

'I'm not talking about Masonry, Mr Lestrade.' Summers withdrew his hand. 'That is the handshake of the Houngan, the Voodoo priest. It is a phallic gesture.'

Lestrade didn't doubt it for a moment.

'Tell me, did you dream of dancing? Of candles in the wind?'

Lestrade nodded. Suddenly, Summers grabbed his arm. 'You didn't dream of riding a horse backwards, did you?' he almost shrieked.

'Mr Summers,' Lestrade confessed. 'I can barely ride a horse forwards.'

'Thank God.' Summers clasped his hands. 'Thank God. You see, Mr Lestrade, today is Friday.'

'Thank God, indeed,' said Lestrade.

'No, no. You don't understand. That means that yesterday was Thursday.'

Lestrade was impressed by the rapier logic of this man's mind.

'Urzuline's night is Thursday.'

'Is it?'

'Of course. She is a sexually insatiable goddess, Mr Lestrade, and she may already have had her wicked way with you.'

'Really?' The black girl with the shiny body gyrated through Lestrade's befuddled brain.

'Five years ago, Celestina, the daughter of the President of Haiti, married a goat.'

'As you do,' Lestrade said.

'That gave official credence to the diabolical practices of the Voodoo cults – and many and mighty are they. You know what a zombie is?'

'Oh, yes,' Lestrade told him. 'I have one in my office at the Yard. His name is Ned Blevvins.'

'Please, Mr Lestrade,' the priest said solemnly. 'No levity. If I am right in my conjecture, then the devil himself is loose among us. There have been rumours for months. Only now am I beginning to close in on their hellish abominations. They dance themselves into a frenzy, these black chappies, worshipping Damballah Ouedo, the snake god. Oh, they cover their tracks by daylight by feigning Catholic adherence to St Patrick.' And he crossed himself. 'He who rid Ireland of the snakes, or so it is said. But by night, they copulate with their women surrounded by a thousand candles. Your dream will not have included a white cockerel, because the ritual slaughter of that poor animal only takes place on Wednesday, Damballah's day.'

'A bit like Sheffield,' Lestrade observed.

'You may have seen – and I'm just glad you can't remember it – the testicles being hacked off a pig or a dog. The dancers would have writhed around, naked, foaming at the mouth, with their eyes rolling, utterly under the demonic possession of the loas, the spirits of Voodoo. Then the priestess, the Mambo, would have screamed out "What is truth?" and would have exposed herself to the men. When she collapsed on the floor, a few privileged men would have been allowed to kiss her private parts.'

There was a strange look in Summers's eyes. Lestrade had no recollection of any of that in his dream, although all his working life, of course, he had been looking for the truth. How ironic that he might have found it under cover of darkness somewhere in deepest Middlesex.

'This man Morant.' Summers seemed to have got a little more of a grip on himself. 'And this man Toussaint are from Haiti?'

'Morant has estates there,' Lestrade told him. 'Toussaint, I assume, was born there.'

Summers nodded. 'Mr Lestrade. I want you to rest here until

you feel strong enough. Then, I want you to use your no doubt considerable powers of arrest. This black evil among us must be eradicated. Had they made you ride backwards on a horse, then your soul would be utterly lost. You would be a zombie. I've only seen one once, at a freak show when I was a boy, but the horror of it stays with me. A tall, black man with mad, staring eyes. His keeper ran red-hot needles through his flesh and he did not wince, did not flicker. The lights were on, but no one was home. I warn you, Mr Lestrade, unless we act – and quickly – the whole of Middlesex will fall prey to this evil, like an all-consuming drug that devours a people. We must crush it – or perish in the attempt.'

'Well, we had a bit of a bash, certainly.' Charles Morant looked different out of uniform. The field-drab of the Devil's Own had been replaced by a sharply cut suit of pin-striped black, the obligatory scarlet braces of the City flashing beneath it now and then as the great tycoon leaned back in his office chair. 'I'm sorry, Lestrade, if I'd known you had an aversion to strong drink, I'd never have invited you.'

'Strong drink?' Lestrade queried. 'I think there must be some misunderstanding, Mr Morant. Mr Summers here . . .'

'Father Summers,' the priest reminded him.

'Quite. Father Summers is accusing you of devilish practices. I believe there is still a law against witchcraft in this country.'

'Witchcraft?' Morant roared with laughter. 'Come, come, Lestrade. You accepted my invitation to a post-manoeuvres party at my country house. It may have been the champagne talking, but you said – and Toussaint here will bear me out – "Lead me to the black women".'

'Is this true, Lestrade?' Summers was horrified.

'No,' the Superintendent assured him. 'Most cataclysmally not.'

'Well, all I could offer you was Miss Johnson from the typing pool.'

'Miss Johnson?' Lestrade frowned. He had no recollection.

'Yes. You must realize, gentlemen,' Morant explained, 'that coloured folks at home are a little unusual. I suggested a professional lady and lots of burnt cork, but you were adamant – and rather politically incorrect, I'm afraid, when you said, "A real nigger or I'll arrest every man Jack of you!" Well, luckily, Miss Johnson of the typing pool fitted your exacting category, being descended as she is from Gold Coast slave-stock via Moorfields, Bristol. However, as the evening wore on, you weren't content with that, were you? "Candles!" you demanded "and a white cockerel". I must admit I was rather surprised at a senior officer from Scotland Yard. God forbid that the newspapers should get hold of this.'

'You drugged my champagne,' Lestrade insisted.

'The Special Reserve?' Morant raised an incredulous eyebrow. 'Oh, come on, Lestrade. You saw me down that with you, glass for glass. Even Toussaint here had a sippette, didn't you? Toussaint?'

'As you say, sir.' The chauffeur was suddenly impeccably spoken. 'A sippette. I confess, I don't know what my father, the Methodist minister, would make of it.'

'Why are you talking like that?' Lestrade rounded on him. 'Yesterday, it was "massa" and "lordy, lordy".'

'That's an appalling racist slur, Lestrade,' Morant commented. 'I had expected rather better of the Metropolitan Police. Gentlemen, I am fascinated by your fancy stories – what is it, Father Summers – voodoo in Middlesex? But, unfortunately, I'm afraid that these are the delusions of a sick mind – yours, Lestrade.'

The Superintendent took stock of the situation. He hadn't expected for a moment that Morant would come out and admit it, but the man was so sure, so suave in his denials, it would take a lot more than the frankly deranged Montague Summers to break him down. Here was a formidable opponent, an accomplished liar, up to his neck in money. Lestrade needed the full weight of the law. 'You wouldn't object', he said, 'if I had a few of my lads go over your country house with a fine-tooth comb?'

'You know perfectly well I would.' Morant smiled, leaning back in his swivel chair and clasping his fingers over his gold lamé waistcoat. 'Really Lestrade. This is London, 1913. Such police brutality went out with Robert Peel.'

'Did you know him, sir?' Lestrade could change tack with the deadliness of a cutter.

'Don't be fatuous, Lestrade.' Morant scowled. 'Robert Peel died in a fall from a horse in 1850. I wasn't even a twinkle in my father's eye.'

'Not that one, sir.' Lestrade stood his ground. 'The Robert Peel who was a victim of a hit-and-run back in January of this year. January 13th to be precise. Tell me, what were you doing on that day?'

'When?' Morant frowned. 'Good God, Lestrade, how should I know? It was months ago. A month is a long time in business.'

'It was a pea-souper, sir,' Lestrade reminded him. 'The worst of the year. Were you, I wonder, anywhere near Hyde Park?'

'Toussaint?'

The huge negro, divested now of his goggles and dusty leather, consulted a large diary on the broker's desk. 'Er . . . let's see,' he muttered. 'Ah, yes, January 13th. Luncheon with Mr Lloyd George at Number 11.'

'Is there a time there?' Lestrade peered at the book upside down. He'd become adept at that over the years.

'Cocktails, eleven thirty,' the negro said. 'I think you'll find the Chancellor's Press Office will confirm that.'

'I'm sure they will.' Lestrade nodded. 'What about August 14th?'

'The 14th?' Morant repeated. 'I was supposed to be grouse shooting with the Earl of Blair Atholl that week, but old Lovell persuaded me to attend these wretched bally manoeuvres. Utter waste of time, of course. Where was I on the 14th, Toussaint?'

'Charity croquet match,' the negro said. 'Against Lord Rockingham's eleven.'

'Oh, yes. Chatsworth. Gorgeous day. Winston Churchill was there – boring little fart that he is. His wife's quite a looker, though.'

'So you were nowhere near Farnborough, then?' Lestrade asked.

'Farnborough?'

'Mr Lestrade . . .' Summers had stood idly by for long enough.

'Not now, Father,' the Superintendent interrupted. 'The grown-ups are talking. Perhaps, though . . .' He smiled at Toussaint. 'Perhaps I'm talking to the wrong person. After all, Toussaint, you're the chauffeur, aren't you? You're the one who oils the gears and cranks the shafts. I bet you could fly an aircraft, couldn't you?'

The black blinked.

'Or at least, find a vital fuel line and saw it through.'

'Toussaint sees most things through,' Morant said, his smile like acid. 'That's why I employ him.'

'Mr Lestrade . . .'

'I can only apologize', Lestrade said suddenly, 'that Mr Summers and I have wasted your time. Should you wish to press charges, sir,' he said to Morant, 'against Mr Summers for defor-mation of character, I shall of course be delighted to act as your witness in any civil action.'

'What?' Summers was dumbfounded.

'Not a peep out of you,' Lestrade snapped. 'You can't go round accusing honest brokers of black magic in the middle of the Sea-son. We are a civilized nation, sir. Now, apologize to Mr Morant.'

Summers pulled himself up to his full five feet three. 'I'd rather rot in Hell,' he said.

Morant turned to Toussaint and smiled. 'I'm sure that can be arranged, Father Summers,' he said.

11

Inspector Francis Dimsdale of the Serious Fraud Squad wasn't exactly one of the 'big three' at the Yard – more of the 'small three hundred and twenty-nine'. He was one of those people whose rise was without trace and whose jobs remained shrouded in mystery. Not the mystery that Sholto Lestrade was enveloped in, but one which the world didn't understand and about which it didn't give a damn. The Serious Fraud Squad had grown out of a marriage made in hell of Forensic, Administration and Accounts on the one hand and Pensions on the other. No one thought of Francis Dimsdale as a policeman at all, but every now and again, there would be guarded phone calls, words between Heads of Districts at the Yard urinals and anxious glances in the direction of Barings Bank.

It was all the more odd, then – one might say incomprehensible – that Inspector Francis Dimsdale, of the Serious Fraud Squad, should be found lying on the magnificent croquet lawn of Edwin Lutyens's Castle Drogo with a bloody pulp where his head used to be. And as if he wasn't busy enough, Sholto Lestrade had a telephone call that morning from his old oppo, Jim Whistler of the Devon Constabulary. And it was only for auld lang syne that a third of the 'big three' made his excuses and left.

The last person he'd expected to see on the platform at Paddington was the Reverend Montague Summers, yet, there he was, biretta in hand, staring anxiously after him.

'They told me you'd be here, Mr Lestrade,' he said.

'Really?' The Superintendent brushed past him. 'Who did?'

'A Constable Tait from your office.'

'He's history.' Lestrade scowled, fighting his way on to the train and down the corridor to find a suitable compartment. He got to one where an old bat sat knitting.

'Hello.' She beamed up at him. 'I'm Miss Froy. Won't you join me?'

'No, thank you,' said Lestrade, tipping his bowler, and he vanished along the corridor.

'Look, I'm sorry.' The priest was still at his elbow. 'But I just couldn't leave things as they were.'

147

Lestrade spun round. 'Mr Summers . . .'

'Call me Monty,' Summers reminded him.

'Mr Summers,' Lestrade insisted. 'I didn't for a moment mean it about Charles Morant suing you. I'm sure it's the furthest thing from his mind.'

'But . . .'

Lestrade had found an empty compartment and threw in his battered Gladstone and bowler. 'But I had to make it appear that I'd made a terrible mistake and look as if I was saving my own reputation – what there is of it.'

'You mean . . .' Summers was confused.

'I mean . . .' Lestrade sat down on the itchy seat-coverings of the Great Western's second-class rolling stock and checked his half hunter. ' . . . that we are already three minutes late and if you don't get off now, the next time you'll see civilization – and I use the word guardedly – will be Swindon. Now, believe me, Father, you don't need that.'

'But you believe me?' Summers had sat down opposite him, the eyes sparkling, the smile gappy. 'About the voodoo?'

'Let's say', Lestrade said, 'I'm keeping an open mind.'

The whistle blew and a man with a flag trotted along the crowded platform. 'Father . . .' Lestrade said.

'No.' Summers sat stoically. 'No, I'm coming with you.'

'I am on a murder inquiry, sir,' Lestrade said. 'I am not allowed to carry passengers.'

'Please, Mr Lestrade,' Summers begged him. 'I need an explanation. Please.' He cocked his head to one side. 'Pretty please?'

The train lurched and began to shudder as the pistons turned. Lestrade sat back. 'Here,' he said. 'You might as well make yourself useful.' And he pulled a large card out of his Gladstone with the words "Labour Party Conference" printed on it. 'Stick this on the corridor-side window, will you? That way, we won't be disturbed.'

Discretion was Lestrade's middle name. Along with Joseph, that is. He wouldn't ordinarily discuss murder cases with a member of the public, even with a carriage guaranteed to themselves. But this member of the public was a Catholic priest. 'Bless me, Father,' Lestrade said, 'for somebody has sinned.' And the Father Confessor sat back and listened.

'Worsthorne Griffin,' said Lestrade. 'Harmless old boy apparently, died as a result of a heart attack. Except that the heart attack was induced by something that frightened him – a calling card with the devil's face.'

Summers sat up. 'Really? Not his arse?'

'Er . . . no,' Lestrade said. 'Unless it was a very bad drawing.'

'No, I only mention it because the witches of old used to kiss the devil's arse in disgusting parody of our Saviour's face.'

'Get away.' Lestrade shook his head. 'No, this was definitely a face. In scarlet with the number "14" on the back.'

'What does that mean?' Summers asked.

'You tell me.' Lestrade reached for his cigars and the flask that Constable Lyall had filled that very morning.

'Well.' Summers's broad forehead creased into a frown of concentration. 'Pythagoras said, "Number is the ruler of form and ideas and is the cause of gods and demons." Isaac Newton spent years studying the numbers in the Book of Daniel.'

'Ah, when he wasn't angling, you mean.' Lestrade thought he might as well show he wasn't a *complete* ignoramus.

'Of course, numerologists do extraordinary things with figures.'

'So do jobbers,' said Lestrade. 'Which is what old Griffin was. Someone sent him that card knowing the effect it would have on him.'

'Who was it?'

Lestrade sighed as the locomotive gathered speed. 'If I knew that, Monty, I wouldn't be sitting here having this strictly entregnu conversation with you. But Griffin isn't the last.'

'He isn't?'

'No. Cigar?' Montague Summers wasn't to know what a rare moment this was in the life of Sholto Lestrade. And he threw it all away by declining.

'Next came Emily Wilding Davison.'

'Ah, that tragic woman who threw herself under the king's horse at the Derby.'

'Threw schmoo,' Lestrade said, blowing rings to the ceiling. 'She was pushed.'

'No!' Summers crossed himself, looking alarmed. 'Well, I wouldn't want to marry one, of course,' he said. 'But I see nothing wrong with the fair sex having the vote. After all.' He chuckled. 'It isn't as if they're asking to become priests or anything outrageous like that, is it?'

'I think you're missing the point, Father,' said Lestrade. 'Emily Davison wasn't killed by a chauvinist. Or at least, she may have been. But the motive was purely personal. The king's horse was number fourteen. Our murderous friend has a sense of poetry.'

'Numerologists would say . . .'

'Of course the irony is that I know the name of the man concerned.'

'You do?'

'No, not really. But I do know the nob-de-plumb he used. Cole. I believe he hoisted Miss Davison up on to the rail on some pretext and pushed her. I know something about him, too. He's a reckless fellow who's not very good at killing. Or perhaps he enjoys taking chances, who knows? Throwing somebody under a horse is actually a pretty dodgy way of killing that somebody. It didn't do the horse or jockey much good, but the victim got up and walked away.'

'Did she?'

'Well, tottered,' Lestrade conceded. 'So our reckless friend doubled up through the horrified crowd and emerged moments later as a handy passing doctor. He drove the injured woman to the nearest hospital and by the time she arrived, she was all but dead.'

'How do you know that?'

'I don't.' Lestrade shrugged. 'That's what makes this case so devilish. But I lied a moment ago when I said that Worsthorne Griffin was the first victim. He wasn't. He was the second.'

'Who was the first?'

'A man named Robert Peel.'

Summers frowned. 'Oh, but surely, he died from a fall from his horse on Constitution Hill . . .'

'Not *that* Robert Peel.' Lestrade sighed. Presumably the dead man had had a lifetime of that. 'This man was run over at Hyde Park Corner, but the driver wasn't sure he'd killed him and he knew he'd been seen. So he doubled back, disguised as a policeman.'

'A policeman?' Summers repeated. 'But how would he . . .'

' . . . have had time to put on the uniform? He wouldn't. He must have planned something like that, and been wearing the uniform under his driving clothes.'

'And how do you know this?'

'I would refer you, as I believe Mr Asquith says in the House of Commons, to my answer of a few moments ago. I don't. But the constable was off his beat and gave his name.'

'Not usual?'

'Unheard of,' Lestrade said. 'This copper made a point of it. Smith. Alexander Smith. Does that mean anything to you?'

Summers shook his head.

'Chummie used the same ploy later at the racecourse. This time he was Dr Cole. Familiar?'

'No,' Summers admitted. 'Not in the slightest. Sorry.'

'His next victim was Samuel Cody, an aviator. His plane crashed near Farnborough earlier this month.'

'I remember reading about it,' Summers said.

'The same tell-tale calling card was jammed into his cockpit.'

'So he'd been visited by the devil, too.'

'The devil with a hacksaw,' Lestrade said. 'Sawed right through his fuel pipe.'

Summers shook his head.

'Victim five was luckier. He survived.'

'Who was that?'

'Tom Allardyce, a reporter turned book editor. This time our killer turned to poison.'

'A talented fellow,' Summers commented.

'Needs must when the devil drives,' said Lestrade. 'For some reason, he couldn't drive this time, so he poisoned instead. He visited the offices of Constable and Company calling himself John Adams – ring any bells?'

It didn't.

'And he laced Allardyce's coffee. Something else we know about our friend – he's not o'fay with poisons. Got the dose wrong.'

Summers's razor intellect was warming to the matter now. 'So, Allardyce was a victim because . . .' But his razor intellect only warmed so far.

'Because he was the eyewitness to the "accident" at Hyde Park Corner.'

'But surely, if Adams and Smith are one and the same and Allardyce recognized him and Allardyce is still alive, then . . .'

'Ah, but Adams was careful to gain access to Allardyce's office when Allardyce wasn't there. The secretary saw him, but Allardyce didn't. And of course the secretary hadn't seen Constable Smith.'

'Our man is a veritable will o' the wisp.' Summers chuckled. 'Elusive as a pimpernel, difficult to catch as leprosy.'

'The secretary!' Lestrade was sitting bolt upright.

'What about her?' Summers asked.

'Forgive me, Father,' Lestrade said. 'I didn't take in all you said to me about voodoo when I woke up yesterday, but you said something about Urzuline's night – Thursday?'

'Yes, that's right. And Damballah's day is Wednesday. What of it?'

'Oh, nothing.' Lestrade sank back into his seat and watched Surbiton flash by.

'You look . . . inscrutable, Mr Lestrade.' Summers smiled. 'Have you solved the case?'

'Solved?' Lestrade smiled back. 'No, Father, not quite. But let's just say I know who did it. And if it weren't for loyalty to a fellow officer, I'd pull the communication cord right now and turn this thing around. As it is.' He fumbled for his half hunter. 'It's nearly three-quarters of an hour to Swindon. When we get there, I'm sending you back by return of train. Now, tell me again about this voodoo nonsense of yours.'

The Drewe family had been building Castle Drogo for two years. From a distance, as you meandered the narrow Devon lanes and peered over the singing hedgerows, it looked for all the world like a medieval pile. In fact it was Julius Drewe who had made the pile, as some of his snobbier friends noted through clenched teeth, from trade and he'd commissioned Edwin Lutyens, the modernizer of country houses, to build him a country seat as befitted a toff; albeit a toff who owned Home and Colonial.

The granite Babylonian lion snarled down on Lestrade and Whistler as they alighted from the Devon constabulary trap and their policemen's feet crunched on the gravel.

'Is it me or is this place made of wood?' Lestrade asked.

It wasn't him. John Walker, his agent, had a full-scale wooden model of the house erected in that long, sweltering summer.

'This is where we found him.' Drewe led the investigating officers up the shallow steps through what would become the rose garden, a threat past its best now that droughty middle August had taken its toll, and into a vast green arena, hedged round by close-cropped conifers like some great emerald Coliseum.

'Gertrude Jekyll wouldn't like it,' Drewe told them. 'Buggers up her plans quite dreadfully, but I had to give Walker's chappies somewhere for recreation.'

The hoops were still in place and there was nothing now to mark the bloodiness of Dimsdale's end.

'Here.' Inspector Whistler squatted on his heels. 'He was lying here.'

'What was he doing here?' Lestrade squatted too, but his left knee rebelled and he stood up again, sharpish.

'Playing croquet.' Julius Drewe was a small, countrified man for all his years in Home and Colonial. And considering this was Devon, the Norfolk jacket fitted him to a tee.

'And he was done to death . . . ?'

'With a mallet,' Whistler told him. 'Possibly two.'

'With mallets aforethought.' Lestrade was talking to himself, noting the lie of the ground. 'Who found the body?'

'Walker, my agent.' Drewe parked himself on his shooting stick. 'What time was this?'

'Look, Superintendent.' Drewe got off his shooting stick again. 'I don't want to seem uncaring or rude, but I have already told your chappie here all this.'

'My chappie?' Lestrade's face darkened. 'Inspector James Whistler is the most decorated policeman West of Lostwithiel . . .'

'East!' Whistler hissed out of the corner of his mouth.

'West of Eastwithiel. A man is dead, sir, on your property, and I think you owe it to the Inspector here to be as co-operative as you can.'

'With respect, Mr Drewe,' Whistler said. 'Chief Superintendent Sholto Lestrade is one of the most brilliant detectives this country has produced.' He leaned closer to him. 'They say he has the ear of the king.'

'Hmph!' Julius Drewe was unimpressed. After all, he had virtually brought Indian tea to the country single-handedly. 'Lucky he hasn't got his poppy eyes as well.'

'The purpose, sir,' Lestrade explained, 'of asking a witness the same questions several times is to jog their memory; unlock those little secrets of the mind that could catch a killer.'

Looking at the sallow, rat-faced man before him, it was patently obvious to Drewe that the Superintendent wasn't likely to catch a cold with any degree of certainty.

'What was Inspector Dimsdale doing at Castle Drongo in the first place?'

'Drogo!' Drewe snapped. 'Castle Drogo. Named after my ancestor, the mailed Drogo de Teigne. I had called him in to check my books.'

'Something was a rye?' Lestrade asked.

'Claude Beaufort, a friend of my eldest son, Adrian. A dabbler on the Stock Market. The idiot's got in way over his head. I warned him but he wouldn't listen. He's in with a pretty rum crowd in London, Lestrade.'

'Your son's friend is a broker?'

'No,' sneered Drewe. 'Just broke. But I suspect him of helping himself from my account.'

'On what grounds?'

'On the grounds that he used to come straight out with it and ask me for money. Point blank. Just like that. I told him. I said he was to bugger off and never ask again. Infernal cheek.'

'And did he?'

'No. But I know from friends that he's still losing heavily. Every investment he makes turns to ashes. He's a Jonah, that boy.'

'Couldn't he be obtaining the money from elsewhere?'

'Where? There isn't a bank in the country daft enough to lend him any more. And he can't have gone to the Jews or he'd have no kneecaps by now. No, he's a crafty bugger is young Claude. Went to the London School of Economics, so he's not only clued up on how to spirit money away via double-entry book-keeping, but he's learned nasty little Socialist tendencies too. Adrian's washed his hands of him. I contacted Whistler here – well, actually I contacted Whistler's mother, didn't I, Jim?'

"Fraid so, Mr Drewe. I can only apologize again.'

'No, no, I understand.' Drewe hooked his shooting stick out of the hard ground. 'My mother was just the same. Gaga as a newt. Luckily she died before they invented the telephone. Anyway, Whistler said – and I admire his candour on this – that there was no one in the Devon Constabulary with sufficient brains to handle fraud and had I thought of the Yard? Well, I freely admit I hadn't, so I telephoned Whitehall 1212 and got a total vegetable who eventually put me through to Dimsdale. To be absolutely fair to him, he was here by nightfall on the same day.'

'You keep your books here, in the Castle?' Lestrade asked.

'God, no. The thing's a builder's yard at the moment. I'm staying in a house in Torquay. The books are in the safe.'

'And who has the combination to the safe?' Lestrade queried.

'Only me and Frances, my wife.'

'No one else?'

'No one. Except, remember, Claude went to the LSE.' Drewe tapped the side of his nose. 'Need I slur more?'

'I should like to see those books, Mr Drewe,' Lestrade said. 'And that safe.'

'Be my guest.' Drewe waved expansively. 'The nearest hotel is nearly ten miles away and I happen to know the beds are lethal. I've got a spare berth at Kilmorie for you. Look.' Drewe checked his watch. 'I'm late already. Potter about by all means, you two, but get some results, will you? Whole building force has got the jitters over this wretched business.'

And he wandered away.

'So, what do you think of Julius Drewe then, Sholto?' Jim Whistler passed Lestrade the sandwiches.

'My God, Jim, your old mum still turning out this wonderful chutney after all these years? How is she, by the way? I forgot to ask.'

'Well, you know, misses Dad still.'

'Oh, yes, the knife-throwing act. Bit unusual that, isn't it? Normally it's the bloke who throws the knives at the girl.'

'You know Mum always wore the pants, Sholto.'

'Oh, yes, at the Wild West Show. You never did tell me who won that stand-up fight, your mum or Buffalo Bill Cody.'

'Well, it was . . . Sholto.' Whistler paused in mid-reverie. 'Much as I'd like to talk over old times, I suppose we *ought* to talk about the case.'

'You're right, Jim.' Lestrade uncrossed his legs and poured them both a glass of good Devon cider.

'That'll put hairs on your chest.' Whistler raised his scrumpy.

'Here's to crime!' Lestrade clinked his glass with the Inspector's. 'Down the hatch.'

'They'd had the good sense to leave Dimsdale's body where it was, then?' Lestrade asked. 'But my question to Mr Drewe wasn't as fallacious as he evidently thought. Here we are surrounded by square miles of foundations and trenches and our victim is casually playing croquet.'

'Julius is a fiend,' the Inspector told him. 'Devon Croquet Champion four years running. And Sussex, I understand, before that. He hasn't had the gardens laid out yet, but he insisted on putting the roses in and having this croquet lawn levelled. See that?' Whistler waved to the cool foliage. 'Instant hedge that is, three quid a yard.'

'Never!'

'Money's no object here.'

'And yet, Drewe called the Yard because of money.'

'Oh, he doesn't mind losing it,' Whistler said. 'He just objects to losing it to Claude Beaufort.'

'What do we know about this man Beaufort?' Lestrade's vision was beginning to swim just a little in the noonday heat.

Whistler consulted his notes. 'Aged twenty-eight. Went to Harrow and the London School of Economics.'

'In that order?'

'That's what it says here. Got a job with Raleigh Harman in the City.'

'Lombard Street!' Lestrade was still able to click his fingers, despite the scrumpy.

'Do you know it?'

'In a manner of speaking. Go on. Well, there was some financial shenanigans, involving the Muriettas.'

'Indian princes?'

'No, the Spanish brothers who lost a fortune a few years back. South American interests collapsed. I don't pretend to understand any of this, Sholto – that's why we called in Dimsdale. Hasn't he got any notes?'

'He has.' Lestrade sighed. 'They're in my briefcase. Unfortunately, I've only had since Swindon to make head or tail of them. Before that I was forced to share a carriage with a religious maniac.'

'Ah, I did that once!' Whistler moaned. 'On my wedding day.'

'Oh, yes, how is Dorothy, Jim? I forgot to ask.'

'Rabid, as usual, thank you, Sholto. So Dimsdale's papers told you nothing?'

'He was a deep one, Francis Dimsdale. Single man. Few friends. Very much a loner at the Yard. You know, the Serious Fraud Squad is only made up of three blokes – Tom, Dick and Francis. It's not exactly a laugh a minute, I understand, on the fourth floor back.'

'No.' Whistler nodded. 'Well, it wouldn't be.'

'Do you know Beaufort? Personally, I mean?' Lestrade asked.

'I met him once. Julius had a big do when Mr Lutyens laid the foundation stone with him. I was invited along with the Rector of Drewsteignton and the Mayor of Torquay. Struck me as a bumptious fellow.'

'The Mayor of Torquay?'

'No, Claude Beaufort. Arrogant little sod. I'd only met him minutes before and he was touching me for five bob. Spent all his time, if I remember rightly, telling me what a rich man he was and how he still might be a millionaire by Christmas, if certain parties kept their nerve. I didn't know what he was talking about. More cider?'

'Why not? What time does this Walker arrive, the bloke who found the body?'

'Not till three. He's out in Okehampton buying brass-headed seven-sixteenth Whitworths.'

'Now, there's a man I envy.' Lestrade sighed.

It did not accrue to the credit of Sholto Lestrade that he missed John Walker utterly that afternoon. It may have been the journey in the company of the rather earnest Rev. Montague Summers. It may have been the curious, dream-like events of the previous night. It may have been the burning sun and the Devon cider. It may have been a combination of all three. But whatever it was, Sholto Lestrade slept through the rest of the day and with him, Jim Whistler.

When Lestrade awoke, it was to the realization that Jim was snoring softly an inch or two from his ear, with his left arm draped over Lestrade's shoulder in a manner not quite befitting senior officers of their respective forces. The workmen had noticed, but they were sensitive souls, Gervaise, Quentin and Piers, and they'd simply smiled at each other and tiptoed away.

The Superintendent removed the Inspector's arm gingerly and clambered to his feet. He toyed with kicking the local man awake, but he looked so peaceful with a buttercup on his nose that Lestrade left him to it and went in search of the agent, Walker. He rounded an instant hedge and was making his way across the iron-hard earth in the direction of the chip-chip of the stone mason's hammer, when an enchanting little girl, not that much younger than his Emma, but with raven curls and deep, brown eyes leapt out of the shrubbery at him.

'Got you!' she squealed, pinning Lestrade's arms to his sides.

'Indeed you have.' The Superintendent winced. 'Miss . . . er . . .'

'Mary.' She let him go and solemnly shook his hand. 'But everybody calls me Daisy.'

'Miss Daisy.' Lestrade tipped his bowler. 'Were you stalking me?'

'Yes, I was rather. It's deadly dull around here. I've been here every day this summer, did you know?'

'Really?' Lestrade's eyes narrowed in the sun. 'Were you here the day Inspector Dimsdale died?'

'He didn't die, you silly man.' Daisy snatched a dragonfly from mid-air and proceeded to pull its wings off. 'He was murdered. Battered to death with a croquet mallet.'

'Or mallets,' Lestrade corrected her.

'It only sounded like one to me,' she said.

'You . . . you saw it?'

'No.' She sprinted over to a pile of rubble and proceeded to do handstands on it, her unmentionables flashing white in the sun. 'Worse luck. I just heard the thud. Well.' She landed on her backside on the pile. 'It was more of a squelch, really, with just the hint of a splat. Oh, it hasn't worked.' She looked at him wistfully, with her head on one side.

'What hasn't?' Lestrade asked.

'Well, when I usually describe it, people go pale. Aunt Evelyn was sick.'

'So you didn't hear anything, then?'

'Are you calling me a liar?' she snapped, her dark eyes blazing.

'Er . . . yes.' Lestrade smiled. 'I believe I am.'

'Well, that's beastly!' She sulked, getting up just to stamp her feet. 'They say', she scampered over to him and looped her arm through his, 'that you solved the Caddis case all by yourself.'

'Do they?' he asked.

'And that you smashed the entire Nibelung Ring single-handed.'

'Well, I . . .'

'I thought you'd be fatter.'

'Really?'

'Well, your photos are.'

'My . . . ?'

'Wait a minute.' She frowned, holding the bowler-hatted man at arm's length. 'You're not Chief Inspector Froest at all, are you?'

'Certainly not,' said Lestrade. 'I'm . . .'

She cuffed him playfully in the ribs with a left cross that would have slowed Bombardier Billy Wells. 'I know who you are, silly.' She laughed. 'I've got something for you.' And she thrust a hand down the front of her frock. 'Well, look away, you horrid old man,' she insisted. 'A lady has to do these things sometimes. Oh, where is it?' And she hauled out a deadly-looking catapult. 'No, that's not it.'

Lestrade was now staring at a clump of trees that marked the boundary of the intended North-West tower.

'Isn't it awful?' he heard Daisy say. 'That's where Papa intends to build a Bunty house for me and Frances. Honestly, you'd think we were children. Here we are. It's really quite spiffing. Wonder who it is? Old Nick?'

Lestrade spun with the hairs on the back of his neck crawling. The girl with the jet curls and the blazing eyes was holding out a red calling card to him. With the devil's face on it.

'Where did you get that?' he asked.

'From a man,' Daisy told him.

'Where? When?' Lestrade was shouting.

'Gosh, you're angry.' Daisy stood her ground, as befitted a little girl who might one day inherit the Home and Colonial Empire. 'Over there.' She pointed to the gravel drive. 'Two hours ago.'

'What did he say?'

'He said.' And she thought for a moment to get it absolutely right. 'He said "Hello" and I said "Hello" back. Well, I didn't say "Hello back"; I mean, I said . . .'

'Daisy!' Lestrade thundered, then calmer. 'Daisy, the gentleman who died . . . was murdered . . . here the other day. I think the man who gave you this card might have been the man who murdered him.'

'Oh, no,' Daisy said. 'He was delightful. He gave me a bar of chocolate. He got a bit soppy, telling me how lovely I was, but when I told him not to, he said it was because he was surrounded by writers all day and some of it rubbed off.'

A klaxon sounded across the sunbaked Devon heathland and a

Silver Ghost purred up the drive, to slide to a halt a few yards away.

'Ah, there's Mansell. I must go . . .'

'Wait, please.' Lestrade stopped her. 'This man. The one who gave you this card – what did he look like?'

'I don't know. He wore goggles and a motoring cap. I couldn't really see his face.'

And Lestrade's face fell. The man he had been hunting for so long had been here, at Castle Drogo, only hours ago, only yards away from where he'd been caught napping. He could have kicked himself.

A liveried chauffeur climbed out of the Silver Ghost, a look of living fear on his hunted features. He saluted feebly, like a man about to walk those last steps to the gallows.

'Are you driving, Miss Daisy?' he faltered.

'Rather, Mansell. Have you had the shockers done since last time?'

'Yes, Miss,' Mansell said. 'And the new camshaft and bumpers. I've had that right wing re-housed and of course a new transmission.' And as he spoke he began to buckle himself into a suit of home-made armour.

'Excellent, well hodge over, Mansell. Where do you want to go? Spin round the lanes?'

The chauffeur winced.

Daisy Drewe clambered into the driving seat and waited until the long-suffering Mansell had cranked the engine into fighting trim. 'Well, don't look so grumpy, Superintendent.' She stuck her head out of the window. 'The man who gave me that calling card was driving a black Fiat Mephisto, licence number 1789. It was a racing model, but I bet he couldn't catch me on the bends!' And she roared off in a cloud of dust, waving frantically while Mansell prayed silently and fervently beside her.

Department B2 of the Metropolitan Police, commonly known as Traffic, was in a state of transition in those days. There was no truth in the rumour that little children in that year of 1913 could point to a horse in the street and say 'Mummy, what's that?' but the day was coming. The internal combustion engine was here to stay and it would usher in, eventually, the garage, double yellow lines and traffic wardens, each one of them a plague on mankind.

But in 1913, Department B2 was still small enough to allow the friendly, warm personal touch and camaraderie between colleagues who oozed mutual respect.

'Who are you calling a useless waste of space, Lestrade?' Jack Fordingbury shrieked, ever a man whose octaves got the better of him.

'You, Fordingbury.' Lestrade left the man in no doubt. 'Never trust a Department – or its nominal boss – whose Assistant Commissioner is a bloody civil servant.'

'We're all civil servants!' Fordingbury blinked furiously behind his semi-opaque glasses.

'Servant you might be,' Lestrade snapped. 'But I've yet to hear a single civil word from you. Now, for the last time, who owns the black Fiat Mephisto, licence number 1789?'

'For the last time, I don't bloody know! Have you any idea how many motor cars there are out there? Hundreds, Lestrade, bloody hundreds! Not to mention the motor buses, motor bicycles, motor . . .'

'I don't want a job description, Fordingbury.' Lestrade leaned on his whitening knuckles on the man's cluttered desk. 'I want information. People are dying around this car and I've got to stop it. If it's a matter of manpower . . .'

'It's not manpower!' Fordingbury tried to be reasonable. 'I simply do not have a listing for a Fiat Mephisto licence number 1789, black, blue or indigo with cream spots.'

Lestrade paused for breath. 'Are you telling me that this is some sort of ghost car? That it doesn't exist?'

Fordingbury shrugged. He could do no more.

Lestrade shook his head, toying for a moment with breaking the man's glasses. Then he thought better of it and made for the door.

'Bentley,' he heard Fordingbury say. 'You might try W. O. Bentley. He might know something.'

'Crisp?' said W. O. Bentley.

'I beg your pardon?' said S. J. Lestrade.

'They're thinner than usual French fried potatoes – sort of *pommes frites manqués*,' the designer told him. 'A Mr Carter has recently imported the idea from America, where they call them Saratoga Chips. I think they're rather good.'

They may have been, but Lestrade wasn't sure how they'd go down with the axle grease covering Bentley's fingers and he declined.

'The Fiat Mephisto?' Lestrade reminded him. It was like a furnace in Bentley's Mews garage that day as August drifted to its close.

'Ah, yes.' The designer had found a battered old ledger under a

160

pile of spare parts. 'Ah, I've been looking for this Napier bit for months. Now, then. The Fiat Mephisto is, of course, a most unusual vehicle. Especially on the road. It's a racer, Mr Lestrade, not a runabout. For God's sake, de Lorean,' he suddenly screamed at a passing mechanic. 'You can't expect to sell a car that looks like that! Get a grip, man. Mephisto. Mephisto.' And he ran his grubby finger up and down the line of names.

'Three.'

'You've made three Mephistos?'

'Oh, I don't make them, Mr Lestrade. They are imported from Turin. No, I make them suitable for my customers – various refinements and so on. But I'm not the only importer, of course.'

'May I have the names?'

'Certainly. There's a Mr Fletcher, of Stockton-on-Tees. A Count Vladimir Varutchin, the Russian Cultural Attaché – oh, and of course, Mr Rufus Isaacs, the Solicitor-General.'

But Lestrade barely heard the last name and he certainly didn't hear the last occupation. Chief Superintendent Lestrade had gone.

12

There was a shortage of manpower that summer. The rumour was on the streets that Sir Almoth Wright's book *The Unexpurgated Case against Woman Suffrage* was about to hit the bookshops. It claimed, with a classic piece of mistiming, that women were inferior to men. At Constable and Company, where they were daring to publish it, the insurance companies were wringing their hands and advice was sought on placing machine-gun nests at the corner of Orange Street. Tom Allardyce, back at work but wary of the coffee, got a quotation from one man to board up his windows and from another to unleash a sackful of mice if the Suffragette army tried to invade.

So it was that Sholto Lestrade could only call on three men to move with silky efficiency and speed on the three owners of Fiat Mephistos. That meant two really, because Tait and Lyall, inexperienced, of a decidedly emerald hue, only counted as one complete copper in the investigation stakes. And Ned Blevvins didn't count as an investigating officer at all. Lestrade couldn't possibly send him to the Russian Count, bearing in mind his earlier history and as for sending him to Sir Rufus Isaacs, Blevvins rather dashed all hope there when he said, 'Yes, I'll sort out the Jew-boy all right!'

But Lestrade was desperate. He sent Tait and Lyall to the Solicitor-General, sent Blevvins to the telegraph office to contact Mr Fletcher of Stockton-on-Tees and he himself went to see Count Varutchin.

It was late when he arrived at the Embassy and a tall, odd-looking man with a wall eye ushered him into a great vestibule. Silver-shrouded icons winked at him from every side and he was led through a candlelit corridor and down a flight of stairs. The odd-looking man, apparently wearing some sort of frock, knocked twice on the studded door they'd come to.

It opened and the strains of a plucked balalaika assailed Les-

162

trade's ears. That was nothing, however, to the smell that assaulted his nostrils. He found himself standing in a darkened room thick with incense smoke. In a pool of candlelight in the centre a beautiful raven-haired girl in a scarlet dress swayed and swung, her long tresses flying wide with the glitter of her ear-rings. Around the wall, lounging on velvet-embroidered cushions, half a dozen men in dressing-gowns sat smoking long, elegant pipes.

'Tovarich!' a booming voice hailed Lestrade and Count Varutchin stood swaying before him, his naked chest flashing with gold pendants and diagonal Russian crosses. 'Welcome, Tovarich, to a little bit of Holy Russia. You know what tonight is?'

Lestrade thought for a moment. 'Tuesday,' he said.

'Nyet, nyet.' The Attaché shook his head and led Lestrade to a cushion. 'It is St Vladimir's day. At home, we feast, we drink – just like every other bloody day of the year, really. Come, vodka?'

'No, really, I . . .'

'What?' Varutchin could have boomed for Russia. His eyes rolled white in the flickering candles. 'You would risk an international incident by not drinking with His Imperial Majesty's Cultural Attaché?'

'Well, no, I . . .'

'Good. Good. Here!' And he handed Lestrade a goblet of clear liquid. 'Down the hitch!' And he quaffed his in one.

'Yes, indeed!' Lestrade smiled and did the same. Instantly, he regretted his bonhomie. His throat felt like fire. His heart leapt and raced. He was vaguely aware of the young men laughing and of Varutchin pouring him another.

'Is this gin?' Lestrade asked.

Another laugh. 'No,' said Varutchin, suddenly serious. 'It is the tears of Mother Russia, the waters of the Don. In that drink my friend, there drips the blood of Alexander Nevsky, the sweat of Ivan the Terrible, the urine of Boris Godunov.'

No wonder, thought Lestrade, it tasted like it did.

'Bottoms up!' The Attaché clinked his goblet with Lestrade's again, now miraculously refilled.

'Absolutely!' Lestrade agreed. This time he drank more slowly, but the effect was the same. The swaying girl swayed his way, her voluptuous bosoms threatening to tumble out into his lap. Then she laughed, hauled her scarlet dress over her bronzed, muscular thighs and was away again, dodging in and out of the circle of light, flirting with the men in the shadows.

'You like?' Varutchin nodded in her direction.

'Very nice,' said Lestrade. 'Is she available for the Police Revue?'

'You have gypsies in your country?' Varutchin asked.

'Yes. Yes, we do. They call them pikies in Kent, I understand. Mostly, we move them on.'

'Ah, you English!' Varutchin spat into the candle circle. 'You have no souls. If you want her, take her! She is yours!'

'Well, thank you,' said Lestrade, wriggling a little on his Turkestan cushion. 'But the Police Revue isn't for ages yet.'

'Revue schmoo.' Varutchin shook his hands in despair. 'I am talking about *taking* her, Lestrade. Having your evil English way with her. Do you not *do* this in England?'

'Well, yes.' Lestrade cleared his throat. 'But a gentleman waits until he is asked.'

'Pah!' And Varutchin hurled his glass at the empty fireplace where it shattered into a thousand pieces. 'Or.' He suddenly had an idea. 'Perhaps I have misread you. Perhaps you are not as other Superintendents.'

'I'm sorry?' Lestrade had lost the Russian's thread.

'Please, my dear friend, do not apologize. God has made us all in mysterious ways. Who are we to wonder at his purposes? You just happen to be a perverted, stinking degenerate. That is no fault of yours. Tell me, did you have an over-loving mother? An absent father? I understand that, from what I have heard, very few British policemen have fathers.'

'No, I . . .'

'Do not despair. For all we have Siberia and the knout and the wheelbarrow and an utterly emasculated parliament and a country that is a stranger to human rights, we are very broadminded about such things. Nikolai!' And the Attaché clicked his fingers.

A tall, slim young man with blond hair and dark eyebrows crawled over, sitting close to Lestrade and smiling sweetly at him.

'This is Nikolai,' explained Varutchin. 'You will find him sympathetic to your needs.'

'What?' Lestrade felt the room start to twirl very slowly. 'You mean he can show me to the lavatory?'

'Lavatory?' Nikolai repeated. '*Nyet, nyet.* I only go there when I absolutely have to. Here at the Embassy I have a room. Shall we take turns? I am very flexible.'

'He is,' Varutchin assured Lestrade. 'Your flexible friend.'

But Lestrade had suddenly caught the drift of this conversation and had stood up. The room bobbed and ducked like a prizefighter and the gypsy girl came back to grind herself against Lestrade's groin. Nikolai pouted and flounced back to a big sailor in the corner.

'Count.' Lestrade prised the girl's arm from around his neck.

'One, two, three,' Varutchin bellowed, then laughed. 'Just my little stock joke. Well, if you don't want Nikolai . . . and you appear not to want Natasha, what do you want?'

'Some answers,' Lestrade told him.

'To what?'

'Can we go somewhere quieter?' Lestrade thundered above the clapping and stamping.

Varutchin sighed, shrugged and waved to a far door. Lestrade led the way, a little uncertainly, and they entered an office, its walls cluttered with photographs of bearded men in huge fur hats.

'I had no idea', the Attaché said, 'that this was an official visit. The correct procedure is to make out a request in triplicate, get it translated into Russian, send it to St Petersburg and hope the Prime Minister has not changed since last week.'

'I don't think I have time for any of that, sir,' Lestrade said. Varutchin dipped a silver fork into a silver bowl that contained glistening black stuff. 'Beluga?' he asked.

'No, sir. We British police hardly ever carry guns and certainly not German ones. Do you drive a black Fiat Mephisto, licence number 1789?'

'A black Fiat Mephisto, yes – although I would be grateful if His Imperial Majesty were not to hear of it.'

'Really?' said Lestrade. 'Why?'

'His Imperial Majesty is not fond of Italians. Their pasta makes him ill. He is decidedly anti-pasta. No, His Imperial Majesty drives Delaunay-Belvilles and your own, your very own Rolls-Royces.'

'And your licence number?'

'What is all this about?' Varutchin asked, applying his second forkful of caviar. 'Are you sure you won't . . . ?'

Lestrade shook his head. He seemed to remember scraping stuff like that off his shoe from time to time. 'I'm afraid I am not at liberty to divulge,' he said.

'And neither am I,' the Attaché told him.

'Why not?'

'It is classified.'

'Classified?'

'If I let my registration number be known to Ivan, Grigori and Nikolai, I would be a sitting target for an anarchist's bullet.'

'You need have no fears on that count, Count,' Lestrade assured him.

'Billhooks!' the Russian scoffed. 'Only two years ago, as I took

165

residency, there was the siege of Sydney Prospekt.' Lestrade remembered it well. He was there.

'And not ten years ago, you gave asylum to Vladimir Ulyanov – and that's where he belongs, by the way, in an asylum. You even let the Jewish dissident Karl Marx use your British Museum Library to write his nonsense. Don't tell me that England is not a hotpot of anarchy.'

'I could simply break into your garage,' Lestrade said.

Varutchin nearly gulped down the fork the third time he swallowed. 'That would be an act of war!' he thundered.

'Count Varutchin.' Lestrade was as patient as he could be with two vodkas inside him and a killer to catch. 'I am on the trail of an assassin. I really don't have time for all the diplomacy you seem to think is necessary. For the last time, what is your licence number?'

Varutchin fumed for a moment. 'Very well,' he said. 'But I am putting in an official complaint against you. It could mean sanctions.'

'Sanctions?'

'Yes. No more vodka. No more caviar. Your economy will disintegrate by Christmas.'

Lestrade leaned towards him, but the combination of liquor and those little black nibbly bits drove him back. 'The number?' he growled.

'CCCP 1924,' the Attaché told him.

'May I see it?'

Varutchin hurled his fork into the dish. For a moment, his eyes blazed like a madman's, then he relented and hauling open a drawer at his desk, pulled out a key. He marched in his heavy Cossack boots to a sliding door and ushered Lestrade in. The Superintendent found himself in a lift, jolting downwards into the bowels of the building. When it stopped, Varutchin wrenched back the metal gates and the two walked through the echoing subterranean chamber. The Mephisto was parked at a rakish angle in a corner, gleaming from every orifice. Lestrade checked the number plate. Varutchin had been right. He also checked the front wings. No sign of damage. And then, for good measure, the rear, in case the Russian had *reversed* into Robert Peel at Hyde Park Corner. Nothing. No dent. No scratch. The bodywork of the Mephisto was immaculate, although Lestrade didn't care for the fluffy dice hanging from the roof – obviously a Russian icon.

'Thank you, sir, you've been most helpful – and I'm sorry to have intruded on your party.'

'*Nyet, nyet,*' the Count said. 'St Vladimir's night goes on until

166

week Monday. Time for a few more vodkas yet. Tell me.' He closed to Lestrade. 'Am I on the clear?'

'The clear?'

'Yes. You Okhrana chappies do not muck about – this I know. You would not waste your time on all this unless you had me as a suspect that is prime.'

'Your car, sir,' Lestrade said. 'Has it been involved in an accident, say, within the last eight months? Well, to be more specific, last January? January 13th in point of fact.'

'Certainly not,' Varutchin said. 'This is out of the question. If my driver had transgressed I would have had him shot.'

'Oh, good.' Lestrade smiled and had to be content with that.

Sir Rufus Isaacs had beautiful hands. The rest of him was quite trim too, as Lestrade discovered when he visited the Solicitor-General in a dawn raid. Tait and Lyall guarded the doors, one at the front, one at the back. It was a well-established policy with the police – hit 'em early, after dawn, with the sleep still in their eyes and their brains befuddled. Haul them out of bed; depending on their social class, give them time to pop on the old dressing-gown, then launch into a series of unpleasant and hostile questions, designed to throw, overawe. It never failed.

Well, almost never. Except that this time, when Lestrade arrived, barging his way unannounced into the Solicitor-General's study, the Solicitor-General was already on his eighty-third press-up of the morning. He glanced up at the sallow man in the bowler and shook his hand with his left while continuing to pump up and down on his right.

"Morning,' he said cheerily. 'Superintendent Lestrade, isn't it?'

'It is, sir,' Lestrade said. 'And I apologize if I've caught you at a bad time.'

'Not a bit of it. Ninety-eight, ninety-nine, one hundred. There!' And he bounced upright, reaching for a jug. 'Guava?'

'Church of England,' Lestrade assured him. 'This is an official inquiry, sir.'

'Yes, I rather thought it would be. You clearly weren't happy with the answers I gave to your constables – who, by the way, look a bit conspicuous, I think, at my front and back doors. Although I assure you, if I chose to make a run for it, neither of them could catch me.'

Looking at the man's quadriceps femoris under his short bath-robe, Lestrade didn't doubt it.

'You have a reputation as an honest man, sir,' Lestrade said.

'I think that helps in a Solicitor-General, don't you?' Isaacs smiled.

'And there is a rumour that you are to be made Lord Chief Justice.'

'Yes.' Isaacs crushed a lemon in his left hand and deftly caught the juices in a glass. 'Honesty is a little less necessary there, I'll grant you. I remember you in the Seddon case.'

'An excellent piece of prosecution, sir, if I may say so.'

'Well, it is my only murder trial to date, but I must say I enjoyed it like hell. Egg-nog?' He shook a silver decanter.

'No, thank you. Now, about your car . . .'

'Ah, yes. Your constables intimated a traffic offence. Speeding, perhaps. I could not recall.'

'I'm afraid it's more serious than that, sir,' Lestrade told him.

'Yes, I guessed it might be from the time of your arrival this morning. Celery?'

The fresh green stalk interested Lestrade not one jot. 'Thank you, no,' he said. 'You own a black Fiat Mephisto?'

'I do.'

'What is its licence plate number?'

'Lord. Now you've asked me. Er . . . B 1403 I think. Can you tell me why you want to know?'

'A black Fiat Mephisto killed a man last January. I have reason to believe that what at first appeared an accident was actually wilful murder and that the vehicle has been involved in other deaths.'

'And you think it was me?' Isaacs poured himself a tomato juice with lashings of Worcester sauce.

'There are only a limited number of such cars in the country, sir. Yours is one of three that I know of.'

'Is it?' Isaacs smiled. 'How gratifying. Who owns the others?'

It was Lestrade's turn to smile. 'That', he said, 'I'm afraid I can't tell you.'

'I didn't think for a moment you could. Tell me, is Mrs Pankhurst somehow involved in this? And the woman known as Boadicea?'

Lestrade blinked. 'You are very well informed, sir,' he said.

'Of course,' said Isaacs. 'I'm the Solicitor-General.'

'You remember the death of Miss Emily Davison?'

'Tragic.' Isaacs tutted. 'I have often prosecuted Suffragettes because that is currently the law of the land. I do, however, have a great deal of sympathy with their cause.'

'I believe that Emily Davison was murdered.'

'Murdered?'

168

'She was *thrown* on to the Epsom course. I've seen the moving pictures. Merely stunned by the king's horse, she was taken to hospital where she died a few days later.'

'But . . .'

'Exactly.' Lestrade could see the way the Solicitor-General's mind was working. 'She was taken in a black Fiat Mephisto from the racecourse by a doctor called Cole. No one at the hospital knew that name and he has subsequently vanished without trace.'

'I see. So you believe that I am this Cole?'

'It is possible, sir,' Lestrade said.

'It is possible that the moon is made of green cheese, Superintendent, although science teaches us not. Where else has this car appeared?'

'At the scene, for instance, of the murder of Inspector Dimsdale of the Yard Fraud Squad.'

'Fraud?' Isaacs's impassive features scarcely moved.

'Yes. He was battered to death with a croquet mallet in Devon a few days ago.'

'What was he working on?'

Lestrade chuckled. 'Now, now, sir,' he said. 'There are *some* things I couldn't possibly comment on.'

'But you surmise Dimsdale's death had to do with his job?'

'It would seem likely,' Lestrade said. 'A policeman's lot is not, I am told, a happy one.'

'Well, I hate to disappoint you, Superintendent, but I did not own my Mephisto last January when such a car killed a man. I did not acquire it from Mr Bentley until early May.'

'You have proof of the Bentley purchase?' Lestrade asked.

'Of course. My secretary has all the documents. But I fear he will not be in for another two and a half hours.' He sighed. 'You can't get the staff any more.'

'Indeed not, sir,' said Lestrade. 'Well, I'm really very sorry to have troubled you. I will call back when your secretary is in.'

'Not at all,' said Isaacs. 'You're sure I can't tempt you to a carrot soufflé for breakfast?'

A girl's voice answered the telephone. 'Hello?' But it was replaced immediately by a man's. 'Put it down, you silly little minx.'

'David?' Isaacs was on the other end of the line. 'Was that Margaret?'

'Er . . . yes,' the man said quickly, clamping his hand over the receiver. 'Get back to your blackleading, girl, or you'll feel my hand on your backside.'

'But I've been feeling that all night, Mr Lloyd George,' the maid said.

'Do you know what time it is?' Lloyd George demanded of the receiver. 'Decent folk are still in their beds. I was having an Early Day Motion.' And he kicked the maid hard so that she hit the floor with a thud.

'What was that?' Isaacs asked.

'Oh, nothing. Just my red box falling off the bed. Cares of state, you know.'

'Yes, I see,' Isaacs said, lifting a pair of dumbells with his free hand. 'Look, David, you ought to know, I've just had a visit from Chief Superintendent Lestrade of Scotland Yard.'

'So?'

'He's snooping.'

'Of course he's snooping. That's what he's paid for.'

'He mentioned Dimsdale.'

'Dimsdale?' Lloyd George suddenly sat up, fumbling in the bedside cabinet for his false teeth. 'I thought he was dead.'

'He is,' Isaacs said. 'But I didn't know that.'

'I am a Minister of the Crown,' Lloyd George reminded him. 'I *have* to read newspapers. And the death of Dimsdale just happened to catch my eye.'

'Well, I thought you ought to know,' Isaacs said.

'Yes, yes, of course, Rufus. Good of you. I'll be in touch.'

'Right. Oh, love to Margaret.'

'Who?'

'Your wife.'

'Oh, yes. Yes, of course.' And he hung up.

The maid had picked herself up and was undoing her nightie thongs.

'Not now, Maisie,' the Chancellor of the Exchequer snarled. 'Now I have to make a few telephone calls.' He saw the early sun filtering through the net curtains of Number 11 Downing Street, outlining the tilt of her breasts and the curve of her hips. 'Don't go too far away, though.' He twinkled at her. 'I shan't be long. I am, after all, accountable for my telephone bill to the Great British Public.' And he winked at her and slapped her bum.

'Hello, operator? Give me Welbeck 451.'

Sergeant Ethelstan Douglas stared straight ahead as Lestrade swept past him. No cheery 'Morning'. No 'Hello, guv'. Not so much as a kiss-my-arse Lestrade noticed. You didn't get to be a Chief Superintendent *without* noticing. But it was known that the desk man at the Yard had his difficulties. He'd married Attilla the Hun years ago under the guise of a woman called Bertha. The Germans had named a piece of field artillery after her. And if, sometimes, Sergeant Douglas seemed to have lost the will to live, well, it was understandable.

Ned Blevvins met the Chief Super face to face on the first floor landing South, but even that backbone of the Force, never at a loss with a scurrilous remark or a cruel jibe, merely looked in the other direction.

And when Frank Castle Froest looked straight through his old oppo, Lestrade *knew* something was up.

It was. Tait and Lyall were not in his office, buried in paperwork, suffocated by shoe-boxes. In his office stood Inspector John Kane and Detective-Constable Jenkins, ashen-faced, grim-mouthed.

'John?' Lestrade threw his bowler at the hat stand and missed dramatically. 'Has someone died?'

'Sholto Joseph Lestrade,' Kane said. 'I am arresting you on suspicion of the murder of Mrs Millicent Millichip on January 13th last in the City of Westminster. You are not obliged to say anything . . .'

It was just as well. Lestrade was speechless.

'. . . But anything you do say will be taken down.' Constable Jenkins stood poised with his notebook. 'And may be given in evidence.'

'Bollocks, John!' Lestrade laughed when he'd recovered. 'Not April 1st, is it, by any chance?'

'I don't need the cuffs, guv, do I?' Kane asked.

Lestrade just stood there. He'd never been arrested before. It was a weird experience. He who had arrested more felons than the rest of them had had hot dinners. It was indeed a weird experience. John Kane was holding out his hand.

'What do you want?' Lestrade asked.

'Your chiv, sir, please – the brass knuckles. And for you to come quietly.'

For a moment that seemed eternity, Sholto Lestrade stood stock still, waiting, his head slightly on one side as though listening for something – for an explanation. Kane shifted uncomfortably. It was the exact angle a man stood at when his neck was in the noose and there was a white hood over his head, the material billowing in and out of his open, terrified mouth as he fought for breath, gulping in the air they would soon deny him. Then Lestrade fished in his pocket and handed over the brass knuckles with the secret blade and John Kane took it.

'This way, guv,' Jenkins said. 'If you please.'

The grey day was over and night lay over the sleeping prison. In the long, grimy corridors outside, the measured tread of the warders tolled the hour, the minute, the second. There was no clock in the condemned cell. No reminder of the time, of the precious, little time left.

The Reverend Ashley Congleton had been idly flicking the cards as Lestrade told his tale.

'The rest you know,' Lestrade said, leaning back in the hard, upright chair. 'You've read the trial notes.'

'Many times,' the Chaplain said. 'The case against you was circumstantial at best.'

'I didn't know Millicent Millichip,' Lestrade told him.

'So you said.' Congleton nodded. 'But the letters. They found the letters under her floorboards at the Phlebotomist's Arms. Letters in your handwriting.'

'Accusing her of blackmail, yes. Do you know what I'm worth, padre?' Congleton shook his head. 'Nearly six thousand pounds.'

'No!'

Congleton shook his head again.

'I've married a rich woman with her own house and my Superintendent's pay isn't at all bad. Why would I need more? Why would I need to be on the take?'

Congleton shook his head. 'They said the same about Alan Aitcheson, from L Division.'

'Alan Aitcheson had more form than a National School,' said Lestrade. 'Everybody from the Home Secretary down to the newest rookie knew about Aitcheson. He was a byword for a bent copper. Even other bent coppers despised him.'

'Greed, my son,' Congleton mused. 'It's an irrational emotion, but a powerful one.'

'And how, if I was taking all this money, did Millicent Millichip find out about it?'

'The prosecution rather fudged that, I'll grant you,' the Chaplain said. 'But Isaacs was devastating in his cross-examination. The knife clinched it, of course.'

'The knife!' Lestrade tutted. 'Bernard Spilsbury is an idiot. I've always known that. The blade of my knife is four inches long, which happens to be the depth of the wound that killed the publican. Who's to say, however, that the knife that killed her wasn't five inches long, or ten or eighty-three – and that only the first four inches penetrated?'

'Yes, I must concede that Curtis-Bennet fluffed that one, didn't he? Still, what can you expect from a Radley and Trinity man? I'm still frankly astonished you put your life in his hands. So that's it, then? All we can do is to trust to God's divine mercy.'

'And the Appeal Court,' said Lestrade. 'Let's not forget that.'

The Appeal failed. Their Lordships sat there like the three wise monkeys, but the Radley and Trinity man was no more impressive with them than he had been at the Old Bailey.

'I see no reason', mumbled the eldest of the wise monkeys, 'to overturn the judgement in this case. Take him down.'

And they did.

For a man of six foot three with the build of a brick privy, Harry Bandicoot could move like a cat. The wisteria presented no problems, neither did the drainpipe. Once on the leads, he had the moon for an enemy, gilding his curls as he ducked behind the twisted turrets and spiral chimneys. Below, on the frosty gravel, he heard the measured tread of the Metropolitan Security Patrol and the occasional snatch of grunted conversation. It was nearly Christmas now and biting cold, but he couldn't trust his gloves on the narrow parapet and he couldn't feel his fingers at all.

At Bandicoot Hall now, he knew, what ought to have been all happiness and light, with candles and the spitting Yule log, was sorrow and long shadows and everyone afraid to look at the clock. Thank God Emma was spending Christmas with cousin Edwina in Munchen-Gladbach. She would miss Ivo's coming of age, but the old girl had not seen her adopted niece for years and was so very insistent. She would miss her father's hanging, too, and although she would probably never speak to Harry or Letitia again because of it, it was for the best. Letitia had insisted that Fanny come to Bandicoot Hall, as had been planned those months before.

Anyway, there would be no hanging. Not if Harry Bandicoot had anything to do with it. He swung around the gargoyle that leered out over the West entrance, catching sight of the bobby's helmet fittings twinkling in the frosty night below. His numb fingers slapped uselessly at the edge of the parapet and he swung back. All those years in the gym at Eton had set him in good stead, but he was older, heavier now, the night was cold and one slip could mean death. He braced himself and launched all the harder, this time catching it and somersaulting over the top.

Here another Etonian skill was needed. A door faced him,

locked and barred. But Harry held the record for breaking into the tuck shop at Eton and the old know-how had not deserted him. He slipped his tiepin into the lock with the instinct of a cracksman who had lost his way in life. There was a click. Two. And he was in.

In, but not there. The attic rooms were dark, but his way was illumined by the druggets glowing in the frosty phosphorescence over chair and rocking horse. His knee collided with a particularly sharp what-not, and he clenched his teeth hard to stop himself from crying out. He found the door and eased it open. Down a flight of carpetless stairs he went from the attic until he felt the familiar tread of Persian. He'd been to this house once before and he thought he remembered every nook, every cranny. He was wrong. Hauling open one door, he found himself staring into a face. For a moment, panic seized him. Then he realized it was his own face and he'd found the bathroom, complete with mirror. He'd be more circumspect the next time. Chances were a house like this would have dogs. He eased open what must be the Master Bedroom door, only to discover a lapful of mops and brooms, which he caught desperately before they hit the floor.

Suddenly, there was a bark from below. Bandicoot flattened himself against the wall and peered as best he could over the banister rail. A large Irish setter was padding excitedly along the corridor below, twisting round occasionally, its tail thrashing madly to and fro.

'Go on, Seamus, you deaf old bugger. You're not sleeping with me tonight and that's it. Now let's hear an end of it.' The apparition in the dressing-gown pointed vigorously and the loyal, hapless, useless beast slunk off to a well-chewed mat at the end of the passage.

Bandicoot waited until his master had retired beyond the elm-panelled door. Deaf dog, oblivious master. Things were working well. He dashed along the landing and down the stairs, jerking back as he realized Seamus was lying on his side, staring down that very passage where the room lay. He crouched on the stairs, waiting in an agony of indecision. Then, as he heard the clock in the great hall below strike one, he chanced it. Again, luck was with him. Seamus had turned over in his rabbit-hunting sleep and had his back to Bandicoot. The Old Etonian braced himself, dashed across the gap and into the room.

The nightshirted man had come out of the closet now and was sitting up in bed surrounded by red boxes, his bald head gleaming in the light of his bedside lamp.

'Don't scream, Reggie,' Harry ordered, closing the door behind him.

'Harry Bandicoot!' the bald man gasped. 'I haven't screamed since I rowed for Tit Hall and matriculated rather earlier than I'd intended. Now, do you want to tell me what the devil you're doing creeping around a man's house *before* or *after* I summon the police?'

'I've come to talk to you, Reggie. It's urgent.'

The bald man blinked at him, then reached across and put on his glasses.

'Harry,' he said patiently, hugging his knees under the bed covers. 'This country house of mine has thirteen bedrooms, eight bathrooms and an ice house referred to by Roger Ascham, tutor to Her Late Majesty, Queen Elizabeth. It also has a front door and – though I'm sure Ascham would be appalled – a telephone. One you knock on, the other you pick up and speak through. You don't have to sneak around like Burglar Bill. Do you know how silly you look in that scarf, by the way? My God, your hands are blue.'

'It's cold out there, Reggie,' Bandicoot told him.

'Here.' The bald man fumbled under his covers and hauled out a hot water bottle. 'Hold this for a bit.'

'This isn't a social call, Reggie.' Bandicoot declined it. 'I didn't use the phone because you'd refuse to talk to me. I didn't use the door because your bobbies would be jumping all over me.'

'Would they?' the bald man asked. 'Why?'

'Because you're the Home Secretary, Reginald McKenna, and you're their boss.'

'And before that I was First Lord of the Admiralty and before that President of the Board of Education and Financial Secretary to the Treasury. I have a long and glittering career behind me. You and I have known each other since schooldays. Why have you waited until now – and used this rather bizarre fashion – to pay your respects and express your unbounded admiration?'

'You are the Home Secretary,' Bandicoot said again. 'The man who rations mercy.'

'Ah.' McKenna realized the situation and put aside his red boxes. 'You're here about Lestrade.'

Bandicoot closed to the foot of the bed. 'He didn't do it, Reggie,' he said levelly.

'A body of twelve men and true decided he did,' McKenna parried.

'They were wrong!' Bandicoot insisted.

'Harry, Harry.' McKenna scrambled out of his bed and crossed to warm his hands by the dying embers of the fire. 'Our system of justice has its faults, but it's still the finest in the world. Sholto

Lestrade had a fair trial. I know. I've read the transcripts. Incriminating letters in his hand were found in the dead woman's house. She was blackmailing him because he was taking bribes. Yes, I know all about his illustrious career – the OM, undying gratitude from His Late Majesty, blah, blah, blah. The man had a motive, Harry, and he was found holding the body.'

'Exactly!' Harry clicked his fingers. 'Why? What kind of idiot would wait at the scene of the crime to be arrested?'

'The kind of idiot who's on the inside.' McKenna tapped the side of his nose. 'What Lestrade doesn't know about the criminal mind I can write on Winston Churchill's IQ. It's called the double bluff. If a distinguished Chief Superintendent with an impressive record tells you a dying woman fell into his arms, stabbed fatally, you simply accept it as one of those freak incidents that are stranger than fiction. What you don't do is to suspect him. We have John Kane to thank for that.'

Harry Bandicoot reached inside his black coat and pulled out a sheaf of papers.

'What are they?' McKenna asked him.

'The deeds to Bandicoot Hall,' Harry said. 'As you know, it has twenty-four bedrooms, eleven bathrooms and a stable slept in by King Arthur. It should fetch nearly a million on the open market. Oh, and these are all my shares, worth another two or three hundred thousand. Take them. They're yours.'

'Mine?' McKenna was staring at the man. He'd clearly gone mad.

'In exchange for one thing,' Bandicoot said.

McKenna laughed. 'I see,' he said. 'I understand now. All this for the life of Sholto Lestrade. You're a generous man, Harry Bandicoot, and a loyal friend. But you're also a bloody fool.'

'You're the man who rations mercy,' Bandicoot shouted. 'You're the only one who *can* save him now.'

'I have to have grounds, man!' McKenna shouted back, whirling around the room. 'I can't just release a man because he's a copper or because he's a friend of yours. I . . .'

Reginald McKenna stopped in his tracks because Reginald McKenna found himself staring into the barrel of a silver-chased Smith and Wesson held firm and level in the right hand of Harry Bandicoot.

'Harry, Harry,' the Home Secretary said softly. 'I remember teaching you to shoot that at Bandicoot Hall. Do you remember? In the cherry orchard there? I even remember what it says on the barrel – it's engraved on them both – "To H. B. May You Always Have The Last Shot".'

Harry wanted to shout, to scream, to blow off the bald head of the unflinching, principled idiot who stood before him. But he was Harry Bandicoot, Old Etonian and friend of Home Secretaries. McKenna's commutation to life elicited under duress would be meaningless. And anyway, Harry Bandicoot couldn't live with himself. He flung the revolver down on the bed, where it bounced harmlessly.

'Harry.' McKenna reached up and put his arm around his old boyhood chum. 'Take your pistol. Take your deeds and go home. You've done all you can. You've risked imprisonment coming here tonight. Breaking and entering is an offence, you know. Not to mention pointing loaded revolvers at Home Secretaries. And up on the leads there, you probably risked your life as well. Now be a good chap and leave by the door, there's a sensible fellow.'

'Don't patronize me, Reggie,' Harry growled. 'You were my last chance. There's a man sitting in a tiny cell in Pentonville tonight and although he'd never show it, he's scared to death. And he's going to die in two days' time. That man and his daughter mean all the world to me . . . And there isn't a damn thing I can do about it.'

He picked up his gun and slipped it into his pocket. He filed away his deeds and share certificates. He looked sadly into the face of Reginald McKenna and he saw himself out.

The Home Secretary returned to his red dispatch cases and adjusting his glasses, wrote on the bottom of Fanny Lestrade's plea for clemency in the case of her husband – 'I can see no reason why the law should not take its course.'

13

Letitia had wanted to help. To be there. To do something. But Harry had told her the best service she could render the Lestrades now was to be with Fanny. Fanny wanted to see Sholto. Every day. Every minute. But the cold, sad walls of Pentonville kept her out. She walked the cherry orchard with Letitia, she looked into the dark, memory-filled waters of the lake. She saw him running to her, swinging her round, kissing her. She heard his laughter and felt his warmth beside her in her empty bed.

Harry didn't sleep, either. Harry went to the Yard.

'I've been expecting you.' Inspector John Kane looked up – and up – at the earnest face in front of him.

'You have?'

'It's not many Inspectors of the Metropolitan Police who get phone calls from the Home Secretary. You have friends in high places, Harry.'

'Not friendly enough, unfortunately, John,' Bandicoot said. 'What did he say?'

'Just two words.' Kane was still bemused by it. 'Help Bandicoot.'

Harry smiled. Old Reggie hadn't abandoned Sholto after all. 'Where do we start?' he asked.

Kane slid a shoe-box across the desk to Bandicoot, then a second, then a third, then a fourth.

'What's this?'

'The evidence.' Kane sighed. 'Or rather part of it. The rest I'll have to get up from the basement. Close your mouth, Harry, you didn't think this would be easy, did you?'

'I've read the trial transcript.' Harry scraped back the chair and huddled with Kane over his desk. 'Isn't that enough?'

Kane leaned back, chuckling.

'Damn it, man!' Bandicoot thumped the desk. 'You arrested him in the first place.'

'I did what I had to do.' Kane thumped it back. 'I want you to understand something, Harry. I love that man as much as you do.

178

Everything I know, everything I do, everything I am, I owe to Sholto Lestrade. But what I am is a copper – he taught me that. We found damning evidence, evidence that pointed at him. Do you think he would have hestitated if the shoe had been on the other foot? If I'd been in the frame – or you? Because if you do, you don't know Lestrade very well!' Kane relented. 'As a matter of fact, I damned well nearly didn't go through with it.'

'What?'

'I nearly burned the letters we found at the Phlebotomist's Arms. I'd even struck the match. But something – conscience? – made me blow it out.'

'All right, all right.' Harry leaned back in the cluttered office. 'Look, John, I'm not very good at this. Logic and all that. Deduction. I became a copper by mistake a long time ago and I wasn't here for long. But this much I do know. If something niggles, if something smells, then you worry it. You tease it and you wrestle with it and you finally sort it out.'

John Kane had never heard so many metaphors in one sentence in his life, but he wouldn't dream of telling Harry Bandicoot that. They were like drowning sailors clinging to a piece of wreckage, a piece of wreckage that was the truth, tiny and isolated in a sea of lies and hatred and indifference.

'So where do we start?' Harry looked blanker than ever.

'All right,' said Kane. He jerked suddenly to his feet and wrenched open the door. 'Jenkins, no calls. No interruptions. I'm out, savvy? On a case and you don't know when I'll be back.'

'Right you are, guv,' Jenkins said.

'Yes.' Kane closed the door and stared into the glowing coals. 'But not this time, I fancy.' He turned to Bandicoot. 'First principles.' He spun his chair around and straddled it. 'What do we know about the guv'nor's involvement with Millicent Millichip?'

'She died in front of him.' Bandicoot was starting to count on his fingers. This was a bad sign.

'Stabbed to death with a chiv which might have been his, but equally might not. A chiv he lost.'

'Lost?' Bandicoot repeated.

'Yes. He claimed that Fanny had lost it somewhere at home.'

'Is that significant?'

'It might be,' Kane said. 'If that knife was the murder weapon and the guv'nor was guilty, he'd want to lose it, wouldn't he?'

'Then why find it again?' Bandicoot asked.

Kane stroked his impressive chin. 'Because the moment had passed. Months had gone by since Mrs Millichip died and he felt safe. I told him the case was shelved – he could afford to relax.'

'John!' Bandicoot thundered. 'The last thing Sholto needs now is a devil's advocate. He's had the devil against him since the case began. Where are the letters, the ones Sholto supposedly wrote to Mrs Millichip?'

Kane fumbled through one of the shoe-boxes. 'Here,' he said. 'Two of them.'

'No prints, I suppose.' Bandicoot asked.

'Clean as a whistle.'

'Interesting.' Bandicoot took in the scrawl. It certainly *looked* like Lestrade's hand.

'What is?'

'That Sholto wrote wearing gloves.'

'Standard blackmailer's or poison pen letter writer's precaution these days.' Kane shrugged. 'Even your stupidest felon has heard of fingerprints.'

'Is that why Mrs Millichip wore gloves, then, because she was a felon and knew the letter was from her blackmail victim?'

Kane blinked. That thought had never occurred to him.

'You mean . . . ?'

'I mean, John.' Harry was getting carried away now. 'Why aren't Millicent Millichip's dabs all over these letters?'

'My God!' Kane just sat there.

'When did you find them?'

'Last month,' Kane said. 'When we searched.'

'You only got round to searching last month?' Bandicoot was incredulous.

'Ah, that was the third search.'

'The third? Is that usual?'

'Well, no,' Kane bluffed. 'We normally hope to find something conclusive the first time.'

'But you didn't.'

'No.'

'And the second time?'

'The money. Nearly three thousand in notes. And the devil's calling card.'

'But no letters.'

'Er . . . no.'

'Where did you find the money and the card?'

'Under the floorboards in the snug,' Kane told him.

'And where did you find the letters?'

'Um . . . the same place.' A cold, clammy realization was dawning on Inspector John Kane.

Bandicoot leaned back, never once taking his eyes off Kane. 'Who told you to search for the third time?' he asked.

'The Solicitor-General,' Kane told him. 'Rufus Isaacs. It was his suggestion.'

'The man who is now the Lord Chief Justice,' Bandicoot mused.

'Indeed.' Kane nodded, for a moment losing his grip, doubting himself. 'No, wait. Wait. The guv'nor was so vague about where he was going in Oxford Street the day Millichip died. He was altogether travelling in the wrong direction.'

'Of course he was.' Bandicoot threw his hands in the air. 'This is Sholto Lestrade we're talking about. Dear as he is to me, I wouldn't trust him to take me across the road. He couldn't see his hand in front of his face that day. He was just in the wrong place at the wrong time.'

'He was that,' Kane conceded. 'I tried to tell Isaacs at the trial that Millichip was linked to the other victims. She'd worked for Robert Peel at one time and she saw George Griffin, old Worsthorne's son, throw himself into the Thames. The irony was that the guv'nor and I were working on the same case.'

'So.' Bandicoot's face was a study in effort as he tried to work it all out. 'Whoever killed Mrs Millichip doubled back along Oxford Street to hit Robert Peel at Hyde Park Corner?'

'The other way round,' Kane told him. 'Peel died first. Our man, almost certainly wearing a policeman's uniform, drove his Mephisto at Peel and killed him. But he realized he'd been spotted, even in a pea-souper, by a witness.'

'Allardyce.'

'Exactly. So just to make sure, he dumped the car around the corner somewhere, leaving his motoring clothes, his goggles and so on, there. Then he happened to stroll past as the beat copper – for two reasons – to make sure Peel was dead and to make sure Allardyce hadn't seen anything.'

'That took some nerve.' Bandicoot nodded.

'Oh, chummie isn't short of that,' Kane said. 'Unless . . . '

'Unless?'

Kane was on his feet with a light in his eye like St Paul must have had on the Damascus Road. 'What day is it, Harry?'

'Er . . . December 21st,' Bandicoot said. 'Thursday.'

'Thursday!' Kane clicked his fingers. 'Got your motor outside?'

'I've got the Panhard, yes. Why?'

'Because', said Kane, grabbing his hat and muffler, 'it's a lovely day for a little spin to Orange Street.'

The man they sought was not at Orange Street, but his light o'illicit love was.

'Where is he?' John Kane loomed over Jessica Fry, who had first been coy, then tried to file her nails and finally resorted to whistling 'Dixie'. It was only when John Kane threatened to arrest her, complete with force-feeding tube whether she ate or not, for attempted murder, that she helped the police with their inquiries.

'Brooklands,' she said quickly. 'It's the Christmas race meeting. Selwyn Edge, you know, the racing driver, is writing his memoirs.'

Harry's foot was to the floor as the Panhard-Levassor roared its way out of London. It was nudging fifty past Roehampton, nearly sixty as he screamed around Richmond Park. The coppers' speed trap at the Star and Garter absolutely failed to stop him and three bewildered bobbies could only stand scratching their heads at the audacity of the maniac who'd just crashed through their barriers, leaving two of their number sprawling in a particularly soggy hayrick.

In the back of the car, Jessica Fry clung on for dear life, her eyes shut most of the time as Surrey hurtled by. The Panhard's radiator was belching steam by the time they got to the gates of Brooklands and the three of them abandoned it by the roadside and dashed through the milling crowds sauntering in for the third and final race of the day. There were feathered hats and silk toppers everywhere, interspersed with alien-looking men in leather duster coats with fur gauntlets and goggles that reflected the weak December sunshine. They'd put up a huge Christmas tree, covered in car headlamps that flashed on and off and the Surrey Regiment in their winter greatcoats were thumping out all the Christmas tunes to the delight of young and old alike.

'Where would he be?' Kane was shouting above the din, dragging the hapless Jessica behind him, past the milling crowds.

'He's driving', she shouted back, 'in the third race. Wants to see how Mr Edge does it.'

'The pits are over there!' Bandicoot roared and took off through the throng. Kane found a patrolling constable, flashed his warrant card and parked Miss Fry with him, with strict instructions not to let her out of his sight.

But there was no sign of their man at the pits, merely mechanics tinkering and tuning in their greasy overalls and ceaselessly tweaking the underparts of the Peugeots, Singers, Mercedes and Delages that coughed and rattled on the concrete start.

'The Mephisto!' Kane shouted to one of the mechanics. 'Is a Mephisto driving in this race?'

'Yes!' the man yelled back, cupping his mouth with his hands to make himself heard. 'Number 14.'

'I thought it would be,' Kane bellowed. 'Who's driving?'

'Fryer'

'Where is it?'

'In the shed still. Engine trouble.'

Kane was no slouch, but Harry had sprinted for Eton and he reached the huge double doors first. He and Kane hauled them open and there before them stood a sleek black killing machine, its front nearside wing showing signs of repair, its headlights staring like mad, terrible eyes. The driver, crouching over the bonnet, stood up. He was in leather from head to foot, his goggles blanking out his face. A mechanic's head popped up from the other side and another from underneath.

'We're doing our best,' one of them said. 'Another five minutes. That's all we ask.'

'Thank you, gentlemen,' the driver said. 'I can manage now.'

'But, Mr Fryer . . . ' one of them began.

'Thank you,' he said again, his voice echoing around the vaults of the garage.

The mechanics looked at each other and wandered away, muttering.

'Mr Fryer,' Kane said. 'Or should I say Mr Allardyce? It's good to see you back on your feet, sir. I had no idea you drove.'

'A motor car is essential these days, gentlemen, isn't it?'

'It is if you're short of a murder weapon, certainly,' Kane said.

'Who is this gentleman, Inspector Kane?' Allardyce asked. 'I don't believe I've had the pleasure.'

'My name is Harry Bandicoot. And the pleasure's all mine.' And he took a stride forward, his fists clenched. No one, least of all Harry, was ready for what happened next. The leather coat parted and Allardyce's right hand was holding a revolver. The gun crashed once and Harry lurched sideways, losing his balance as the bullet smashed his shoulder.

'Stand still!' Allardyce roared as Kane knelt to help him. 'And don't worry. No one will come to investigate that shot. Not at Brooklands, where backfiring is like the ticking of a clock. You're Lestrade's friend, the major with the North Somerset Yeomanry. Brave of you to fling yourself on Kitchener like that. I could have squeezed off a second shot.'

'But you weren't aiming at Kitchener, were you?' Kane straightened. Right now, he'd kill for Lestrade's knife and knuckles, the ones old Waverley was lovingly polishing ready for inclusion in his Black Museum. All he had was his regulation ebony truncheon. It was no match for Allardyce and his bullets.

'No, I wasn't,' Allardyce told him, climbing on the Mephisto's running board and adjusting the ignition. 'But I did toy with it for a moment. Well, when you've got a gun in your hand and a bastard in your sights, why not? And now', his snigger sounded hollow in the cavernous gloom of the shed, 'I've got two bastards in my sights. Before I kill you, though, humour me a little. How did you get on to me, with dear old Superintendent Lestrade about to take his last short stroll?'

'One case,' Kane told him. He was standing behind Bandicoot now, wondering how badly he was hurt, whether he'd be capable of anything. 'That's what I never fully appreciated. Lestrade and I were working on the same case and yet we went our separate ways. What threw me – threw us both – was that you killed twice on the same day. That pea-souper last January. I've always thought it of course. Ideal opportunity, fog. Why the police uniform?'

'Insurance,' Allardyce said. 'Oh, I was a relative novice in those days. I'd only killed twice before and never with a car. I wasn't sure how easy it would be. Oh, I could knock Robert Peel down, of course, but could I actually kill him? I needed to be sure.'

'And then, of course,' Kane said, 'you gave the game away. You fell for that oldest of sins, Mr Allardyce, the sin of pride. You had to announce yourself, didn't you? How many days did you wait there, I wonder, at Marble Arch, for Lestrade to turn up? But when he did, you were in your element, weren't you? You invented the policeman because you'd hired the uniform. You even invented a ridiculous name, knowing we'd check, knowing there'd be no Alexander Smith in F Division. You'd be laughing all the way to the bank, wouldn't you? Knowing that we block-heads on the Force had fallen for it. And that's what all this has been about, hasn't it? Money and arrogance.'

Kane saw Harry try to rise.

'Don't move!' Allardyce's hand was rock steady, the muzzle of the revolver in a straight line with Bandicoot's head.

'Of course,' Kane kept talking, his throat bricky dry, his hands like lead, but the tone was calm and matter-of-fact, 'you made one *very* bad mistake.'

'Really?' Allardyce yawned ostentatiously. 'What was that?'

'You got your dates wrong. You said you were in the Hyde Park area because you were visiting Dame Vera Krupskaya about her memoirs. You said you were there on January 13th, which is indeed the day Peel died. But Dame Vera told us it was January 2nd.'

Allardyce's laugh echoed in the high-vaulted garage. 'You utter buffoon,' he said. 'The Gregorian calendar and the Julian calendar. The Russians use a different dating structure from us. The old girl thinks Old Style. I don't.'

'Ah.' Kane refused to be outmanoeuvred. 'But then of course, you made another mistake. You told little Daisy Drewe that you were poetic and flattered her because you were surrounded by writers and that – and I quote – "some of it rubs off".'

Allardyce chuckled. 'Me and my big mouth,' he muttered and cocked the revolver again.

'And of course,' Kane shouted, desperately playing for time, 'your biggest mistake was the coffee.'

'It was?'

'Oh, yes.' Kane eased the weight to his right leg. If only somehow he could signal to Harry to do the same to his left, the sudden movement in opposite directions might throw Allardyce off balance; long enough, anyway, for Kane to get that gun. 'Yes, the coffee was a bad one. You see, our man – you – had been very efficient that far. Millicent Millichip wasn't your normal weapon, but you handled it well. The car, you tell us now, was your first, but it was smoothly done. The devil's card – you've got a whole pack, presumably – to old Griffin Worsthorne was a master stroke. So why, suddenly, should our man fail with Tom Allardyce? Unless, of course, he *was* Tom Allardyce.'

'Yes, Inspector Kane?'

The voice came from nowhere. Tom Allardyce had crept in via a side door. 'I heard talking. Mr Edge was wondering if Mr Fryer . . . My God!' The startled editor found himself facing a madman with a gun and another man crouching on the ground was covered with blood. In fiction, that would have been John Kane's moment, that split-second loss of concentration which he'd been hoping for. But this was not fiction. It was reality. And in reality, nobody moved and the moment was gone.

Fryer hauled off his goggles and helmet in one deft movement. 'Well, well.' He chuckled. 'Just like midnight at a masked ball.'

'Alaric Bligh,' all three men chorused.

'Ana, as Sergeant Blevvins would say, PC Alexander Smith, Dr Cole, John Adams and of course "Burner" Fryer, the hero of Brooklands – he who is always very careful, you will notice, to be photographed in his helmet and goggles. It's a harmless pastime, driving. A bit like killing, really. Some of us do it faster and better than others, that's all.'

'I don't understand,' admitted Kane. 'Mr Allardyce, I'm sorry. I thought . . .'

'No, you didn't, Kane,' Bligh snarled. 'That's the trouble with

Scotland Yard. No one does. Oh, I admit that Lestrade gave me a few sleepless nights, but nothing I couldn't live with.'

'Why?' Allardyce said. 'You tried to kill me. Why?'

'I wasn't sure about you. You saw me run down Robert Peel. You also spoke to me when I came back as PC Smith to make sure he was dead. You could recognize me again, even in that pea-souper. In the end, I couldn't take that chance. There was too much at stake.'

'What?' asked Kane. 'What was at stake?'

Bligh waited, still standing as he was on the Mephisto's running board. 'Well,' he said. 'Why not? Bandicoot is bleeding to death and I've got more than enough bullets for the two of you. Besides, the third race will be starting soon and the engine noise will drown all the dying in here. The world's police will be looking for Burner Fryer, the legendary driver, but they won't find him. Not here. Not anywhere. You should have listened, Kane. You should have listened to Inspector Dimsdale. Oh, the man was as dull as dishwater, of course, and that's why you didn't; neither you nor Lestrade. But Dimsdale knew his figures – that's why he had to die. Numbers, Kane, that's what this whole thing is all about. Numbers. Numerologists could have solved it in a twinkle of a cash register. They apply numerical values to letters. Take, for instance, the letters of my surname. B is 2, L 3, I 1, G 3 and H 5. Add them up, Mr Allardyce. What do you get?'

'Fourteen,' Allardyce told him.

'Fourteen. The same number as Broker Morant's Middlesex Regiment – the Inns of Court Rifles, the Devil's Own. Do you know, they had the infernal cheek to blackball me once? Me! It's outrageous. Well, I bided my time. You see, to kill is easy, but to kill and get away with it, well, that's trickier. So I invented a few red herrings as the crime novelists say – threw a few clues out, like sparks from a weld.'

'What was it', Kane asked, 'that they had in common, your victims?'

Bligh checked his hunter. 'Well, I may have to miss the race, gentlemen, but, well, why not . . . Very well.' He cleared his throat. 'In the beginning, there was a Chancellor of the Exchequer who was very, very greedy.'

'Lloyd George?' Kane and Allardyce chorused. Harry, bleeding, shocked, couldn't remember his name at that precise moment.

'The same.' Bligh beamed. 'The brother of a friend of his, the Solicitor-General as was . . .'

'Rufus Isaacs.' Kane and Allardyce had got into something of a rhythm now.

'Precisely, they heard of a fortune to be made in the Marconi Wireless Company and they bought shares in it. Illegally, of course. Now these gentlemen are brilliant in their respective fields, but neither of them had *quite* the finesse to handle the market end of the transaction. That's where I came in. Now of course, I couldn't exactly apply for these shares in the names of D. Lloyd George and R. Isaacs, could I? So I used aliases. I ran my inky little finger down a Kelly's directory and hit upon one Robert Peel and his former housekeeper, Millicent Millichip. I vaguely remembered Peel in fact from the City. It wouldn't matter if he were caught. If the balloon went up, my aliases would be visited by the long arm of the Fraud Squad, not the Chancellor of the Exchequer, the Solicitor-General and my good gentleman self. I used poste restantes, of course, so that I could collect the shares and the dividends, before discreetly imbursing my colleagues. That's when it all went wrong. That gaga old duffer Worsthorne Griffin in my offices sent the first dividend payments to the addresses of the *real* people. Millicent Millichip was suddenly rich, so were Robert Peel, Herbert Wilson, the others. That maniac Emily Davison would start splashing it about on her futile Cause; Wilson would have bought a theatre in his name; that little turd Withers would have bought a regiment. All too showy, too public. So we were losing money.

'Then that damned Frog newspaper got hold of the story, or part of it, and Lloyd George and Isaacs were in the frame. My name, mercifully, was kept out of it, although my partners in crime were quick to remind me that one little word from them . . . I was left with the job of patching it up. And that was fine. I started with Peel. I sent Millichip a message to come to Oxford Street urgently on the day of the pea-souper. I hadn't bargained for the fog and I couldn't see a damned thing beyond Marble Arch. It nearly threw my timing. I waited on foot for the tram she said she'd be on. She was late in fact. I waited for three. When she arrived I walked past her, stabbing as I went. As I glanced back, some Samaritan was trying to help. When the papers told me who he was, I could have wept for joy – a scapegoat, a man in the frame. It couldn't have been more perfect.

'I told you a moment ago that I had killed before. So I did. George Griffin was a lawyer meddling into my affairs. I pushed him off the Embankment near Vauxhall Bridge. It was sheer coincidence that Millicent Millichip had seen him go. What she hadn't seen, of course, was me. I quite enjoyed old Griffin moping about Raleigh Harman every day, but then that's the sort of bastard I am. I put it about that George had received a calling card from the devil on the day he died. When I sent one to old Worsthorne, it broke his heart, poor old lad. Serves him right for sending out those dividends in the first place. He should have stuck to guano.'

'Emily Davison . . .' Kane prompted him.

'All right.' Bligh smiled. 'I confess her name was not chosen at random. For a start she lived in Northumbria, and was not in Kelly's at all . . . No, it was her obvious link to my old adversary that nudged me in her direction. Old Charlie Davison was a business rival way back – but not for long. He went the same way as George Griffin. She was horrified when I lifted her up on the rail like that, but as I looked back, I saw her get up. It was unbelievable. I took the biggest chance of all there and doubled back as Cole. No one seemed to notice – the stupidity of the common racegoer.'

Outside the engines were revving on the starter lines, the crowd cheering already before the flag was up.

'Cody was easy. A saw through the right pipe. That simple. Herbert Wilson likewise. I sat through the whole of that turgid tosh he was in at His Majesty's, then went backstage to leave flowers. I also left a tin of live ammunition. Had a spot of luck there – the Properties man was an imbecile. I have to confess, Allardyce, I bungled you. Poisons are a closed book to me. Still, you can't win them all. At first I decided to put Morant in the frame, then, when Lestrade didn't seem to go along with that, I toyed with Dimsdale, but Dimsdale was too close. He could have got to me through Drewe's dealings. Drewe is honest as the day is long, but as you will have gathered, I'm not, and neither is Claude Beaufort, who is in over his head . . . But then, I got the call.'

'The call?' Harry spoke from the floor. Kane sensed something was afoot. No one moved.

'From Lloyd George. The cunning old Evangelist was being pestered by Lestrade. So Lestrade had to go. I'd already pointed in his direction once by planting that suspicious manuscript at Constable. I laced your coffee, Allardyce, as John Adams and I doubled back, in suitable uniform, when I realized that Miss Fry had called an ambulance. In fact, she called four. That's what gave me time to change and join the others. I rather enjoyed writing Lestrade's memoirs. One of our professionals of course forged your comment, Allardyce.'

'As he forged Lestrade's letters to Mrs Millichip,' Kane said.

'Indeed. It took quite a bit of persuading, Kane, to get you to search her premises a third time, but the Lord Chief Justice has a silver tongue, does he not? Now, gentlemen, I have been very patient, very accommodating. But now, I believe, the race is about to start.'

'Now, John,' Bandicoot shouted and from nowhere, a monkey wrench was in his hand and out of it, hurtling through the air to smash the Mephisto's flimsy windscreen. Bligh fired wildly, the shots crashing in the half-light as everyone dived for cover. Then he was in the Mephisto and revving for the door.

Kane leapt on to the running board as the car smashed through the closed doors. He was still hanging on as it screamed in a blaze of burning rubber out on to the track, carving up the drivers who had just put foot to pedal. Allardyce and Bandicoot staggered out into the daylight, Jessica and the constable rushing to their aid. There were screams from the crowd as the Mephisto, gleaming black with the scarlet devil's face glowing on its bonnet, snarled through the leading cars, forcing a Peugeot on to the side. Kane's knuckles were white on the doorhandle as he saw Bligh cock his revolver and point it at him. Neither man was watching the road as the car hit the fierce camber on the first bend and the shot went wide, to ricochet off the concrete.

Kane took a deep breath and let go with one hand, fumbling in his pocket for his truncheon. Bligh aimed again, this time steadying the car as it came out of the chicane. Kane hurled the hardwood and it bounced on the driver's forehead. His eyes crossed as the blood flowed and Kane hurled himself clear to roll on the muddy track and break his ankle on impact.

He saw as if in slow motion the Mephisto take the second bend. Was Bligh mad? He wasn't braking. He was accelerating into the curve, sliding with the camber. For a second, the Mephisto did the impossible and broke the laws of Physics, then it slewed to one side and ploughed into the rail, splintering the white wood in all directions before coming to a stop beneath the tall, lone cedar. There was a silence that John Kane had never heard before. The cars behind him had stopped. The crowd's chattering and screaming were still. He hauled himself to his feet and dragged his dangling leg to the buckled wreckage of the Mephisto.

Alaric Bligh lay with his head thrown back, his throat sliced through by the shattered glass of the windscreen. The Mephisto's engine ticked and shuddered until the only sound was of its front wheels still turning.

So, Boadicea was right after all. Lloyd George *was* responsible. No move was made against him. Nor against Rufus Isaacs. The Marconi Scandal had had its day and top-hatted men walking the corridors of power and flat-capped men walking their whippets all agreed that there was no smoke without fire. But Alaric Bligh had done his work well. He had left no links with his puppet masters. And in the years that followed, as Chancellor of the Exchequer and as Prime Minister, David Lloyd George was to preside over vastly more murders in the killing fields of Flanders.

Ashley Congleton shook Lestrade's hand as the Superintendent climbed into Harry's Silver Ghost outside the grim, grey walls of Pentonville. The thing looked like an ambulance, with Harry in the back with his arm in a sling and John Kane on crutches. Only Constables Tait and Lyall seemed to be in one piece.

'It's good to see you out, guv.' Tait beamed.

'It's good to be out, Constable,' Lestrade said, easing his collar.

'Sir.' Lyall was looking a little sheepish. 'I . . . er . . . I've got something to say, sir.'

'Oh, yes.' Lestrade looked at the boy behind the wheel.

'Well, you won't know this, sir, but at school, I won the History prize.'

'Well, never mind, lad,' Lestrade said. 'That's nothing to be ashamed of.'

'No, sir,' Lyall said. 'It's not that. It's these names – Alexander Smith, John Adams, Cole, Fryer.'

'What about them?' Lestrade asked.

'They're all blokes who mutinied on the *Bounty*, sir, you know, Captain Bligh's ship back in 1789. Do you think that could have had any relevance, sir, to the case, I mean?'

Lestrade exchanged glances with Harry and John in the back.

'No, Constable.' He smiled. 'I'm sure it has no relevance at all. Now, step on it, Lyall. Bandicoot Hall for Christmas. Oh, and if you see a little bloke with a rope under his arm and a disappointed look on his face, drive like the devil!'